These Dark Things

Also by the Author

A Few Drops of Blood

These Dark Things

A Novel

JAN MERETE WEISS

For Dave

⌐

Copyright © 2011 by Jan Merete Weiss

Published by
Soho Press, Inc.
227 W 17th Street
New York, NY 10011

Library of Congress Cataloging-in-Publication Data

Weiss, Jan Merete.
These dark things : a novel / Jan Merete Weiss.

ISBN 978-1-61695-076-7
eISBN 978-1-56947-939-1

1. Women detectives—Fiction. 2. Murder—Investigation—
Fiction. 3. Catholic Church—Fiction. 4. Camorra—Fiction.
5. Organized crime—Italy—Naples—Fiction. I. Title.
PS3623.E4553T44 2011
813'.6—dc22
2010045686

Printed in the United States of America

10 9 8 7 6 5 4 3 2

With special thanks to Juris Jurjevics for his guidance and vision. And to the wonderful team at SOHO—particularly, Mark Doten, for his editing genius. As well, Bronwen Hruska and Justin Hargett.

And with gratitude to Laura Hruska, *in memoriam.*

*In October the sowing of the wheat
begins, and November honors that which
lies beneath the ground awaiting
rebirth; the dead return in a ritual visit to
the cult of the dead, and the whole period
between the beginning of November
and Epiphany, is tempis terrible, in which
the gates to the Afterworld remain open.*

FRANCO CARDINI,
I giorni del sacro: il libro delle feste

1

A large cypress tree arched over the graves, and a few clouds the color of peaches. The horizon glowed. The Neapolitan sun hadn't yet begun her climb. Gina Falcone surveyed the newest additions beneath the burlap on her cart. Besides the midsized tibia, a rib cage, and a large femur, there was a child's skull. Male or female, the bone cleaner didn't know. Nor did she care. The recent dead troubled her no more than the bones of the plague victims from centuries ago.

At Via della Piazzola, she entered the old section of the city. Most of the red paint was chipped off her cart. The bare metal wheels ground against the black flagstones. Walking past tiny dark alleys, the *vichi,* she imagined the omnibuses draped in black that had waited, centuries ago, for the priests and stretcher-bearers to carry out the cadavers during the plague epidemic.

It was a block more to the Church of Santa Maria delle Anime del Purgatorio. Outside the flower shop, a middle-aged tourist, her hair rumpled from sleep, was bent over the buckets, inhaling the jasmine. Gina passed like a shadow come loose from a building. She adjusted the bag on the cart as it banged along the cobblestones. Market stalls clustered under medieval arches. The fishmonger dumped mussels onto a bed of ice. Across the way, the cheese man hollered up to his wife, who scowled and lowered a basket from their window. He removed keys and substituted butter and a loaf of bread.

" *'Giorno*, Signora," called a robust man arranging burnt-orange apricots in his shop.

" *'Giorno*, Nico," she replied.

Near the back of the shop, Nico's mother sat crocheting. Everyone knew not to touch the fruit. You pointed to what you wanted and he made the selections, weighed and bagged the apples or grapes, and you paid. Gina Falcone disregarded the convention. Nico didn't like it but never objected, even when she ate a piece of fruit without paying. Or grabbed a pear to test its ripeness and sent a half dozen others rolling across the ground.

That she did holy work and could intercede for souls waylaid in purgatory—like Nico's grandmother—kept him from saying anything to her. Gina Falcone was among the last of the bone cleaners. Officially, second burials had ceased decades ago. It was an ancient practice going back to the Egyptians. The mourners waited a year for the flesh to decompose, then disinterred the bones. Some placed them in an ossuary, a bone box, for the second burial. Or the few remaining bone cleaners, like Gina, collected them from the grave keepers and carried them to their rest in certain Naples churches where the practice was still quietly tolerated.

"*Ciao*, Gina," Nico said, charging her a token for the fruit she'd taken.

She crossed the street to the church, a dark structure amid the crumbling ochre buildings that surrounded it. A sunflower, a rose, and a stem of mimosa rested in the iron gates. Four bronze skulls and femurs sat atop four short columns. The skulls gleamed, polished daily by the passersby who touched them. Santa Maria delle Anime del Purgatorio. Vagrants dozed in the shadows of the black stones, the Church being too stingy to invite them in but not heartless enough to forbid them a concrete bed outside its doors. The odor of urine was strong.

Purgatorio was four centuries old, built around the time the Cult of the Dead took hold in Naples, when Jesuits celebrated sixty masses a day on its altars. They preached among skulls and skeletons laid out on black cloth. The priests hadn't held ecstatic services here in many years. Gina missed them and the large crowds of parishioners carrying torches and flashlights in procession, descending to the crypts where each would select a skull to pray over.

The faithful still climbed down into the crypts to wash bones and privately pray for those in limbo, souls that had left this world but not yet reached the next.

At the end of the Second World War, Gina Falcone had dug up the remains of her young husband and another fallen soldier and prepared them for their second burial. She felt called to continue, and her work began. For a long time, business was brisk, but it had slowed during the past decade. Signora Falcone survived on a small stipend from the Neapolitan Burial Society and donations from the bereaved.

Church bells tolled eight times. The madwoman on Vico del Sole screamed "*Attenzione*," as she had every morning for years. "*Sono malata!*" I am ill. "*Il pericolo. Il pericolo.*" The danger. The danger.

A dozen people waited to enter the sanctuary—two women for every man. Some fingered their rosaries, prayed under their breath. Tonio the Dwarf stood at the front. A gang of pigeons pecked at scattered breadcrumbs around their feet.

"Away!" Gina cried, waving her arms. They warbled in protest, ruffling their wings, lifting a foot before alighting again. She knew who was responsible: Uccello Camillo. "Bird" Camillo's pockets bulged with crumbs.

The bone cleaner mumbled and grabbed her cart. The faithful moved aside to let her through to deliver the new bones before they entered and descended. Tonio stepped out of the line to help lift the cart up the steps to the narrow church entrance. Gina handed him a key. Tonio was barely taller than the keyhole.

"Needs oil," he said, working it into the lock. He pushed open the wooden door in to the dark interior. The only bright spot was the white altar. At its foot, purple and white chrysanthemums wilted in a vase.

Gina rolled the cart inside and leaned it against the last pew, a simple wooden bench without a cushion. She made the sign of the cross and took the bag from the cart. Gina Falcone could find her way anywhere in the church with her eyes closed. She dragged the bones past the altar and through a small door that led to the crypt. Bones in one hand, with the other she felt her way down the long narrow staircase. Her eyes adjusted. At the very bottom was a faint light. Candles, left perhaps by someone the previous day.

The crypt comprised several rooms. In the first, skulls were piled and stacked everywhere: on the ground, in niches cut into the walls. A shrine with a lone skull strewn with dead flowers rested atop a mound of leg bones. Gina Falcone shifted a decayed sunflower to a flat tin tray layered with finger bones and more skulls. She passed through a hallway of tombstones into the larger burial room. This gallery was filled floor to ceiling with yet more skulls and bones piled neatly in niches. Some eye sockets held slips of paper: messages from worshippers, personal information about the deceased gleaned in dreams about them.

In the room's center was a bench carved from volcanic stone. There was an armrest and a hole in its seat. In times past, the body was placed there, for the flesh to rot away, the putrefied fluids to pour into the drain below. *Puozzà Sculà!* May you drain away—a taunt still heard in the streets.

It was quiet. Dank and peaceful. Gina stopped short before a stack of skeletons. Half reclining on the bench, resting her chin on her hands, was an angel, her face pearly and framed in wavy red hair. Lovely, all in pink. At her pale throat, a beautiful necklace glinted with rubies and pearls. Gina stepped closer to gaze at the red blossom near her heart. There were no petals, only the hilt of a large knife.

The call came in to the Carabinieri regional station on Via Casanova, as Captain Natalia Monte finished her twenty-four-hour sleepover duty. She swung her feet to the floor and tried to clear her vision.

"Why not the police?" she demanded of her dispatcher.

"The body was found at a cultural shrine."

"Damn," she muttered. Protection of cultural institutions was one of the Carabinieri's odd areas of responsibility, answering as they did partly to the Ministries of the Interior, Exterior, and Defense.

Cursing, Captain Monte pulled on her uniform jacket and closed the knot of her tie, splashed water on her face, wet her fingers again, and tamped down her curls. They had sprung back up by the time she descended the three flights to the street and her duty car and driver. Getting in beside him, she closed her eyes and tried to doze as they headed for the crime scene.

Father Cirillo, the monsignor, was waiting for her at the entrance to the church, his ample stomach straining against the mended cassock he'd donned for this task.

"Thank God you're here," he said, coming up to Natalia as she buckled on her holster. "I was at breakfast when I heard the commotion."

Together they entered the church. Near the altar, he pointed to a door, hardly noticeable. Natalia ducked to avoid hitting her head passing through. "Careful," he said, turning to her as they felt their way down the dark stairs toward the lantern light below.

"Wait," she ordered. Someone was coming up the stairs toward them. Natalia drew her pistol as a small man came around a turn in the stairwell.

"Don't shoot!" he screamed.

"Luca, you idiot. I ought to put you out of your misery. If you've disturbed anything—"

"Nothing, Captain. Not ever."

Natalia holstered her weapon. Luca was an old freelance photographer with a lens for a brain. A nocturnal creature, he lived for a good murder. Half the time, he arrived at the scene before the police or the Carabinieri. Luca pressed past them in the stairwell.

"Monsignor," he touched his cap. "Captain Monte."

Natalia glared at him.

"Oh," he said, stopping. "Where was she killed?"

Natalia pointed upward, saying nothing. Luca scurried toward the surface.

They passed through a large cavernous room, through a long hallway, and into a third room, each decorated with centuries of bones piled onto one another, some organized into categories, some arranged in eerie patterns.

"She's in here," the monsignor said. Natalia paused to brush dust from her uniform. Despite the Armani design, it was wrinkled from the long night and now covered with grit. The red bands running down her pant legs were grimy, like her, like the cuffs and collar of her white shirt.

A beautiful girl sat on a stone bench in the center of the

room. Ethereal. Pre-Raphaelite. She did look like an angel—a bloody one.

"As you may have gathered," Father Cirillo said, "this chamber was used several hundred years ago for burials during the plague outbreaks. She's posed like someone might have been in the seventeenth century. I've never seen anything like this except in illustrations."

He was babbling. Natalia wished he wouldn't. She stepped closer, examining the ground.

Communing with the dead. Many in Naples still did it. When Natalia was a girl, her mother's mother—Natalia's *nonna*—had gone weekly to the crypt where her sister's bones were displayed. Sometimes she took her granddaughter. Nonna made herself comfortable on a chair provided there. If there were no other visitors, the clicking of her knitting needles was often the only sound.

Such a gloomy city, Natalia thought, but what could you expect in a metropolis where people actually dressed in black so as not to be mistaken by the dead as living souls ripe for haunting? A miracle that anyone got out of bed in the morning at all.

The monsignor was still lecturing. Cirillo was an amateur scholar and led occasional tours of his church and the surrounding neighborhood. Natalia had seen him holding forth outside the church just the past spring.

"You're too young to remember World War II. Bombs dropped on Naples every day. Twenty thousand people took refuge down here and in passages and cisterns carved by the Romans in the volcanic rock beneath the city."

"Yes, Monsignor."

There was not much evidence of blood anywhere in the room. Murdered elsewhere. Maybe choked at the same time, given the marks under her jawline. And seriously stabbed. Twice. The back of the dress was as red with dry blood as the front was pinkish white.

Skulls ringed the victim in a half circle. Lilies rotted near her feet, their scent cloying. A candle burned. The victim was fair with a smattering of freckles, traces of lipstick visible on her mouth. A girl adorned for life's pleasures.

Natalia walked the perimeter of the room, peering behind stacks of leg bones, wrist bones, finger bones, and skulls. No weapon; only bones and crumbled rock. Something glinted from the rubble. Natalia stepped closer. She slipped her gloves on and picked it up. A small silver heart, untouched by the dust—an ex-voto, a votive offering. Sixteenth-century worshippers had left them as offerings to the saints in gratitude for healing a broken limb, a diseased lung. Clerics as well as laypeople believed in them. Nowadays, most considered them quaint. Most, but not all.

Ex-votos were usually miniature replicas of hands and feet or lungs. A heart was unusual. It suggested someone unsophisticated. Or was that a ruse? Did this poor girl's death cure someone of heartbreak? A spurned lover? Or a mad person? Maybe both and the same.

"'The Cult of the Dead,' the worshippers of the bones were called," Father Cirillo began.

When Natalia had been a girl, on All Souls' Night her father would put a bucket of water outside their front door. "So the dead can drink as they enter the house," he'd say. The next morning, when she would point out that the level of the water was unchanged, her mother had spat to make sure her daughter hadn't aroused the evil eye.

"They get thirsty," her mother scolded. "Mix this." She pushed a bowl of dough to her daughter.

It was to make *fave dei morti*—the broad beans of the dead, the dough molded into the shape of bones. Not a Neapolitan tradition. Natalia's mother had learned to make the cakes from her cousin Rosalia, married to a carpenter from Tuscany. Long after Cousin Rosalia passed and every November until her own death, her mother continued baking them. To honor Rosalia's memory, she said. And hedge her bets, Natalia thought.

Before they kneaded the dough or enjoyed the tasty cakes, Natalia's mother repeated the prayer from the Cult of the Dead: "*Sante Anime del Purgatorio pregate per noi che pregiamo per voi.*"

Holy Saints of Purgatory, we beseech you to pray for us as we pray for you.

2

Sergeant Pino Loriano yawned as he descended the old-fashioned stairs of his apartment house. Great white plaster patches marred the walls, but they were otherwise in good repair. In the foyer, he collected his bicycle and guided it out the door and through the courtyard to the street. On Via Bianchini, he stepped over garbage rotted beyond recognition. The landfills were full, and garbage festered all over the city.

The Camorra, Naples's local criminal organization, refused to collect it—or allow anyone else to collect it—because the prime minister had vowed to see the state-of-the-art incinerator at Acerra finished. That would seriously interfere with the Camorra's business. The prime minister also threatened to force open some of the closed landfills ten kilometers out of town.

The citizens of Cicciano and Marano mounted round-the-clock protests to keep any more refuse from coming into their neighborhoods. Various Camorra-owned garbage-collection companies were warring over who would haul the garbage, if it ever got hauled again. Meanwhile, they were moving toxic industrial wastes, burying them on farmland.

It was a nightmarish mess. Pino dreaded the Carabinieri's role as environmental protector and did not envy his colleagues mandated to deal with it. A murder in a landmarked church would do him just fine.

He got on his bicycle and pedaled down the broad, empty lanes of Via dei Tribunali toward the crime scene. Widows and clerics navigated the dark streets past high stone walls that encased narrow alleys. A vendor was putting sunflowers out on the flagstones. Slivers of blue water gleamed between the aged buildings; ferries and freighters eased from the Bay of Naples out into the Tyrrhenian Sea.

A standard four-door blue Alfa blocked the alley en route to the crime scene. One uniformed carabiniere stood on the cobblestones, arms folded. The other lay across the hood, half asleep. Pino didn't recognize either. He flashed his sergeant's identification, and the conscious one moved out of the way to let him through with his bike. The carabiniere punched his snoring partner, then directed Pino down the alley, toward the Capuchin monastery.

Most nights, drug addicts congregated in the alley. At the moment, it was empty.

Pino squeezed his bicycle through the narrow space between car and wall and entered the worn cobblestone lane. It curved away from Via dei Tribunale. He shouldered the frame and carried the bike down a small flight of stairs. A sleepy resident leaned over her balcony, smoking.

A crowd milled around a street shrine outside the Capuchin monastery. Several votive candles surrounded a large pool of blood. The candles blazed. Catching their flickering light, the pool glistened. The shrine was a crude box nailed together from scrap wood. The collection box was missing.

Pino leaned closer to its cracked glass cover. Inside the box, before a carved figure of the Savior, lay an offering of a cigarette pack and a wrinkled apricot, a prayer card depicting the Sacred Heart of Jesus, and the small porcelain figurine of a female saint too weathered to identify. Pressed to the glass, a yellowed photograph of someone's relative. Left long ago, back when there was still hope. Behind it, a page torn from a magazine. Pino slipped the clipping out. A model's face scratched over with black marker, THIEVING BITCH scrawled beneath it in red. Meaning the dead girl? Pino dropped it into an evidence bag. More police arrived.

Just then, Monsignor Cirillo came out of the church, followed by Captain Monte, Pino's supervising partner. Her hair was even wilder than usual and her blouse untucked, jacket open, her smoky eyes wide with adrenaline.

"There was a note in the shrine," Pino announced, holding up the plastic bag. "It may refer to the dead girl."

"Give it to Dr. Francesca when she gets here. Maybe it has prints." She turned to the bystanders crowding in. "Who lit all these candles?" she said.

No response.

"This is an investigation area," she announced. "If you have no information, you need to keep back. Except you," she said, indicating the elderly bone cleaner, Gina Falcone.

Roof lights whirling, Dr. Francesca Agari, Naples's leading forensic pathologist, made her entrance in one of the department's vintage Fiats. She was halfway out of the vehicle before it stopped rolling. Despite the hour, her two-toned blond highlights were perfectly smooth, like the mauve-and-gold powder glistening above her eyes.

"Christ," Francesca Agari said as she took in the scene. "Hey!" she called to her waiting photographer halfway down the alley. "We need you here!"

An aspiring fashion photographer. His worn leather jacket hung open. His thick hair grew to his shoulders.

"The victim," Natalia informed them, "is in the crypt of Santa Maria del Purgatorio."

Dr. Francesca nodded and dispatched three forensic criminalists into the church. They looked like spacemen in their puffy suits. Pino accompanied Dr. Francesca and the photographer into the church while Natalia ordered the attending carabinieri to canvass the neighborhood.

A fragment of Chopin drifted from the music school nearby. Natalia turned toward it. Someone practicing this early?

There was more light in the sky now, and swallows.

"If you don't need me. . . ." Father Cirillo kicked at broken bottles and syringes not a foot from the pool of blood.

"No, that's fine," Natalia said. "You can go. Thank you for your help."

The monsignor paused to pray over the reservoir of blood and made the sign of the cross, recorded by Luca with one of his three cameras. Natalia approached the bystanders, neighbors who might have overheard the killing if not actually seen it. No one would speak. She circled the puddle of blood, hoping to find a footprint. Nothing.

Pino returned from the crypt, slightly flushed from the climb. Natalia took her partner by the arm, turning him away from the onlookers. They conferred for a moment, agreeing to question the bone cleaner together. The elderly woman was consoling a *monachello*, a novice, encouraging him to go back inside the monastery. He was blind, Natalia realized.

Pino and she walked over to them.

"What were you doing in the crypt this morning?" Natalia asked.

"I bring the bones. From the cemetery, like always. Every week, I come. I have a key to the church." She pointed to Father Cirillo at the end of the alley. "From him. Can I get my cart?"

"Was anyone with you, inside the church? Were you alone in the crypt?" Pino asked.

"Only the angel and me."

"We found a bowl of oil by the shrine here. For the evil eye. Did you put it there, Signora Falcone?" The bone cleaner reminded him of his Aunt Zia Annunziata, a witch who dispensed amulets and planted such bowls to ward off evil.

"Yes," Gina said. "I put the bowl there."

"What do you know about the dead girl?"

"I'm a bone cleaner, not a detective."

"You put the bowl there to protect her," Pino said. "What did the water tell you?"

"The girl was dead. Dead. I didn't do anything wrong."

"What shape did it take?"

"The *jettatori*, so I said a prayer."

"What witch did she need protection from? Who wished her ill?"

Pino's Aunt Annunziata had famously spat when an envious neighbor told her that Pino was a dear little boy. Thereafter his *zia* had insisted that he wear his undershirt inside out to block the woman's evil intent.

"Maybe you saw something that could help us."

"I saw nothing."

"If you did, and you're withholding information, we can take you in."

"Me, an old woman? I'm over eighty." Gina Falcone looked away. "She was a good girl."

"Did you know the deceased?"

"That's not what I'm saying. No one that young deserves such a death."

"We need to find her killer."

"Here." She dug in her pocket and pulled out something wrapped in tissue paper. It was an amulet, a twin of the one Zia Annunziata had insisted Pino wear as a boy; his mother had hidden it in her underwear drawer instead.

"You think I need this charm?"

"I am not a fortune teller. I look after souls. You young people think everything is yes or no. Right or wrong."

"We are sworn to uphold the law," Pino said.

"The Law!" Gina spat. "Yesterday the Law was Mussolini. Today you want to put an old woman in jail."

"You may leave," Natalia said, "but we will talk again."

The bone cleaner retrieved her cart and clanked away.

"The men found the victim's purse," Pino said, holding up a bright red handbag. "It was by the shrine. And these were next to it."

He handed her several photographs—the dead girl mugging for the camera, and then one with a man, his arms around her, face turned away. Posed on a dock, the sun in the girl's eyes.

"She dwells with Beauty—Beauty that must die;" Pino quoted from memory. "And Joy, whose hand is ever at his lips / Bidding adieu."

Natalia looked at him. "Why do you know that?"

"Keats? We had to memorize it because Keats loved Italy so and died in his little room by the Spanish Steps. If we missed even a word, beautiful Sister Mary Frances rapped us with her stick."

They divided the photographs, lingered for a moment on the steps of the church. The beginning of March. Not yet spring. But the sun was already warm. A lovely morning, with birds singing.

Natalia emptied the girl's purse into her lap, and they took inventory. A large zip-lock plastic bag. A lipstick and cell phone, a wallet with identification: Teresa Steiner, twenty-three. From Ulm. German. Studying at the University.

Natalia scanned the faces of the onlookers, who were waiting for any crumb of information, which they'd convert to gossip and transmit across the old city in minutes.

She recognized a few of them—Falcone Gaetano, the caretaker of the government offices around the block on Vico San Paolo. And Falcone's retarded brother, Paolo, with his amazing cauliflower ears.

"If you have no information regarding the crime, we'll have to ask you to leave."

"Public street," a shopkeeper hissed as she passed.

"I'd like to know how the killer got into the locked church with a body and got it down there," Natalia said when the crowd had gone.

"It's not much of a lock. It's ancient, easily picked." Pino stared at the shrine, the light of the massed candles steadily surrendering to the dawn. "You think the killer lit all those candles?"

The palazzo where Teresa Steiner lived was only two blocks from where she had been murdered. Natalia and Pino decided to walk. Something scurried nearby as they set out, a rat edging past the wall.

Pino said, "A politician from the North once called Naples a sewer inhabited by rats."

"There are no rats up north?" Natalia asked.

Laundry hung like banners from lines strung across the alley between the residential buildings. Giant brassieres beside tiny skirts. Underpants of varying sizes; trousers and shirts. To clean what is dirty—to purify. A major preoccupation of her city. On the sidewalk in front of an open doorway: a tiny rack with the clothes of an infant lovingly laid out to dry. Innocent. As if the wearer could escape growing up into the hard life of Naples.

A prostitute stood her post in front of the seedy Hotel Internazionale, across from the railroad terminal, waiting for the next surge of travelers off the Rome train. Checking her watch, the woman took a drag on her cigarette, then threw it down, adjusted her cleavage, and nodded at Natalia and Pino as they passed. Her red wool skirt stopped just below her ass. She wore gold heels. They had to be nearly four inches high—a hazard on the uneven cobblestones. A hazardous profession. Not to mention AIDS and kinky johns, both on the rise. Where were the Jesuits now? Today only a few Carmelite nuns reached out. A few years earlier, Natalia remembered, she had given this same woman a card with the name of their clinic. "*Grazie*," the streetwalker had managed in a tone that conveyed: *You've got to be kidding!* Sad, a prostitute of fifty. But somehow she had stayed alive.

Natalia admired the bold choice of shoe. No doubt she had a closet full. Natalia's mother had owned only three pairs at any one time. Two were sensible—flats with laces. The pair with low heels she wore once or twice a year for special occasions. Natalia's grandmother, who had worked in a sardine cannery, never wore heels in her life.

How has she avoided breaking a leg? Natalia wondered.

A block later, they found Teresa Steiner's former residence. The building wore decades of grime and diesel fumes. By the door, written childlike under the name Lucia Santini, was the word *pensione.* Natalia pressed the caretaker's buzzer and they waited. She was about to ring again when the intercom crackled.

"*Pronto?*"

"Carabinieri."

The door clicked and Natalia pushed open the small door cut into the massive one. Climbing three flights, they arrived out of breath. The landing was dark, one door open—a woman with a dog beside her. The dog was a husky, one eye green and the other blue. She stepped aside to let them in.

In the hallway, a table and a chest of drawers. On top of the drawers, magazines and a vase of dusty-looking plastic flowers. Lucia Santini wiped her hands on her apron. Her eyes were swollen, the flesh around them red.

"They came. They told me already. She's dead."

"Sorry to disturb you again," Natalia said, "but we'd like to ask you some questions. Can we come in?"

The dog sniffed Natalia.

"*Basta!*" Lucia Santini grabbed his ratty collar and pulled him away.

"No, it's okay," Natalia said, "I like dogs." Lucia, however, was already dragging the creature down the corridor, soothing him as they went. "Everything is all right, my sweet baby." She bent down and kissed the dog on his large woolly head.

Lucia Santini was a big woman, arms puddled with fat. Close to seventy, yet her hair was blue-black, pinned up on her head like the Leaning Tower of Pisa. A few hairs of a moustache stuck out above her upper lip. The living room looked to be where Lucia spent most of her time. A cigarette burned in an ashtray by the couch, and the TV droned. Lucia trundled over and turned it off.

"Was Teresa Steiner here last night?" Natalia asked.

"She was in her room, studying. Armando—he rents a room in the back—Armando had gone to bed. He works on the freighters and gets up early. My sister was here. We stayed up watching television. I knocked on Teresa's door and asked if she'd like to watch with us. Sometimes she would. But she said she had to finish a paper for the next day. She seemed tired, not her usual self."

"What was her usual self?" Pino asked.

"Cheerful. And with energy, like young people. Not like us—eh, Osky?" she said to the dog, creeping toward her. "Teresa wanted to know everything about Naples. She wanted to try new things. She loved to go dancing. Can you imagine: she wanted me to go tango dancing with her. But she was a serious student. Sometimes her light would be on till two or three in the morning. I'd look in and she'd have her nose in a book."

The dog wandered back to its mistress's side. She patted him on the flank, starting up his tail. Natalia took out her notebook.

"Do you remember what she was wearing when she went out last night?"

"Nah, but I can tell you she was dressed up in something pink. And high heels. I thought she might have been going dancing." She pulled her housedress closer. It was missing buttons. A pocket hung limp.

"How late were you up?" Pino asked.

"My sister left at ten, or just after, when the TV show finished. I cleaned up and went to bed."

"Did the girl receive any phone calls?" Natalia's pen was poised.

"No. Not on my telephone. But she has one of those mobiles they all carry. My room is at the other end of the apartment, so if she did go out, I wouldn't have heard her. You want to see her room?"

They followed her across the dim corridor. The door was open, towels and sheets folded on the bed.

"Excuse the mess. I was just taking them in from the line."

"Don't worry," Natalia said, looking around. A sad-looking room. Maybe the walls had been white once. The bed was like the one Natalia's *nonna* slept in after her husband died. It was barely big enough for one. The mattress sagged and it had an iron frame. As if she were doing penance for still being alive.

Teresa Steiner must have used the small table to study. The overhead bulb didn't look like it provided much light. Natalia imagined the TV or radio going constantly in the adjoining living room. She wondered how the girl could concentrate enough to study here anyway. Probably she spent some time at the library. Natalia remembered how she had adored the library's quiet when she was a student.

Lucia sighed. "I was born here." She crossed to the unmade bed and smoothed the sheets.

Natalia sifted through a drawer crammed with colorful silk scarves.

"My mother didn't like hospitals," Lucia added. "She had a friend who died in one, giving birth. I was her only child, the only one who survived."

"I'm sorry." Natalia closed the drawer. Pino was down on his knees, looking under the bed.

"It was God's will that she live with me her last year," Lucia said. "Hot in here, isn't it?" She opened the louvered doors to the balcony. The men working on the church across the way shouted to one another.

"Would you like coffee?" Lucia offered. "I was just going to make myself a pot."

Pino looked at Natalia. "I have to get going."

"I'd like some. That would be great," Natalia said.

"I'll see you out," Signora Santini said to Pino. "I can tell you about the dog."

"The dog?" Natalia asked.

"Not a big deal," she said. "He'll give you the report."

Pino winked at his partner. She frowned and proceeded to explore Teresa Steiner's room.

In a plywood cabinet against one wall hung Teresa's expensive designer clothes. Gucci and Prada. Apparently Teresa could have afforded a better room, even an apartment in an elegant palazzo. Why did she rent a seedy room here?

Natalia closed Teresa's door and walked back into the living room. She sat down at the end of the couch. Lucia put their coffee on the table and sat herself, tugging her raveled sweater into place. Natalia was reminded of crazy Maria, who sold the only bad-tasting tomatoes in Italy at a table on the corner of Via Capozzi. She sheltered three or four dogs under it. Her hair never combed, face dirty, clothes scavenged from the garbage—but her dogs were always bathed and groomed.

Petting Osky, who had settled at her feet, Natalia could imagine coming home to a soft friendly creature rather than to empty rooms. A dog would generally be glad to see its owner. Men were another story.

Lucia pushed a plate of biscotti to Natalia. The coffee was surprisingly good.

"Did Teresa Steiner have gentlemen coming to her room?" Natalia asked as she reached for a cookie.

Lucia bit into hers, scattering crumbs. Whiskers spiked from her chin.

"She had a lot of boyfriends, but the professor was the one she saw most. Said he was her thesis adviser, and they were going to her room to work. I'm making coffee in the morning when he slinks past without even a *buongiorno*. I can always tell when they're married. They bring me sweets the first time and then they don't want to have anything to do with me. Far be it for me to speak ill of the dead," Signora Santini added, "but your boss is gone and you're a woman. You understand."

"He's not my boss," Natalia said. "Actually, I'm his."

The dog jumped up and stretched out between them.

"I seen her with Gambini."

"Zazu, the mob boss?"

"Yeah. Aldo Gambini. Twice. Signor Rocco, he called himself—like I was stupid! So I got suspicious and followed her. Guess what? I watched her open a collection box at a shrine and stuff money into her fancy bag. She had a key. Right in the alley where she was killed. It figures. But still, it did surprise me. She was a nice girl. Brought me treats."

"Are you sure? Taking money?"

"Sure I'm sure. That hair. You couldn't miss it. One night she came home late. Said she wanted to talk. Did I mind?

Of course I didn't. I thought she was gonna confess to a broken heart. Instead, she says she's working for Gambini, collecting shrine money. Told me her mother had cancer."

Usually even the Camorra hesitated to commit crimes near the shrines under the eyes of the saints or the Madonna and Jesus. In the old days, thieves had strung ropes across the dark alleys to trip people at night and rob them. A Dominican friar had persuaded the Bourbon king to sponsor oil lamps, but the thieves destroyed them. So the king installed votive candles before statues of the saints. People loved the shrines. But the Camorra took over and the shrines became one more business, like bingo or festival games: a cooperative venture between the Camorra and the Vatican.

A small man with black hair walked into the living room carrying a bucket. Without a greeting, he set it down by the television and set to his task. The TV occupied a place of honor on a metal rolling cart surrounded by artificial plants and silk flowers. He dipped the rag into the bucket, squeezed it, then proceeded to wash the screen in smooth strokes.

"Armando," Lucia offered finally. He looked at Natalia but didn't say anything. A tidy man, obviously, but today he'd missed a wedge of shaving cream crusted on his ear. "From Chile," Lucia added, as Armando turned back to his chore. Lucia set down her cup and continued the discussion.

"'Don't tell anyone,' Teresa said. And the next day, she brings me a bottle of Giorgio perfume. Must have cost fifty euros!"

"What is the boyfriend's name?"

"I don't remember."

"What did he look like—the professor?"

"A peacock. Old and vain. You know—fancy."

"Did Teresa Steiner seem frightened recently?" Natalia noticed Armando watching them now.

"She *should* have been frightened," Lucia said, lowering her voice. "Gambini isn't some puppy you tease," she whispered close to Natalia, a scent of garlic on her breath.

Lucia Santini and her dog walked Natalia to the door.

"Thank you for your help," Natalia said. Signora Santini turned, stoop shouldered, and the door groaned shut, leaving Natalia alone on the landing.

On the street, Natalia dialed Pino. "You still in range?"

"*Certo.*"

"See if you can get an ID on the man in the photo we found with his arms around the victim. Try the University. According to Signora Santini, she had an admirer, a *professore.*"

3

Once on the street, she showed Teresa Steiner's photo around the neighborhood. Maybe someone had seen something or someone with her. A man next to his motorcycle was on the pay phone at the corner, hand cupped over the mouthpiece. His black jeans and shirt were unbuttoned to show off his thick gold cross and hairy chest. He had a diamond stud in his right ear. He smoked and talked, ogled women as they walked by. He didn't believe in shaving or haircuts. Mama's favorite boy.

Call finished, he winked at Natalia even though she was in uniform. He swaggered by, jumped on his bike, and sped off. Exhaust burned Natalia's ankles.

She tried to read the license plate. Low on the totem pole, no doubt, hardly worth pursuing, but you never know. Natalia walked into the alley whose stairs led to the *policlinico*. A woman was sweeping the passage, a fat little boy huddled beside her on the cobblestones.

" *'Scusi,*" Natalia said to her, holding out the photo of the late Teresa Steiner. "Do you know this young woman?"

The woman was sorry, but no, she didn't. Natalia thanked her and climbed the stairs to the street above. It was nearly lunchtime. A cluster of doctors in white strolled across the courtyard of the Hospital for the Insane. A woman screamed behind them and pounded on the iron gate. Ignoring her, a straggler unlocked the gate and slipped out to jog after his colleagues.

The usual crones were gathered on a bench beneath the statue of Saint Francis. The saint was surrounded by his angels, stone features worn away, wings cracked. A vendor sprayed his lettuces, a cigarette hanging from his mouth. Workmen took seats on the ground under their scaffolding, opened lunch pails, and pulled out enormous sandwiches wrapped in paper. The madwoman screamed again; the workmen smoked, even as they ate and drank, and commented on the beautiful women passing in review.

Two nuns in full gray habits took each other's arms as they crossed the street. Once, Natalia had wanted nothing more than to become a nun. Lots of her schoolmates did. On the cusp of adolescence, afraid of their sexuality, the girls had adored and worshipped the nuns. Marriage to God seemed preferable to the prospect of union with a hairy man.

The wind gusted. Clouds rushed past the roofs and church spires looming over the orange and lemon trees. The clouds were blowing out to sea. As a kid, Natalia had imagined mermaids flipping their tails in the harbor, as they were reputed to have done in ancient days. A decrepit old woman sat on a wooden chair on the sidewalk. Natalia had never known her name. She'd been known as a *strega*, a witch, since Natalia was a child.

Just then, a young mother wheeled her baby carriage up to the old woman, who pulled two sewing needles from her jacket and inserted one needle into the eye of the other, chanting, "*Vacchi e contro e perticell agli vocchi, crepa l'invidia e schiatton gli ochi.*" Eyes against eyes and the holes of the eyes, envy cracks and eyes burst.

Protection against the evil eye.

The next corner brought Natalia onto a market street. The vendors signaled to one another in case one was doing something that would arouse the law.

"I have lovely peaches. No charge for the carabiniere." The woman was not five feet tall—a muscular *nonna* in torn sneakers. She was missing her front teeth. Probably dealing numbers from her "office"—the folding table behind the cantaloupes and tomatoes. An orange-and-white cat dotted with black peeked out from below a saw-horse table heaped with fish. Of particular interest were the sardines, silver and sleek, their tiny bead-eyes open and shiny.

All around, sellers hawked their wares—cherries and oranges, sausages and cheeses, pinwheels, underwear, shoes. Natalia sensed items being covered, boxes hidden, but she didn't look.

The hungry—mainly gypsies—lurked all day, waiting for vendors to be distracted or to step away for a moment so they could vanish a melon or a plum. Failing that, they would even salvage discarded spoils or the odd onion that rolled into the gutter.

"Look at those." The *nonna* pointed to a mound of purple blossoms fallen from the trees still flowering all over Naples.

"Every week I sweep and every week they come back. What are you gonna do? They say they cure mental problems. I don't need the blossoms, but I should. You're young. You don't know. When I was growing up, after the War, life was terrible. People were hungry. They broke into the aquarium for food. My father brought home a bag of goldfish. And now we got this garbage." She pinched her nose. "Speaking of garbage, you heard? Last night. They got Franco Tozzi. He was a piece of shit, but a little boy was playing next to the car when the bomb went off. Burned so bad, his mother didn't recognize him." She made the sign of the cross.

Natalia paid for the grapes and peach and strolled on, glad to move away from that particular stretch of street. Patches of gold stained the buildings. Sheets of laundry lines billowed like synchronized swimmers.

Natalia recognized Pino's curly head bent over a display of figs.

"Have you ever seen any as beautiful as these? Try one," he said when he saw her.

"Delicious," Natalia said.

The vendor was filling two bags. "I got some for you," Pino said.

Not everyone could work with Pino. He had a reputation as an eccentric, refusing a car, even a motor scooter, attached to his old bicycle. He was a Buddhist, which intrigued her. He looked at things from unusual angles. "Lou Scarpetto," Pino said, introducing the fruit man. Pino didn't mention Natalia by name.

"Delighted," Scarpetto said. "Your boyfriend and I went to school together. Way back."

"Boyfriend"? What was her partner thinking?

"Smartest in the class," Lou said. "A real brain."

"Lou—" Pino protested.

"Nah. It's true. And it figures. Pino Loriano is a carabiniere, and I end up selling fruit!"

Scarpetto. Natalia put the name through her mental file. The Scarpettos ran all the produce in this part of town. This pudgy, unshaven man with a ratty apron was more than a millionaire. And, in spite of his genial face, he had killed or ordered killed more than one unfortunate soul.

"We played football together," Scarpetto continued, handing them the figs. "I used to weigh the same as him, can you believe? Married life!" He slapped his belly.

Pino reached for his wallet.

"No." Lou held up a hand.

"Lou, we have to pay. Otherwise—"

"Otherwise what? Your bosses give you a hard time? Anyone bothers you, you let me know. No disrespect, Miss," he addressed Natalia.

"So," he said, hands on ample hips, "the hermit finally got himself a girlfriend. When's the happy day?"

"You'll be the first to know," Pino said. He took Natalia's arm and pulled her away.

"Nice meeting you!" Scarpetto managed before they were swept into the stream of shoppers.

"What was that about?" Natalia asked. Pino was still holding her arm.

"The less Scarpetto knows, the better."

"Have you used him as an informant?"

"A couple of times."

"Okay. I get it. Now can I have my arm back?"

"No," he said.

"Have you lost your mind?" Natalia pulled away, acting as if he were teasing.

The two partners lingered on Via Toledo, looking in the windows of an antiques emporium, and next door the bridal shop, unchanged since Natalia and her best friend had haunted it as young girls. The same mannequins displayed two gowns—one of lace covered in pearls, the other a heavy cream-colored silk.

A juggler performed in the street out front. A *marginale*—one on the margins. A few robbed for a living too, but most contributed their varied talents to society. Some were circus performers, or barkers. A few were hatmakers. The knife grinder pushed his sharpening wheel through neighborhoods, announcing his services with a singsong cry. When she was a child, her mother had hired one-eyed Pietro to repair her copper pots. Amazingly, Pietro could read and write, while many of his clients couldn't.

Pino rifled through a bin of tarnished knives, banded with twine, and boxes of beaded flowers outside the antique shop. In the doorway, the proprietor held up a ripe pear and a fresh pastry, displaying them to a woman leaning out her window across the street.

Although she was only two years older than Pino, she felt as if she'd lived decades longer. They walked out of their district and passed a group of palm trees near the harbor. Gulls circled the docks, scouting for a meal.

The commander of the 10th Carabinieri Battalion, Colonel Donati, leaned back in his chair. Natalia was afraid that one day he would lean too far and tip over. A miracle it's never happened, she thought. He reached into a green glass bowl to grab a lemon drop.

"I'm trying to stop smoking. These are Elisabetta's idea. Try one?" He pushed the bowl across the desk. Donati's wife must have chosen the bowl. Its modern design was unlike anything else in the room.

"No, thanks," Natalia and Pino said at the same time.

"Any progress in the case?"

"Some," Natalia said. "The victim was a German citizen, born in Ulm. Her maternal grandparents were from Palermo. She's going to be buried there whenever Dr. Francesca releases the body."

"Beautiful girl, judging from the photo in the paper." He handed his copy to Natalia. "What do you know so far? What are your concerns about the case?"

Luca had outdone himself: the dead girl looked mythic, a character in a fairy tale in deep slumber.

"The murderer killed her in the street near a shrine," Natalia said. "Carried her through a locked door into the church and down a narrow passage into the crypt beneath. Yet forensics hasn't found so much as a drop of blood along the route, none in the tunnel descending to the crypts. Not a drop, not a smudge, although at least the killer's hands must have been bloody, his clothes stained. And no one saw the assailant come or go."

"Perhaps he came prepared," Donati said, "and wore gloves and one of those suits Dr. Francesca's people wear. Though that wouldn't explain the absence of a blood trail." His eyebrows arched. "Perhaps she bled out before he carted her off."

"Perhaps," Natalia said, without much conviction. "Tell me what you need."

"Help. Support here."

"We're strapped for manpower, but I'll give you Corporal Giulio to assist. He's still on light duty, but he can anchor the investigation desk for you." Donati touched the side of his nose. "Be prudent," he said. "There is the possibility of the Camorra in this." He glanced at his Omega. "Get some lunch."

In the hallway, Natalia said, "Camorra? Hell, no wonder the day shift vanished and we caught this killing. What have they got for local manpower? A couple of hundred thousand to our thirteen hundred?"

Pino only nodded, not meeting her eyes. If they annoyed the criminal clans, trouble was almost guaranteed. Carabinieri died or disappeared as easily as anyone else—prosecutors, witnesses, judges. Colonels, even. No wonder Donati was nervous at the possibility of Camorra involvement.

"Lunch where?" she asked.

"El Nilo. The waitress there recognized Teresa's picture. Said she came in almost every morning. Sometimes again at the end of the day. Recently with a young man. The waitress recognized him too."

The jukebox was going when they walked in: a local instrumental with lots of accordion and mandolin. The girl behind the counter wore purple lipstick. Punk-looking, but pretty, her eyebrows plucked thin. She carried trays of creamy *sfogliatelle* with her tongue sticking out, concentrating hard on not dropping them. She shook powdered sugar over them and laid each in the case, next to the biscotti lined up in neat rows. Pino and Natalia sat on the banquette. The proprietor polished the espresso machine. He nodded at them.

A man in kitchen whites came out from the back, his hair as white as his uniform.

"Tina!" He wiped his hands on his apron as the waitress scurried over. He asked if an order was ready and retreated through the swinging doors. He looked so familiar, Natalia thought. Could that old man have been Turrido, once the proprietor of Vesuvio's Bakery?

When she was young, Natalia had stopped there on her way home from school almost every day to pick up a loaf of *pane nero*, the black bread her mother had sworn by. Not just her mother, in fact: most of the neighborhood bypassed the rival fancy shop, even after it invested in chrome tables and chairs. Their bread didn't hold a candle to shabby Turrido's.

Turrido, with white hair? He'd never been thin, but he'd been fit, his hair bottle-black. He lived above the store with his mother, a beautiful sweet-natured old lady dressed always in black. She cooked for her son in the kitchen behind the shop, the smell of her meatballs tantalizing.

An old woman squeezed past their table and plunked down her shopping in a wide arc around her table. Her gold earrings swung like tiny chandeliers. The proprietor hurried over with her coffee, to which she added sugar.

Natalia and Pino grimaced. They both liked it the traditional way—not so sweet. How coffee is prepared is a local obsession. The sugar went in first, then the inky coffee oozed from the nozzle of the espresso machine. If you didn't like your coffee too sweet, you'd have to catch the bartender early. If he respected you, you got the coffee you ordered.

The owner's grandfather was Don Calo Gero Vizzini, the *Capo di tutti Capi,* a gangster so powerful that he'd greeted the American troops in 1943 wearing an apricot silk foulard Lucky Luciano had taken from his own neck and given him because he had admired it. Vizzini's son was a small-time hood, but as far as Natalia and Pino knew, the grandson who owned El Nilo had never been involved in anything remotely illegal.

The baker came out with a tray of pastries. Natalia tapped Pino's arm.

"That's Turrido, isn't it? Anthony Turrido, the baker?"

"It looks like him," Pino said. "I remember his picture on the front page of *La Repubblica* after he refused to pay protection and they burned the bakery down."

Natalia nodded. "They didn't want to kill him. Watched his shop for weeks, waited until he was out on deliveries. But the mother was in the back, cooking. Turrido's father took off when he was five. I don't think Turrido ever had a girlfriend. Mamma and the bakery were his world. I went to her funeral. One of Gambini's captains came in. Gambini hadn't intended killing the mother. He wouldn't come himself, but his man tried to press an envelope on Turrido. Turrido ripped it to pieces, torn *lira* spilling all over the floor.

"Afterward, Turrido wandered the streets, lost. I always wondered what happened to him. I was a teenager the last time I saw him."

"A courageous man," Pino said. "It makes sense that he's here. The proprietor also disdains the mob. If his father hadn't been one of them, this place would have been trashed a long time ago."

Natalia remembered asking, when she was small, why Turrido lived with his mother. And didn't have children. Because he's a good boy, her mother had insisted. An only child. So he couldn't leave his Mamma.

"Me too," Natalia had said. "I'm an only child. So I can't get married either, or ever leave you."

Her mother had laughed and kissed her, saying, "No. It's different for girls. Besides, I have your father."

Yes, different, Natalia reflected bitterly nearly thirty years later. A woman was still not considered much of anything if she is without a man. Yet it couldn't have been easy for Turrido. What if he'd wanted a wife and kids? What if he'd been in love? And after the tragedy, he'd been like a madman. What woman would have settled for him then? Was he still bitter? How could he not be?

"At least he's baking again," she said.

Pino beckoned the waitress over. He smiled at the girl. "We have a few questions about the photograph you identified of Teresa Steiner to our colleagues. How is it that you know the man who came in with her?"

"Benito? We grew up together. I heard he was becoming a priest, so I was surprised to see him with a girl."

"Has he been blind from birth?"

"He can see a little. He got sick when he was fifteen. A virus."

"Are you sure it was Benito—the man with her?" Natalia asked.

"He knew me, all right. I said, 'It's me, Tina.' He pretended he didn't know me. I didn't want to embarrass him, so I said, 'My mistake.' It didn't seem like he and the girl knew each other that well, but. . . ."

"When was this?"

"Months ago. He didn't come back, either. I figured it was because I was here. Did something happen to Benito?"

"No. To the girl."

"The girl in the crypt," Tina gasped. "Oh, my God." She made the sign of the cross, then kissed her fingers—a proper daughter of Italy, despite appearances.

"What can you tell us about him?" Natalia asked.

The girl bit her lower lip.

"Anything you can tell us will be in confidence," Natalia reassured her.

"I don't know." She scraped at her thumb. Green nail polish flaked off.

"A young girl is dead. And there may be others if we don't catch her killer."

"Even before he lost his sight, he was teased a lot because of his thick glasses. Plus he was short. And he didn't talk much." She ran her tongue over her lips. "I was his friend. For a while. Excuse me. I have customers."

"Please take my card," Natalia said. "We may need to talk with you again."

"I don't want Benito in trouble," she said, taking the card, frowning, and the next second smiling at Pino. "I'm Tina. Prada, like the designer," she added, flouncing away.

Natalia's partner seemed oblivious to the flirtation.

At a table near the door, the owner enjoyed a cup of his own coffee.

"Your baker, Turrido," Natalia said, "I knew him as a child."

"Vesuvio's. Best bread in Naples, I have to concede."

"Do you know where he lives these days?"

"Off Piazza Gaetano, by the docks. He's got a room there. He could afford better, but. . . ." He shrugged. "Did you find out anything about the dead girl? I saw her here a coupla times, but Tina waited on her."

"We're working on it, thanks."

"*Scusi*," said a familiar voice behind her. "Natalia Monte?"
It was Turrido. He showed the wisp of a smile.

She smiled back. "So you did recognize me."

"The uniform threw me. I wasn't sure. How is your mother?"

"She died. A few years after your poor Mamma."

"I'm sorry to hear," he said, making the sign of the cross.
"She's in heaven." He stepped back. "Eh, eh? Whaddya
know? One of the first women on the force, no? And a captain. Mamma would have been proud of you."

"So, how are you?" she asked. "You disappeared from the
neighborhood."

"People don't know me around here. They leave me
alone. What about you? Married? Kids?"

"No. Just the job."

"Little Natalia Monte. Who would have thought?"

"A girl was killed this morning. You must have heard
about it."

He looked pained. "Yes."

"She was a student, a beautiful girl. She came into the
café a few times, according to Tina."

"I don't wait on customers."

"But you come out sometimes, to look after the orders."

"Sometimes."

"She was tall, a redhead. One time she was with a priest."

"Sorry, I can't help you. Come by some time. For a visit."
He told her his address. "My bell is number five."

"That would be nice—for old time's sake." They smiled
at each other again, and he left.

"Turrido," she said to Pino. "He played the harmonica.
Did magic. He could make his thumb disappear. And
found coins in our ears."

Pino nodded. "You know Tonio the Dwarf? He didn't do
tricks, but he threatened us with curses. We were terrified.
We thought we'd stop growing like he did. What time is it?"

"Time to go."

"You're a million miles away," Pino said as they walked out. They were jostled on all sides by lunchtime traffic. Gates clanked down in front of the shops.

Natalia said, "Did you notice? The small *corno* around her neck? I wouldn't have taken her for the type. Tina's kind of cute."

"Whose neck? That girl's?" Pino said, putting on his sunglasses.

"Yes, that girl. Tina. My mother had a huge horn in our living room. She was convinced that our neighbor was a *jettatore*. What made her think the woman was a witch, I don't know. She'd been our neighbor forever. A pretty lady, she always wore lipstick, even when she was old. My mother couldn't very well shun her, so she bought this giant coral horn. I'm sure your aunt had one. It wasn't until recently that it occurred to me that my mother was jealous because the woman made my father blush."

"Jealousy," Pino said, steering his bicycle around a bald German doing push-ups next to a handwritten sign: *Will Work For Food.*

Truth be known, Natalia's best friend wore a *corno,* and she herself said "*buongiorno*" to the spirits upon entering her own house.

4

When Pino reached Posillipo, he chained his bicycle to a post and entered a fashionable apartment building. He mopped his face with an old handkerchief in the elevator. On the twelfth floor, a beautiful woman opened the door when he knocked.

"*Si?*" Not unpleasant—formal.

"Carabiniere." Pino showed his ID. "Sergeant Loriano."

"Oh." She stepped back to let him in. Her white pleated skirt matched the pristine apartment. The apartment was filled with fresh-cut daisies. A nod to Pino, a quick kiss for her husband who was sitting on a white couch, and she was gone.

"Please, sit down." Professor Marco Lattanza pointed to a white couch that was the twin of the one he was sitting on. "Can I offer you something? Lemonade or a drink, Sergeant?"

"Lemonade would be nice, thank you."

Professor Lattanza went to fetch refreshments. Through the picture window, ships as small as toys zigzagged in the bay.

Professor Lattanza returned with the lemonade.

"You know why I am here," Pino said. "You are Miss Teresa Steiner's thesis adviser, yes?"

Lattanza closed his eyes and pressed a finger against them. "Teresa Steiner was a thrilling student. She was working on a monograph of our neighborhood street shrines. She wanted to know everything about the history of Naples. Since I am an expert, well. . . ."

Pino reached into his bag for the photographs. He handed Lattanza two of them.

Professor Lattanza put down his glass. He looked at one and then the other. "My God, the photos, of course. You'd think the worst. But believe me, we weren't intimate with one another any more. Teresa took a short leave of absence after her mother was diagnosed with cancer. When she came back, she hardly smiled. She'd been an incredibly sunny girl. She also changed her thesis topic. I had the feeling someone else was mentoring her and helping with her project. She stopped confiding in me. She is"—he took a deep breath—"she *was* such a beautiful woman."

"Were you home last night?"

"Am I a suspect?"

"Routine questions. Everyone who knew her will be questioned."

"Certainly I was here. I worked late, but that is normal. Marissa can vouch for me."

"Anyone besides your wife?"

"I find that insulting."

"Again, merely routine."

"Of course. Forgive me. It is upsetting news. I can't imagine anything more horrible for a parent. If there's anything I can do. . . ."

"We'll need a statement as soon as possible. If you could come by? Later today or tomorrow would be best."

"Certainly."

Nice to be rich, Pino thought, back on his bike, coasting downhill past large, elegant houses. He swerved to avoid a fat gold caterpillar inching its way across the street. If it could survive another ten feet, it might end up a butterfly and dance among the roses in the *Orto Botanico* for the balance of its brief life.

He didn't need to pedal until he reached the cobblestones along the waterfront. An ocean liner floated out of the harbor, its horn bellowing. A melancholy sound of departure. He closed his eyes. For a moment, there was only the wind, the goddesses, and the sea.

"*Campesino!*" a driver screamed at him out the window of a Mercedes.

"Watch where you're going!" a woman's loud voice assaulted his ear as she raced by in a convertible. She had a nasty face, and a bony arm, which she waved at him. "*Bastardo!*" she yelled, gunning the engine.

So much for goddesses, Pino thought, and headed for the Carabinieri station.

⁓

On Piazza Borsa, students tipped their faces toward the sun. A few were reading. Girls and boys in jeans, scruffy T-shirts, and wearing backpacks; a few girls in short tops, their gorgeous midriffs on display. Had she ever been that young?

Natalia reached the Quartiere Porto, and then Largo San Giovanni Maggiore. There was the Bar Université, where she had spent countless happy hours daydreaming and reading her textbooks. Across from it, the Dante and Descartes Bookstore, another favorite destination where she had wasted many afternoons browsing. Today there must have been fifty silver scooters clumped in front of the bookshop, the popular color this year. She'd forgotten the beauty of the Cappella dei Pappacoda, the small chapel opposite the school, with its gothic marble portico and shabby door.

A monk scurried out. His heavy brown hassock must have been uncomfortable in this heat, but his only visible acknowledgment of such earthly concerns was that he was barefoot in sandals, instead of wearing the traditional heavy shoes. His rope belt swung as he walked past.

The scent of marijuana was strong in the outer court-yard. There were one or two cars parked there, but mostly bicycles. Not much had changed. The same beat-up bulletin boards and plain stone stairs, a wide balustrade, the classrooms open to the courtyard, overlooking a few neglected plantings.

A professor passed—an older portly man in a linen suit and gray straw hat. A briefcase stuffed with books and brimming with yellowed papers was clutched to his side. How many times had he delivered the same lecture? He'd probably been teaching when Natalia was a student, though she didn't recognize him.

Her first year at the University, Natalia was one of hundreds of students streaming into the shabby gray and white stone building. She did well in her studies—the first year, her paper on the female iconography of the Church won a prize, and in her second year she was honored with an invitation to a conference in Rome. She had only been to Rome once before, on a religious pilgrimage with the nuns when she was thirteen. When her professor told her she was going, her mother made a special outfit for her. She hadn't thought of it in years. Lemon-colored, the dress had a fitted bodice and a full skirt. Her mother made a little jacket to go with it. They even found shoes to match. Afterward, she never wore the dress again. Natalia felt a stab of anxiety as she entered, for the first time in years, the place where she had suffered her disgrace. She walked across the marble foyer, feeling badly until she remembered Teresa Steiner.

Bypassing the elevator, she went to the stairs. A group of students was discussing the latest Almodovar film: "What do you mean, gay theme? There is no such animal!"

Maybe there was progress, after all. One could not imagine this discussion when she'd been a student. She climbed the stairs to the third floor. At the end of the corridor, the Titian poster was a little more faded than when she'd last seen it. The Olivetti typewriter had been replaced by a computer. The same cactus with the deceptive, soft-looking growth sat on the sill.

"*Buongiorno.*" A woman looked up from a pile of papers.

"*Buongiorno, signora,*" Natalia said, holding up her ID. "Is Professor Massone in her office?"

The red lipstick bled into the cracks around the mouth, and her face had a few more wrinkles, but it was the same department secretary. A devoted Catholic woman, she began the majority of her sentences with "If God wishes it." Or was it "If God wills it"? She still wore her signature high heels. When she stood, the crooked seams of her stockings marked her thin calves.

The day Natalia's thesis was refused, she had taken her, sobbing, into an empty office, brought her coffee, and sat with her until her friend Mariel arrived.

Professor Massone was reading a journal as Natalia was shown in.

"Excuse me," Natalia said, "I'm here about Teresa Steiner."

Professor Massone stood up. "Come in." She extended her hand, "Please, sit down. Terrible. I can't believe it. She wasn't my student officially, but she came to me to talk about her work. She didn't want her thesis adviser to know. Most of the male faculty is hostile to the idea of feminist studies. I am in the enemy camp."

"Please elaborate, if you will."

"She felt terribly alone. She'd just found out that her mother had cancer. Her mother responded well to treatment, but the prognosis wasn't good. She had taken some time off and had come up with an idea about our street shrines, that they represented the female."

"Female?"

"Yes, because they were originated by men but were female iconography and tended by women from the earliest days. Her work was cutting-edge. She would have been an academic star. She was on to something. We Neapolitans take the shrines for granted. We don't see them really. Teresa was—how can I say this? She refused the compromises that become necessary as we get older. You know better than I, the Camorra involvement with the shrines. If you think about the thousands of shrines that exist, you realize how lucrative they are. At the very least, a way for the women tending them to ease their poverty, feed their families, maybe start a bank account. There wasn't a day my mother didn't toss a few coins into the shrine on our block."

"My mother too," Natalia said. "We think Miss Steiner was collecting for Gambini."

"You know, I was afraid of something like that. I tried to warn her without spelling it out, but she had a beautiful enthusiasm and you didn't want to clip her wings. Whatever she was doing, she knew Professor Lattanza would disapprove of her decision to use the shrines for her thesis topic. He's not a mobster, don't get me wrong: he's a snob."

"And her lover?"

"Yes. To make matters worse. But you know that already." She made a fist, then stretched her fingers. "Teresa Steiner was one of the most interesting students we've had in a long time. Are you all right?"

"Maybe a glass of water."

Professor Massone opened a drawer and pulled out a bottle of Pellegrino and a glass.

"Here. It must be the heat."

"Probably," Natalia said. "Thank you."

Teresa Steiner's thesis adviser and her own years ago were one and the same man. Natalia too had been close to completing her doctorate, until the same Dr. Marco Lattanza pressed against her as they rode alone in an elevator at the conference they were attending in Rome. She pushed him away, refused to sleep with him. A month later, he scrawled *Indefensible* across her black-and-white title page in blood-red ink.

Too ashamed to tell her parents what had happened, for a year she lived at home, not doing much of anything. It was Mariel who'd finally rescued her from depression, encouraging her to join the force.

"Better?" Professor Massone asked.

"Much. Thank you."

"I'd like to publish Teresa's thesis—posthumously—as a tribute to her."

"Anything else you can tell me about her?"

"She was a nice girl. Polite. Ambitious. If she had lived, she would have commanded attention."

"Ambitious enough to use Dr. Lattanza to advance her own career?"

"Hard to say. I had the feeling she came from a poor background. I never saw her in a pair of jeans. Always a skirt or dress. They were colorful but cheaply made. We are—were—about the same size. She was slimmer, but close enough. I had a couple of Prada pieces I couldn't fit into any more. I didn't want to offend her, but I took a chance. I needn't have worried. Like a child, she was so excited. She ran around the desk to kiss me. . . . oh, God!"

"I'm sorry," Natalia said.

"No, it's okay. We have to find out who killed her," Professor Massone said firmly. "I feel confident with you on the case. It will not be 'overlooked,' as so often happens when it is a female who is killed. Meanwhile, will you excuse me? I have a class in forty-five minutes, and I have not even peeked at my notes."

"Of course. About Teresa's paper? I'm curious."

"Professor Lattanza will not facilitate its publication, I can assure you of that. But I am persistent when I want to do something."

"Would jealousy of her work upset him enough for him to kill, do you think?"

Professor Massone laughed. "Well, if academic jealousy led to murder, the halls here would be strewn with bodies. I am not fond of that man, but murder. . . ."

"That was Dr. Francesca," Pino said to his partner, who had just walked in as he put down the phone. "She's established the time of death—between three and four A.M."

"You're not going to believe this," said Natalia. "Teresa Steiner's adviser was Professor Lattanza."

"I know. What about him?"

"Mr. Adviser, the one I told you about?"

"Jesus. He's coming in to sign a statement. You may not want to be in the office."

"I wouldn't miss it, but no, I don't want him to see me."

The phone rang. Pino answered. "Yes, perfect," he said and hung up. "Speak of the devil."

The professor appeared an hour later. Pino escorted him to an interrogation room. Natalia stood behind the two-way mirror. It had been ten years. Lattanza's hair was mostly gray now, but he was thin as ever. He probably still got up at five A.M. and jogged several miles from his home in Posillipo to the University. And sewed the pockets shut on his suits and sports jackets. To avoid unsightly bulges in his clothes and be confident of the figure he cut.

Today he sported an orange silk tie and a lavender shirt. Bold, you had to give him that. He was still showing off his sartorial splendor. And he was still pulling the same shit. Wait until she told Mariel.

The collar of his shirt was flipped up. The day was hot, but he was prepared for intense air conditioning.

"Professor," Pino said, taking the chair opposite. "I hope you don't mind a few questions."

"Not at all." In spite of the air conditioning, suddenly he was sweating.

"Teresa Steiner's landlady said that Teresa asked her if she could keep a dog. Teresa said she'd found it in Pompeii, that she wanted you to take it. She was angry because you wouldn't. She told Signora Santini she didn't want to see you any more. Her landlady let her keep the dog overnight, but she couldn't have another dog in the apartment because her own is quite old."

"The stray we found in Pompeii. It was a mangy thing, for one. And for another, how would I explain it to my wife? Teresa was furious. She took the dog and left me at the station. I heard she found a woman to take it. She stopped attending classes and she refused my calls. This sounds trite, but I missed her. How can I say it—I was, am basically a lonely man. I even went to the lady, Signora Lucci, and tried to buy the dog back."

"If you didn't have any contact with Teresa, how did you know what had happened to the dog?"

"The students talk."

"Did the other students know about your affair with Teresa?"

"I don't know."

"You didn't care if people knew?"

"It's not that I didn't care. I just couldn't live without her. Haven't you ever felt that way?"

"We've located the person who left a bowl of water near the body to ward off the bad spirits."

He rolled his eyes. "Ah, yes. The evil eye."

"We also have someone who might have seen the murderer."

"Who is that?"

"We are not at liberty to give out such information. Did you see Teresa Steiner any time after she broke up with you?"

"No. I volunteered to continue as her adviser, but she refused."

"That didn't bother you?"

"It broke my heart, but I only wanted the best for her."

"I'm sure your wife will be pleased to hear that."

"Marissa is a mature woman. She understands I have need, sometimes, to go outside the marriage. If you must know, it was Teresa who insisted we become lovers, not I."

"You were in love with Teresa Steiner. And when she broke up with you, you threatened her."

"That's ridiculous. No. You're wasting your time. There was someone else she was involved with—after me."

"How do you know that?"

"She as much as told me."

"You're lying."

"I'm trying to help you. Let me come clean. A confession, if you will. She broke my heart—but only a little. I was obsessed—for a week, maybe two. She wouldn't take my calls. I wasn't used to rejection. But let me speak man to man. There is an endless supply, don't you agree?"

"An endless supply?"

"Girls. Women, if you want to be 'politically correct.'"

"I suggest you didn't get over Teresa Steiner. That you followed her, up to and including the night she was killed. It was you who killed her."

"Absurd. The week before she was killed, I did follow her, but that's all. She was walking out of the University ahead of me at lunchtime. I remember it was a Monday and I'd just given my first exam of the semester. She met a man outside Cappella Sansevero. They slipped into the alley and kissed. I pretended interest in the antiques in the window of the little shop across the street. But they wouldn't have noticed me if I'd walked right past them. I waited, and they went in together. As far as I know, only clergy have the key when the chapel is closed, as it usually is on Tuesdays. But obviously I am wrong about that. When the door didn't close fully, I thought of following them in, but the chapel is small and it would have been more than obvious.

"I was curious, though, so I waited. I wondered if she'd taken up with one of my colleagues. But she came out alone. I was going to try to speak with her, but she rushed away. I knew she was interested in Sansevero. In fact, I was going to take her there myself, but she broke it off. Frankly, I was surprised she was interested. The Sanmartino Christ, of course, magnificent. But the ghoulish reproductions of the blood vessels in the anatomical models—and that two servants may have been murdered to create them. Barbaric! I thought she was more sophisticated. She was raised Catholic but didn't go to church. I guess that made her even more curious. You know how that goes.

"After her mother died, she said she hated God. As if God was a magical creature who could grant our wishes. She was a child in some ways. A gorgeous, lost child. You wanted to protect her from something. It was as if she wouldn't recognize evil or danger, even if it came up to her face."

"And you weren't that danger?"

"Hardly."

"Could you identify him—the man she was with?"

"I was too far away to get a really good look, but he seemed about my height and build. I'd say he was close to my age."

"How convenient for you."

"I'd take a lie detector test on it."

"Until the case is solved, you are under suspicion."

"This is such a waste. I am due at the University. I have a lecture this evening."

Pino stood up. "We're going to need your passport, Dr. Lattanza."

"You're joking."

"Under the circumstances, you're lucky that's all that is required."

"You are young, Officer Loriano, and perhaps you don't yet realize how things work in Naples."

"Are you threatening me?"

"How could I threaten *you*—a carabiniere, an officer of the law? I am, after all, a lowly university professor."

"You can drop it off downstairs with the officer on desk duty any time within the next three hours."

Natalia watched him read the transcript and the report, and then sign both.

"Thank you for coming in," Pino said. "We'll be in touch."

As Lattanza's footsteps faded down the linoleum corridor, Pino came to Natalia in the observation area. "You okay?"

"Do you believe him? About the other man?"

"Maybe he's telling the truth."

"That liar?" Natalia said. "But if it's true, which I doubt—only someone with seniority would have a key to the chapel. A city official, or a priest. Not that I believe Lattanza's story for an instant."

"Unless someone lent him their key."

"Unlikely. San Severo has been moved up to the top of the list of treasures the mayor made up last year to deflect attention from her poor ratings. I remember, because the Fire Department had to get an injunction to obtain access. That brouhaha didn't do anything for her popularity. What was she thinking?" She nodded. "I hope he did it, the son of a bitch."

Natalia waited at the front door of Professor Lattanza's apartment. She could swear that the woman who opened the door to her had recently cried, but her makeup was fresh and she attempted a social smile.

"Yes?"

Even though she was in uniform, Natalia flipped open her identification wallet.

"My husband is not here."

Natalia nodded, knowing he was on the way to the University to teach a four-hour graduate course.

"I am Captain Monte. May I speak to you then, if you don't mind?"

"Sure. Come in."

Natalia was sweating from the walk up the hill. Her uniform trousers were held at the waist with a safety pin under her jacket. She felt less than elegant. Then again, next to Marissa Lattanza, with her pencil skirt, tailored blouse, and high heels, most female mortals felt like slobs.

"A glass of water, Captain?" Madame Lattanza asked.

"Thank you, yes."

Natalia listened to footfalls receding. Nice to be able to afford this large a space. A carabiniere's salary was not much, but even she could afford some fresh flowers once in a while.

Marissa returned with two black glasses and yellow coasters, which she put down on the glass top of the coffee table. Natalia drank and carefully placed her glass on the coaster. She took out a notebook. "According to my partner, Sergeant Loriano, you said your husband was home last Thursday, the night Teresa Steiner was killed, is that correct?"

"Yes."

"He didn't go out?"

"Not to my knowledge."

"We have a witness who places him on Via dei Tribunali after eleven P.M."

"They must be lying."

"Are you sure, Signora Lattanza? This could be important. A young woman is dead."

"I know. Yes, it's terrible," she conceded. "But people die. This is Naples, after all."

"Did you know your husband was having relations with Teresa Steiner? Sleeping with her? That he was serious about her?"

"I seriously doubt *that*. It's an occupational hazard, working at the University. All those young girls. They don't mean anything to him."

"He took her on holiday to Procida. We have it from several sources that he was very taken with her."

She didn't say anything as she smoothed her perfect hair.

"Signora Lattanza."

"Ruttola. Signora Ruttola. I kept my own name."

An opening, Natalia thought. "That's commendable, that you kept your own name. You have your own profession, I understand."

Marissa Ruttola adjusted one of her diamond earrings.

"Yes. I'm an architect, as I'm sure you already know. If that's all, I have a meeting with a client in half an hour."

"Thanks for your time." Natalia slipped her notebook into her bag. "Beautiful flowers," she said, getting up.

"Yes, they are," Marissa Ruttola said. "We have a different kind every week. Marco—my husband—chooses them. They are always a beautiful surprise."

"Signora Ruttola, I feel I must tell you. I was a student of your husband's years ago. He made a play for me and I refused. He got me kicked out of the University."

For a moment, Signora Ruttola didn't say anything. Then: "Shouldn't you disqualify yourself from investigating him?"

"I have. At least from that part of the investigation."

Ruttola threw back her hair. "Okay. Enough polite talk. My husband was obsessed with that girl. There were always young girls, you can imagine, but this was different. The week before Teresa Steiner was killed, Marco told me he wanted to leave us and live with her. I wanted to kill him then, and I probably could have, except for the children. I found Teresa Steiner's phone number. I called her and arranged lunch with her."

"You met?"

"Yes. She was a cool one. Surprisingly sophisticated. Wearing a Prada outfit I had found the receipt for among my husband's credit card charges." Signora Ruttola waved away a thought and went on. "It was ironic. She said Marco wanted to leave me and go with her. In fact, she had broken up with him. She told me he was more of an experiment."

"An experiment?"

"Yes. She said he had told her I didn't mind his having an affair. She apologized. How could I hate her? She told me about her mother's cancer, and about Gambini. She was too open. She said she didn't like taking from the shrines, but she hated the Church as much as the mob. If the people thought their prayers were being heard, then it was immaterial where the money went. All that mattered was their belief." Signora Ruttola gestured at a lone photograph in a gray frame. "She reminded me of my daughter. These young women live life as if it were an outfit, something to try on but not wear."

She fixed Natalia with an intent look, seemingly hesitant to ask her question. Then she did anyway.

"Tell me, Captain. Do you think he stripped her of her life before she could try on her next lover?"

Pino pedaled down Via Toledo in civilian clothes, dismounted, and walked his bicycle into an alley where a few men were flipping cards on an overturned box. Like most of the men around here, they would just as soon have cut his throat as met his eyes. Luckily, they were preoccupied with the cards they'd been dealt.

Naples awakened. Sinner and saved share the same streets. The old saying came to Pino: *Il mare non bagnà Napoli.* The sea does not cleanse Naples.

The alley was so cramped that there was hardly room to hang out laundry. A few women had set up drying racks in front of their doors. A baby's underwear was arranged by color, socks in proper pairs. A woman in a housedress clanged a pot in her ground-floor kitchen visible from the street. Pino made an effort not to stare into her cramped rooms, though it was hard not to do.

He crossed Via Casarti, pushing past a group of boys playing football. One muttered something for Pino's benefit. The youth's gold chain and crucifix, prominent on his torn T-shirt, reminded Pino of Totò Riina, a teenaged thug who had kidnapped an eleven-year-old, the son of a rival gang. For two years they held the boy in the mountains. Neither the police nor the Carabinieri pursued the case in earnest. Finally, Totò strangled the child.

The little fly bumped into Pino and said something he couldn't hear over the shouting footballers.

"What did you say?" Pino asked. "I didn't catch that."

"I said, remove yourself from our game or I'll do it for you." He grinned, a bandanna strapped to his dark shiny curls, greasy with styling gel and sweat from his exertions. He was maybe twelve. Employed most likely to deliver drugs. He turned to strut for his friends.

Pino could see the kid's future as clearly as the Tiber cut through Rome. At fourteen, he'd drop out of school. Hook up with the Camorra proper to begin the tests of loyalty on low-stakes crimes they set out. The steps are as serious as entering the priesthood. He would start out among the *picciotti,* a novice for three years serving the Cause, until he had earned the title *picciotto d'onore.* Formal induction would follow. The novice opened a vein with a dagger, dipped his hand in the blood and swore to the assembled to keep their secrets and to do their bidding. Then he stuck the dagger into the table, picked up a pistol and cocked it. With the other hand, he lifted a glass of poisoned water to his lips—showing his readiness to die for the organization. He knelt in front of the dagger. A chief placed his right hand on the supplicant's head, took the pistol in his left and fired it. Then smashed the poisoned glass and embraced their new member.

Pino ignored the fresh kid. At some point he would meet him again. In his office. In the morgue. The Camorra path was centuries old, older than the Mafia, stretching back to Spain's ruthless rule of Naples that had inspired its rise. Talking to this boy would be a waste of time, much as he'd have liked to try. Besides, he was due at headquarters in an hour and needed to squeeze in a haircut before Colonel Donati could give him another lecture on appropriate appearance.

Pino continued walking his bicycle. The football grazed his calf, ricocheted off the wall and bounced back to him. He kicked it to the runt of the gang and was repaid for his trouble with catcalls. They gestured obscenely to his retreating back. He hopped aboard and pedaled off. A few blocks further along, young men on *motorini* lounged on the walk outside Salvatore's barbershop. Some, no doubt, were more dangerous than the gang he just left behind. But these well-dressed gangsters in their twenties and thirties had at least adopted a civilized veneer. Gentlemen of leisure. Unlike Rome, where each would have a cell phone clamped to his ear, they actually talked to one another. Pino was almost certain that Salvatore paid something every month so his windows would remain intact.

The skinny thug in the red silk shirt who watched Pino, affecting an air of civility, had once been a cherub with wide eyes and fat cheeks, kissed and fussed over by adoring females—his *nonna*, mama, older sisters, aunts, and cousins. But there was a price. No weakness. No tears.

A lucky few escaped their families into the priesthood. Others cleaned streets or waited tables. Others hung out around seedy social clubs like casual laborers, looking to pick up the odd job—collection on an outstanding debt, or the beating of a rival gang member. Some ran errands for a boss—sauntered to the corner store for cigarettes and a lottery ticket. Lucky numbers appeared in dreams.

Walking into the shop, Pino caught his reflection in a mirror. Certainly he was not this weary-looking soul with hunched shoulders! He straightened and took a deep breath. The chair was open. Without conversation, Salvatore cut and styled and trimmed Pino's sideburns, as he had done ever since Pino Loriano had turned twelve. Finishing in the shortest possible time, he shaved the hairline at the back of Pino's head, sprinkled talcum powder on his neck, and then brushed the powder off with the soft brush—Pino's favorite part of the process, though he would never voice it.

"Pino." The barber looked worried.

"Yes."

"There is talk," he said, bending to Pino's ear, "against you and Captain Monte." He rested a hand on Pino's shoulder. "I want you and Natalia should be careful."

"Hungry?" Mariel asked Natalia as they sat down to breakfast outside their favorite café.

Eugenio brought the usual—a basket of bread—and retreated to order their coffees. Eugenio was a boyhood friend and looked after them accordingly.

A girl with a black ponytail walked by, her tiny underpants obvious through her filmy white skirt.

Mariel made a face. "What is it with these skirts you can see through? My mother would have killed me if I ever wore something like that."

"Mine too."

Two girls skipped by in short skirts, arms around one another.

"Cute," Mariel said.

Natalia laughed. "Remember? The crochet stockings?"

"Of course."

They'd worn them under their school uniforms in grade school. Natalia got caught. Mariel waited for her loyally while Natalia did her Hail Marys and scrubbed the rectory stoop. To celebrate their crime, Natalia and Mariel had spent the rest of the afternoon sipping cappuccino in a fancy café.

"You're not going to believe this," Natalia said, buttering a piece of the thick bread.

"What?" Mariel asked. She reached into the basket to tear off a wedge of the same.

"Teresa Steiner, the girl who was killed? She was a student at the University."

"Yes."

"Her thesis adviser. . . ?"

"No!"

"Yes."

"Oh, my God. Lattanza. Did he kill her?" Mariel asked.

"We don't know yet."

"Wouldn't it be great if he did!"

Eugenio brought two coffees. Since they'd been there last, another one of his teeth had gone. A front tooth, unfortunately. No one mentioned it as he put the plates down. To be poor in Naples was to diminish, to grow used to one's losses. Food was a necessity, dentists a luxury. They had tried to slip him the money for the dentist, but Eugenio was proud and always declined.

Two men seated together near the dessert cart stared at Mariel and Natalia. They were in their fifties and wore dark glasses.

"They think you're cute," Natalia teased her friend. Mariel kicked her under the table. Bruno, another waiter, danced by, singing a rhyme about the *bruschetta* he was delivering, the innocent bread and the tomato sauce like blood.

"Compliments of the gentlemen," Eugenio winked, as he put a bottle of limoncello and two glasses on the table.

"What do they think—we're tourists?" Natalia laughed. "Tell them 'thank you' from Carabiniere Captain Monte and her friend."

Message transmitted, the men were suddenly uninterested in the women at the outdoor table.

"Are you going to finish your bread?" Natalia asked.

Mariel slid her plate across to Natalia. "I shouldn't have any more. I'm getting fat! I couldn't button my favorite pair of pants this morning."

"What are they," Natalia teased, "size two? You'll never guess who I ran into!" she added.

"Nick Keroci?" Mariel clapped her hands.

Nick Keroci had been Natalia's first crush when she was seven and he ten. Black shiny hair, black eyes. The summer Natalia turned eight, he'd moved with his family to Palermo, breaking the hearts of many in the neighborhood.

"I haven't thought of him in years. I wonder if he is still as handsome."

"He's undoubtedly a knockout," Mariel said. "Never married, waiting for you to grow up." She spooned the froth off her cappuccino.

"Anyway. Not Nick: it was Turrido I ran into. The baker. Remember him? Vesuvio's Bakery?"

"Of course."

"He's living in a run-down neighborhood by the docks. He's practically a recluse."

"Too sad," Mariel said, dabbing her lips. "Any progress on the new case?"

"The body of the poor girl was posed in the mausoleum under the church."

"How awful," Mariel said. "A religious crazy?"

"Could be, I suppose."

"*Or* your Professor Lattanza. I mean, he's a recognized expert on the Kingdom of Naples. He knows our catacombs certainly. Listen, I have a delivery coming to the shop in a few minutes. Call me later, okay?"

"Will do," Natalia said as the two friends kissed. "*Ciao!*"

Better than a sister, Natalia thought, watching Mariel stride away, her beautiful long legs moving purposefully below the white pleats. Mariel turned and waved. Then she was lost among the crowds.

Natalia owed Mariel a lot. When she first signed on for the three-year course at the Carabinieri Officers Training College in Rome, she had soon wanted to quit the male-dominated organization and avoid the persecutions visited upon its first female members. Mariel forbade her to. "What message does it send, *cara*, if you give up? That would be their victory. No. You can't." She wouldn't hear of it. So Natalia had stuck it out, painful though it was, and graduated second in her class, earning an assignment to the Corazzieri Regiment, which protected the president. Or administering its logistics, anyway, as the honor guard was all male. The other reason she had endured was Sergeant Pino Loriano.

When Natalia arrived for her first day of work at the nondescript yet intimidating six-story building on Via Casanova—the Stazione dei Carabinieri—Pino was the other most recent hire and already paired with the notorious Marshal of the Carabinieri Tommaso Cervino, famous for his work on the Nicholas Green case. Though he was pudgy and going bald, he'd informed Pino that: "A good playboy makes a good Carabiniere. And a bad playboy makes a bad Carabiniere." He was serious, and a serious misogynist.

When Natalia walked in, Marshal Cervino threatened to quit. He wasn't the only one. Dirty pictures and obscene cartoons appeared on walls in the office, on her locker, remarks were whispered and complaints made about the inconvenience of having to accommodate a female. The men's club closed ranks. Natalia felt like an outcast. A couple of times she went home in tears.

Slowly things improved. Colonel Donati partnered Pino Loriano and Natalia Monte in the elite ROS investigatory unit, and the lewd comments died down. True, Natalia and Pino were assigned the smallest office, the one without air conditioning and with the flimsiest cabinet for files. Jesus watched from his cross on the wall as the manual typewriter was carted away to make room for the computer Natalia insisted on, and they were in business.

For their first formal ceremony together, Natalia invited Mariel. Natalia wanted to show off her black Armani uniform and Mariel was properly impressed, carrying on about the polished hats and the leather belt with red trim. As plainclothes investigators, Natalia and Pino rarely had the opportunity to wear their uniforms, which were constricting. The boots, the hats, and even the holsters needed to be shined each time they were worn.

After they had worked together for a month, Pino brought her a present: a book of ancient Japanese poems.

"How beautiful!" she said. "But what's this for?"

Her partner was busily straightening a pile of papers. He blushed. The phone rang before he could answer. When he got off, he told her it was for "toughing it out."

"In that case, *I* should bring *you* a present," she laughed. "I couldn't have made it without you. Really."

"That's ridiculous," he said, not looking at her. But it was true.

Soon they were assigned a small mob murder in Castelnuovo. Forchetti territory. The dead man might have been trying to muscle in. A hard case to investigate, as no one was willing to talk. When she arrived home that night, her downstairs neighbor, Luigina, was outside her door with her ghost-like cat.

"You didn't hear it from me," Luigina said, rubbing her hands on her apron. "Carlo Forchetti, that dog. He's at his sister's. Thirty-eight Via Villari."

It was not the last time Luigina slipped Natalia valuable information before anyone else tracked it down. Forchetti's arrest and others got her promoted to a rank above her partner's. He was the only male in the force not bent out of shape about it.

The church bells tolled the hour. Natalia counted eight.

She took out a lipstick and reddened her lips. The mayor had called a meeting of the crime council. Every couple of years, after a particularly bloody week, a panel of experts from the North convened to discuss the problem of crime in Naples. For two or three days, they converged on the city. Bodyguards surrounded them, glinty eyed, ready to use their assault rifles. They even stood outside the restaurants where the experts dined on their expense accounts and caught up on gossip. A few came up with clever theories, a solution or two were bandied about. They would be put into a report. The mayor always made a point of seeing them off at the train station. And nothing changed.

The morning's meeting was a hodgepodge of experts. The Americans were familiar with the Mafia but knew little about the Camorra, so Natalia was asked to brief the assembled. She hoped she wouldn't be lectured in turn. The last time, she'd been treated to an academic's monologue on the connections between the poverty of the inhabitants of Naples on the one hand, and organized crime on the other. As if they hadn't figured that out for themselves long ago.

She was delighted to find that the group consisted of no more than two visitors: one from Berlin, one from Washington, D.C. The colonel introduced her.

"Is the Camorra in the States?" the tow-headed agent from Washington asked.

"They first surfaced in Brooklyn, New York, in the early 1900s, led by the Neapolitan extortionist Alessandro Vollero. By 1916, Vollero was *capo di tutti capi*, boss of the eastern seaboard. Eventually, the Camorra and the Black Hand—the Mafia—went to war for control. Vollero ended up in Sing Sing and the Camorra lost their upper hand. Here in Naples, the Camorra dominates, as the 'Ndrangheta does in Calabria at the toe of Italy, and the Sacra Corona Unita runs Puglia."

The gentleman from Germany wore green glasses, which

he liked to whip off when making a point and whose ear-pieces he liked to nibble when contemplating. "Your local chieftain,"—he consulted his notes—"Mr. Gambini, has interests in our country that are expanding rapidly enough to concern us. He is in the construction business in Germany, for instance, and is getting into the sanitation field."

She nodded. "Here too, of course. He holds a very lucrative contract from the city for garbage removal. One source here told us Gambini is also moving drugs into Europe through Poland and Latvia."

"Great," the American said. "Which varieties?"

"A little cocaine. A lot of heroin. He's testing the markets in those countries too."

"How big is his market here?"

Donati's cheeks puffed as he pondered. "About half a million euros a day." He raised his eyebrows and chin, signaling Natalia to continue.

"Recently a front company of Gambini's shipped some cheap wine to Berlin. Over eight thousand cases. Before it arrived, it was decanted into luxury-brand bottles and re-priced."

She was uncomfortable saying it in front of Colonel Donati, but she said it anyway: "Gambini's hold over his territory is growing, and the Camorra's over the city. The cartel's profits increase daily. They are endlessly inventive. Recently, our police shut down a mob-run radio station in Palermo after it discovered secret messages being transmitted to imprisoned *Mafiosi*."

"Secret messages?" The American actually smiled at this, flashing perfect teeth and making Natalia self-conscious about her own.

"Yes," she said, "in song dedications."

"Why am I not surprised?" said the American. "What can you tell us about this Gambini?"

"He's a *guappo*, a senior member of the Camorra. He

specializes in the costly and nonexistent. Pretending to import expensive fresh fish by air for mob fishmongers, exporting various goods that didn't exist, and charging hundreds of thousands of dollars for medical procedures like organ transplants that never occurred."

"*Ja*," the German official said. "Your clever Mr. Gambini is consolidating power, taking advantage of the 'Ndrangheta and Mafia war in our territory."

"I'm not familiar with this 'Ndrangheta," the American said.

"Another secret criminal brotherhood," Natalia said. "It dominates the drug trade at the moment. Takes in about thirty billion euros annually."

The German nodded. "I'd be more than happy to see them neutralize each other. But I'm afraid for innocent civilians. Just a few hours ago there was another assassination. This one in a mall near Düsseldorf. A forty-five-year-old woman out shopping was caught in a crossfire and gunned down, along with four men who were the primary target."

"Monstrous," Colonel Donati exclaimed with accompanying gestures. "No one is safe." He swiveled toward Natalia. "Now we have to worry about Mr. Bagarella's and Mr. Santa Paola's Camorra organizations too. You know this latest?"

"Only that Bagarella's wife committed suicide last year," Natalia volunteered.

"That's right. And Santa Paola's wife, Elena, was killed six months ago. So the two widowers spent some time in prison together. And now it appears they've exchanged wedding bands and multiplied their power, making life for the rest of us even more interesting than it already is."

"Pardon," the German said. "The killings near Düsseldorf? In the pocket of one male victim we found a singed prayer card with a picture of the archangel Gabriel on the back."

Donati gestured for Natalia to explain. "Part of an initiation," she said. "Recruits for the 'Ndrangheta hold out a hand while a prayer card is lit, and recite, 'As this holy prayer card burns, so my flesh will burn if I betray the Family.'"

The visitors thanked her for her time and enlightening talk and retired to morning coffee in the canteen.

Donati waved Natalia closer. "Two bodies were dumped just last night on Torre del Greco, in front of the tax office. Heroin is on the surge again. I'm thinking, the Teresa Steiner murder—what if the murder victim was actually Gambini's accomplice moving heroin into, say, Germany? Can we tie Gambini to the Teresa Steiner murder?"

"Not yet," Natalia said. "Not enough evidence so far."

Or ever, she thought. Gambini was too smart and kept himself too far removed from the actual deeds.

Colonel Donati's phone rang. "I have to take this. Report to me as soon as you have something, okay?"

In the hall, Natalia ran into Carabiniere Doppo. After a long engagement, he was going to marry his fiancée, who was from a small village south of Rome. Natalia congratulated him. The long engagement was a requirement—not from either family, but from the powers that be—to make sure Angelina's family was not connected to the Camorra or another of the secret criminal societies. Carabinieri were not free to pick and choose spouses like ordinary citizens. There had been too many cases of the criminal brotherhood using their pretty daughters as lures to infiltrate the force through unwary lovers. The same waiting period applied as well for the handful of women serving on the force.

What would she do if her superiors told her she was no longer free to pick and choose her friends?

Pino and Giulio were waiting for her at her desk.

"What?" she said.

"Brother Benito, that novice monk? Gambini's nephew."

"Jesus!"

"His mother's best friend? Gina Falcone."

"The bone cleaner."

6

It had been years since she or Pino had stepped into a church, much less attended one. Natalia looked closely at the confessional as they passed. She had only gone to confession a dozen times, the last more than twenty years ago when she'd been thirteen. She loved the red velvet curtain, the privacy of the small dark space, and wanted to tell the priest something dramatic that would require painful penance. She thought it a grownup thing to do. Coveting her girlfriend's boyfriend, however, barely qualified for Hail Marys, much less genuflection. Tired of the daily diet of religion and mandatory chapel attendance at her church school, she refused to attend Sunday services any more. Despite pressure from teachers and clergy, her parents respected her decision.

"How does it feel?" she said to Pino.

"Strange. But familiar at the same time."

"Yeah, me too."

It was dark and cool. Sunlight pressed through the stained glass. Natalia took out her notepad and pen as they made their way to the front of the nave. Jesuit Father Pacelli met them in the small side chapel and led them through toward the living quarters next door. The confessor to this small population of monks, he lived in their community. Pino had been taught by Jesuits at university and felt comfortable with them. They and the school had been a part of the city since the fifteen hundreds.

To attract converts back then, Jesuit evangelizers had adopted local devotional practices. They organized processions and pilgrimages and went out to preach in pairs, using the piazzas as their pulpits. Crowds had gathered, listened, and followed them down into the underground burial chambers of the *ossario*. Over drink and food, the Jesuits preached and the locals listened and were swayed.

Despite the rumor of concubinage and sexual misconduct, the Jesuits had always been the most decent of orders. Members took their vows of poverty seriously; witness Father Pacelli's worn trousers and his dog-eared sweater, mended more than once at the elbows. How different from the majority of clerics, who patronized fancy tailors for their trim black outfits and elaborate robes: like the princes of the Church, they were well cared for by housekeepers and assistants. No sign of such coddling here. In the kitchen, a novitiate cooked greens for a soup. Another washed dishes. The linoleum and tablecloth were worn and stained. A faucet dripped badly above a deep sink.

Natalia said, "We appreciate your arranging for us to talk to Benito."

"Of course," Pacelli responded, brushing back his sandy hair. "Such a terrible thing, murder."

Father Pacelli led them to a doorway. Pino stopped to read the inscription above it: Praise be to you my Lord with all your creatures—especially Brother Sun who is the day and through which you give light.

"A canticle of St. Francis," Pacelli said.

"Father," the dishwasher called after him, "I need to speak with you."

"In a moment, Milo," Father Pacelli said.

Pacelli opened the door leading to their private quarters. "His room is at the top of the stairs, third door on the right."

The stairway reminded Natalia of Catholic School with its strong smell of caustic soap. Together they ascended the steep stairs to the second floor. On the landing, a sagging wooden table with reliquaries and a tray of ex-votos—a child's hand and an adult foot. Someone interested in antiquity. Natalia sighed. Even among the Jesuits, the yearning for symbols, no matter how crude. But maybe she was being unfair. These had probably been abandoned here centuries ago and had remained ever since beneath the melancholy gaze of Jesus.

They found the monk's door. As soon as they knocked, Benito opened it. Had Father Pacelli told him they were coming?

"Benito Gambini?"

"*Sì.*"

"I'm Captain Natalia Monte. This is Sergeant Loriano. We're Carabinieri. We need to ask you a few questions."

The room, as expected, was spartan. A tiny window overlooked a courtyard encircled by a medieval covered walk. There was a bed, a nightstand, and a guitar. In a wardrobe niche hung two pairs of pants and a shirt. Benito sat on his bed. His eyelids, closed, were bruised half moons.

Pino said: "We believe you knew the girl recently murdered in the alley next door—Teresa Steiner."

The monk sat down on his bed. He bowed his head and took a deep breath. "Teresa Steiner was my friend. She was doing research on the role of shrines in Neapolitan society. I helped her sometimes. She was being followed around by her professor, a creep, and appreciated the company. She'd gone out with him for a while. After she broke it off with him, he wouldn't leave her alone, she said. Kept phoning. Waited for her everywhere. Pestered her."

"Did he threaten her?" Natalia asked.

"Maybe. I don't know. He said he'd block her graduate project. Teresa was sure he had stolen students' work before and passed it off as his own. She worried that he was planning to make off with hers."

"Did you see or hear anything suspicious the night she was murdered?" Natalia asked. She looked out the narrow window onto the roof of the meditation walk.

"I did hear something. It woke me. But I slipped back to sleep and was awoken again a little while later by commotion in the street, when I went down to see what was going on."

"How much sight do you have, if you don't mind my asking?"

"Light and shadow. Like when you look through a mist. On a good day I can make out faces. At night I can't see anything."

"And you think you heard something happening in the street and it awakened you, although your room does not face the street and the walls of the monastery are ancient and thick?"

"My hearing is acute . . . God's compensation for my vision, perhaps."

"So you may have heard Teresa Steiner being assaulted?"

The monk's face flushed. "Yes."

"Can anyone confirm that you were here in your room the night she was killed?" Natalia asked.

"Where would I go? We have prayers in community after our evening meals and retire early."

"Did you ever go to the crypts?"

"Yes, sometimes. To help the bone cleaner, Gina Falcone."

"Even with your vision so poor?"

"The dark doesn't bother me, Detective."

"Did Teresa visit you?" Natalia asked. "Was she here the night she was killed?"

"No."

"No? Are you sure you didn't come on to her?"

"What are you talking about?"

"You're Aldo Gambini's nephew."

"I have been forever. Yes. And always will be. What of it?"

"Do you do work for him?"

"No. I am a servant of our Lord."

"Did Teresa meet your uncle?"

"Yes. I asked him to help her out."

"How?"

"A family illness had reduced her funds. She was visiting the shrines for her research and running out of money. He hired her to attend to the donation boxes there. He has a franchise from the Church to gather the donations. She oversaw them in this district and serviced some herself."

"Were you in love with her?"

"What? That is none of your concern."

"I regret to say that it is now."

"Your question is inappropriate and bordering on offensive. Such things are private. Between myself and anyone for whom I may have such feelings."

"It may soon be between you and the State's Prosecutor."

Benito waved off further talk.

Father Pacelli was talking to the dishwasher when they passed through the kitchen again.

"How can I prepare the dinner without the knife?"

"Something wrong?" Pino asked.

"Nothing. A missing knife. Some Japanese thing. I'll ask if anyone has seen it after Mass. Okay?"

"Okay."

"What do you think?" Natalia asked as they stepped back into the street. "About the knife."

Pino looked back at the monastery. "Probably nothing. But I can follow up if you think it might be important. Odd that it's missing. Probably a coincidence."

"Probably."

"But I think our Brother Benito was emotionally involved with the murder victim, whether or not it was consummated or reciprocated. He has obviously been greatly affected by her death. Whether he had anything to do with it, I'm not sure."

"He's a suspect," Natalia said, "any way you look at it. The young woman's mother was ill. She needed money fast. Benito helped. Interceded with his mob-boss uncle, aided her thesis research and shrine collections. Perhaps she showed interest in him as a man. When he realized that she was involved with others. . . ." Natalia turned to her partner to see how the theory played.

"A suspect," he said, nodding. "*Certo.*"

"I'm going to check into him further."

"Let's look into the Japanese knife, too."

As they entered the courtyard, water splashed them on the head. They looked up and found the culprit watering her plants, blooming with yellow flowers.

"*Mi dispiace,*" she said. I'm sorry.

"*Non ce problema, signora.*"

Pino leaned his bicycle against a wall beneath a web of vines, hoping the rusty frame would discourage anyone from taking it. Gold-tinted leaves and drying laundry extended across the courtyard. Pino and Natalia climbed to the fifth floor. The hallway was a tangle of toys. A baby cried nearby. Natalia rapped on the door.

"Not home." A tired-looking woman with lanky ash-colored hair had come out of the door next to the bone cleaner's apartment. She was shaking a mop. Children's voices leaked from her apartment. Pino reached into his pocket for his ID.

"Eighty-two, my mother. Stubborn. She should be home relaxing with her grandchildren, not getting messed up in police business. Whadda you gonna do?"

"She may have some information about a murder case."

"I knew it." The woman pressed her palms against her eyes. "Mother of God." There was the sound of breaking glass. She threw the mop down and slammed into her apartment.

Natalia and Pino had not heard the door open behind them. Gina Falcone stood in her doorway. Her apartment smelled like a chemistry lab.

"We didn't think you were home," Pino said to the bone cleaner.

"I didn't want my daughter pestering me with her problems and her children. She thinks I have nothing better to do than chase after them. Come."

The bone cleaner waved away Natalia's badge and motioned them in. There was a small balcony that would provide light if the curtains hadn't been drawn across the windows. A pile of bones sat on her table. The flat was so full of piled boxes and stacks of everything that ever passed through Gina Falcone's hands that there was hardly a place to stand.

"Nice cat," Natalia said. A musty old tabby was camouflaged on the bed.

"Bobo," Gina said and made a kissing sound. A toddler in diapers and a shirt smeared with something—hopefully chocolate—stumbled in after them. "Christ! I forgot to close the door. Go! Out! Home to Mama. Nonna's busy."

The baby fell over, shrieking. Gina put him out and locked the door.

"We brought you something to eat," Pino said. He removed a plastic container from a bag.

"You shouldn't have," she said. She carried it into the kitchen and cleared a space for it among the bones.

"*Friarielli* and sausage?" she said. "My favorite."

She'd been washing bones in a bucket by the sink. Pino recognized a femur and a thighbone. She poured the contents of the container into an empty pan. "I can finish later."

Bobo jumped on the table, sniffing the pan. "Get!" Gina hissed, clapping her hands. Pino cut off a piece of sausage and put it on the floor. The cat rubbed against his leg, purring.

"Don't spoil Bobo," Gina said.

"We have a few questions," Natalia said.

"No free lunch—is that it? Whaddya want to know?"

"Teresa Steiner's killer?"

"Nobody was down there when I found her."

"You knew the girl was visiting the shrines that Gambini controls."

"Yes."

"You know Mr. Gambini."

"Aldo Gambini and his brother Pasquale and I grew up together. Pasquale is Benito's father. Benito's aunt was my deskmate in school. I'd starve if it wasn't for a few people at the cemetery and Aldo Gambini. Aldo doesn't forget. The government never remembers us unless we cause trouble."

"If Aldo Gambini knew you told us about the shrines, he wouldn't like it. If he thinks you ratted on him—"

"He wouldn't touch a hair on this head." She tugged a clump of hair, her finger crooked with arthritis.

"Family ties have never stopped him in the past."

"What do you expect? He is an important man. He does what he must. God watches over me."

"God may watch over you, but who will intercede if it goes hard for you?"

"Don't be a smartass. You young people don't know what hard is. When there was no work and people set fires in the streets, and when they ate all the exotic fish in the old aquarium during the War—Gambini helped me through all that. Where was the government then?"

"We haven't found the girl's murderer," Natalia said. "I was hoping you might have something to tell us. Her family deserves an answer."

Gina was silent.

"What about Benito Gambini?" Pino said.

"The boy is a *monachello*. And blind. Why would you bother with him?" She lifted a stone absentmindedly. Natalia recognized it. The *pietra del sangue*—the bloodstone. More superstition.

"Who did you see in the alley the night Teresa Steiner was killed?" Natalia asked.

Gina pursed her lips.

Natalia remembered that as kids, she and Mariel had called her *la strega*—the Witch. Now she looked like an ordinary woman—grown old.

Pino cleared his throat. "Signora, we can make life difficult if you won't cooperate."

"I talked to you Carabinieri already," the old woman said and picked up the fat tabby cat. "She was writing something for her University—about the shrines. I warned her. Be careful. You can ask the wrong person a question, and the next thing. . . . But you can't tell young people anything."

A tiny girl appeared, face smudged and wreathed in curls. "Nonna! Nonna!"

"Nonna's busy. Go away. See the lady?" She pointed at Natalia. "She's going to put you in jail."

Gina Falcone swept up her granddaughter and took her out the door. A few seconds later, she was back.

"My daughter thinks I don't have enough to do, without babysitting."

"Someone saw you in the alley the morning the girl was killed."

"So?"

"Did you see anything, anybody?"

"The girl was German, not from Naples. There are no bone cleaners there. She shouldn't have to spend years in Purgatory. I wish I could clean her bones, once they are free of the corrupting flesh." She paused. "Santa Maria del Purgatorio," she said. "I can tell you anything you want to know about the church. I know it better even than old Father Cirillo. I was married there. Decades ago. A lot of people were getting married then. The war. My mother had a piece of silk. She saved it for me from when I was born and made me a gorgeous wedding gown.

"I cherished that dress forever. But my daughter wasn't interested. Miss Fancy-Pants said she didn't want some old rag. I tried to warn her about her fiancé. A ladies' man before they were married. For her, the stars rose and fell on that two-bit thug. Left her when she was pregnant. Died a natural death, I'll give him that."

She made the sign of the cross and kissed her fingers. Natalia decided they'd had enough and signaled Pino with a raised eye. They told Signora Falcone they might be back.

Outside, a turquoise motor scooter backfired; a young girl with rainbow-colored hair clutched the driver around the waist. Street sweepers in lime-green uniforms propped their orange brooms against a wall to take a break. The colors dazzled after the dreary gray of Signora Falcone's morbid world.

⁓

"I'm Teresa's friend, Elsa Halme." The girl hovered by Natalia's office door.

She was wearing boys' pants, charcoal gray, and a rust-colored sports jersey. Her hair was short. It looked as if she'd cut it herself without the benefit of a mirror. It was too short on the sides, and she had it flattened on top. It still had all the elements of a Mohawk.

There were several piercings—one above her left eyelid, just beneath the wisp of her brow, and two in her nose. Natalia tried not to stare, or to think about what must happen when this girl caught the inevitable cold.

Elsa Halme was a large girl, big-boned, who hunched over to hide her height. Her pale blue eyes were her nicest feature.

"Come in," Natalia said. "Have a seat. So you knew Teresa Steiner?"

"We were close friends."

"Oh?"

"I don't know where to start. My Italian is not so good. I'm from Finland."

"You're doing fine. Can I get you something? Some lousy coffee?"

This brought a smile.

"No, thanks. I am having trouble sleeping. I meant to come sooner. I've been too upset."

"Would you feel more comfortable if I closed the door?"

"Perhaps. Thanks."

Natalia did so and returned to her desk. "So?" she said gently.

"Teresa was my dearest friend at the University," Elsa said, looking at her hands. "My only friend in Naples. I'm foreign, for one thing." She looked up at Natalia. "People can't figure me out. I don't dress feminine. It doesn't help that I'm shy. For a while I was very unhappy. Teresa and I were in a couple of classes together. One was a life drawing class. Not to boast, but I'm pretty good at rendering. She was taking it as a lark. She admired a couple of my drawings and invited me for coffee. Said she knew what it was like to feel like an outsider. I was comforted for the first time. Then she took me to see the Caravaggio paintings at the museum. They were just so"—Elsa broke down momentarily and wiped at her cheeks—"exquisite."

When Natalia had been a student at the University, the Museo di Capodimonte was her second home, the Caravaggios her favorite as well. Often she had been the only visitor there. She mentioned them once to Pino when she was filling him in on her aborted career at the University. He had played football in the park on Capodimonte, but had never stepped inside the museum. Natalia took him to that very room with the Caravaggios, and he'd nearly swooned.

"What kind of a student was she?" Natalia asked.

"Super," Elsa replied, somewhat recovered. "Insightful, thoughtful. Teresa was on the fast track academically. She used primary sources almost exclusively, and even went into the streets to research. Her thesis adviser and sometimes other students made fun of her, but she was on to something important. That the early deities were female until the men took over and suppressed them. And she made other connections. Dangerous ones, maybe. Teresa was particularly interested in the Church and the Camorra."

"Ambitious," Natalia said.

"Yes. She was. It took me a while to understand it. We don't have such complications in Finland. We have socialized medicine, not organized crime. Existential questions. We have aquavit. Good and evil? God? No one believes in that stuff. And if they did, God wouldn't be male." Elsa laughed. "My country is cold and quiet. People keep to themselves. Finland is black and white and gray most of the year. I wanted to escape. The Bay of Naples was wonderful and startling after the Baltic. The colors and the people. Sorry. I don't mean to be patronizing."

"On the contrary," Natalia said. "Teresa Steiner was colorful as well, no?"

"Amazing, yes. Wardrobe and personality both. She loved Naples, but she was not like Neapolitans—she was sunny, happy. About a month ago, she said she needed my help. She had to go home to take care of her mother. You know about her mother?"

"Yes."

"That's when she told me she was working for Mr. Gambini, that he had given her a small territory to supervise, meaning the collection of donations left at the shrines. She was making some extra money from it. Not a lot, but something. She wanted me to take over her territory for a few days. She confided in me. I knew everything—even about her affair with her professor. I worried for her, but she said she could take care of herself, and she could. I mean, she did until. . . ."

Elsa started to cry again.

Natalia handed her a tissue. "This can't be easy for you."

"Her professor was in love with her. But Teresa was tired of his power plays. She wanted out of the relationship. When she told him, he got very angry."

"Did he threaten her?"

"Yes. That's when I told her. . . ."

"Told her what, Elsa?"

"That I was gay and knew she wasn't, but that I loved her anyway and would stand by her."

"What did she say to that?"

"She laughed. Hugged me and laughed. 'You'll get over it,' she said. And then we spent the night together." Elsa wiped at a tear streaking her cheek.

"Was she gay?"

Elsa smiled. "No. Just curious. I won't. Get over it, I mean."

She might well not . . . not for a long time, Natalia thought. Whatever else she was, Teresa Steiner had been a powerful personality.

"After she was killed," Elsa said, "Professor Lattanza asked me to stay after class—I have one course with him. He warned me that if I told anyone about him and Teresa, he'd make sure I didn't get my degree. As if anyone in the department didn't already know."

"How did she meet Gambini?"

"She went for a weekend to a resort with Professor Lattanza. They had a fight and he stormed off. Gambini picked her up while she was eating dinner in a restaurant by the waterfront. She thought he was a harmless old man." Elsa shook her head. "Even I knew better. The next day he took her out on his yacht, said he had a nephew her age in Naples. A nice boy she should meet. She thought that was sweet of him. A 'gentleman,' she said. She told him about her mother and her cancer. He offered her work collecting from the shrines. She said it was a great opportunity not only to help her mother, but to see how it all worked with the shrines."

"I noticed she had some designer clothes. Odd, on a student budget."

"Hand-me-downs. Whatever she wore looked stylish, even things she had bought on the streets. She insisted that I keep something when I covered for her, but I wanted her to send it to her mother. She went and bought me a beautiful poster for my room and sent home almost all the rest of the money she took from the boxes. My poor Teresa."

"A dutiful daughter," Natalia said.

Elsa smiled sadly and nodded.

"Yeah. Except . . . Teresa Steiner's mother?" Natalia added softly. "She died when Teresa was a child."

"Excuse me, Captain," Giulio interrupted. "You have an urgent call from Sergeant Loriano."

While Natalia took the call, Elsa scribbled something on a piece of paper, then slipped out.

"Pino. What do you have?"

"What kind of money did we find in Teresa Steiner's room? Anything?" Pino asked.

"Thirty euros in a drawer. A few in her purse."

"She had an account. I'm at the bank now."

"Which one?"

"Banco di Napoli. A month before she died, Teresa Steiner opened a bank account with a cash deposit of 21,000 euros."

7

Pino headed for the Zen Center. He bumped over the black cobblestones past the markets setting up on Vico Nuovo ai Librai. Grapes and oranges beckoned, jewel-like, despite the fact that the morning air already stank with garbage.

The newsstand on his corner was still shuttered: a death in the family. Workers standing at high tables just outside coffee kiosks hurriedly gulped espresso and tossed the paper cups onto the ground. At the other end of the chasm, between the two-hundred-year-old residential buildings, Vesuvius rose in the distance. Pino's mother had been a girl the last time it erupted.

Walking briskly, he soon reached his destination. Inside the Zendo's meditation room, Pino took off his jacket and sat on the floor. All three Buddhist monks in Naples lived in the rooms on the floor above. Rarely did Pino see them. Rarer still to find them floating through town in their cherry robes.

But this morning proved the exception. One of the monks beat on the *mokugyo,* a drum that looked like a blowfish. An offering of oranges sat on a porcelain plate before the shrine. It was only when Pino looped his legs into the cross-legged Lotus position that he realized there was someone else sitting closer to the enshrined golden Buddha.

The diamond sutra. Pino recognized the chant and joined in the Sanskrit, familiar from years of practice. The diamond sutra was a favorite: Subhito asks Buddha about the nature of reality. "Reality is change," says the Buddha.

It was definitely a girl, judging from her voice. Unfamiliar with the chant, she was trying to make sounds that fit in. The sound of her small sobs broke the silence when the drumming and chanting stopped. Pino stood and walked to her.

It was Tina, the beautiful waitress from El Nilo. Her short blond-and-green hair was done up in small batches banded together in stalks all over her head. Even with the bizarre hairdo, she was stunning.

"I'm okay," she sniffled. "Just a romantic problem."

"Anything I can do?"

"No." Tina shook her head.

Then she was standing and running, her unhappiness swirling after her. It was quiet in the room. The monk had slipped out. The incense, a pile of ash, smoked sweetly. Pino inhaled, imagining the sea and a seagull's melancholy song.

When he came out, the sun was bearing down through the rusted leaves of the lone tree on the avenue. He looked for the girl. Silly to imagine she would have stayed around, but he looked anyway. Nowhere. He retrieved his bicycle from behind Tommaso's newsstand and set off.

⌒

Lola's head was already a crown of shiny foil when Natalia was let into Fionetta's beauty parlor. Natalia greeted the proprietress and bent to kiss her childhood friend before taking the chair next to her. The tall window shades remained discreetly closed, as usual, when Lola got together with her old friends for an early-morning appointment before the salon actually opened. Mariel had yet to arrive.

Mariel, Lola, and Natalia had attended elementary school together and survived adolescence sharing the same classes. They got their first brassieres together and gossiped incessantly about their rivals and first beaus. As they grew older, Lola's family proved a problem. The Nuovolettas were Camorra. Her grandfather was sent away during the Maxi trials, after which her father tried to go straight, but the temptations and the pressures proved too great. He got into contraband-cigarette smuggling and expanded into hard drugs. Lola was twelve when he was gunned down. Her mother took over the smuggling.

Signora Nuovoletta was a country girl from a mountain village in Abruzzo. Her parents moved the family to Naples, where she met and wed Lola's dad. A real love match. When Natalia visited, she remembered being embarrassed by their lingering kisses and the gentle slap her father gave her mother's ample behind. Nothing like the physical expressions her parents allowed themselves.

Natalia loved Lola's birthday parties, which grew even more lavish after her father was killed. However, Natalia's and Mariel's parents forbade them to attend any more, and that was the end of pony rides and elegant cakes and presents. Nonetheless, the three of them continued the tradition, meeting secretly to celebrate. They were, after all, distant cousins, Nonna insisted. Family.

At fourteen, Lola—a fat kid with sagging knee socks— turned svelte and augmented her school uniform with a bustier. The nuns sent her home. Within a week, she'd quit school and was serving drinks in her uncle's bar. At eighteen, she married her second cousin, Frankie. As a wedding present, Frankie was given the carting business in the district. Lola and Frankie built a luxurious home in Posillipo but preferred the simple rooms above the bar and remained there to this day, using the other as a vacation house.

By the time Natalia and Mariel started at university, Frankie was the head of the local gang, the *capo paranza*, and Lola was a glamorous young matron holding court at the latest hot café with the other wives and sisters of Camorra captains. But whenever possible, or when the occasion demanded it, the three of them got together quietly to gossip and celebrate.

"What is Madam having done today?" Fionetta said, frowning and holding up Natalia's gray curls. "Some color?"

"A trim," Natalia said.

Fionetta hadn't changed her beehive hairstyle since the three friends first came to her at sixteen, hoping to find the secret to looking older. "Onetta" was fragrant with Chanel and the holding spray that lacquered her hairdo.

"Can you believe the garbage?" she said, peeking out around the drawn blinds.

"What's this?" Natalia said, holding up Lola's wrist.

Lola beamed. "My new bracelet."

"Nice."

"Nice? It's *gorgeous,* is what it is. Twenty-two-carat diamonds set in gold."

"From Frankie?"

"Yeah."

"Special occasion?"

"I don't know." Lola looked pensive. "I think he's whoring around on me."

"Frankie?"

"Yeah. Frankie."

"I don't think so, Lola. The guy worships the ground you walk on. Maybe he just had a success . . . in business."

"Maybe." Lola laughed. "Look, I love the man, but he isn't the brightest star in the sky."

"How are the kids?" Natalia asked.

"Weeds. Nico is this tall." She held out a hand, a meter high. "He's a head taller than the other two. They all pester me about when Aunt Natalie and Aunt Mariel are coming over and bringing more presents."

Besides being discreet, Fionetta was also nearly deaf. Nonetheless, Lola beckoned Natalia to sit in the chair next to hers, and leaned over to whisper. "I had a visit from Aldo Gambini the other day. When Frankie was out."

"No kidding."

"At first I thought maybe he was sniffing around."

"That old man?"

"Old men indulge in sex, too, Natalia. Remember sex?"

"But with one of his captains' wives?"

"It's been known to happen. But that wasn't it: he has babes all over and a serious *amorat* on the side, named Bridget. He wanted advice." Lola leaned even closer. "Gambini is recruiting women."

"Great," Natalia said. "Feminism lives. But he's a little late. Rosetta 'Ice Eyes' Cutolo ran her brother's operation for thirty years while he was in prison. Ermina Giuliano ruled the Forcella section around the train station forever. And Maria Licciardi controlled the Secondigliano district and waged a drug war with rivals. Shot it out with other Camorra women in the streets. A dozen people died, I think."

Lola turned serious. "He was also trying to find out about you. I couldn't tell whether he was expecting me to tell you or not. I'm sure he knows we still see one another from time to time. So I think maybe his asking after you was a message." She screwed up her face. "Don't know for sure."

"Probably."

"Yeah."

Natalia didn't have to ask what the unspoken message might be: stay out of Gambini business. She shrugged. "I have to do my job."

Lola gave her an exasperated look. "Think about yourself for once. You don't see your boss out on the street, do you? He travels with three bodyguards in two cars. Three. Who's looking out for *you*?"

A knock at the front announced the arrival of Mariel, splendid-looking as always in a matching silk blouse and linen skirt, hair a sleek gold cap, perfectly groomed.

"Sorry I'm late. I was trying to cope with the garbage out in front of the bookstore. I had exactly one customer all day yesterday. The stench is horrible. The whole street is strewn with uncollected garbage, from the Porta Alba to Piazza Dante."

"Here too," said Fionetta, and helped her into a salon frock.

"What did I miss?" said Mariel.

"Lola wants to know how many dates I've had in the last half year." Natalia touched a curl descending over her eye. "I had to confess: none."

"Men are overrated," Mariel said. "I prefer my cat."

"Em, you could date anyone you wanted," Lola said.

Natalia agreed. Mariel was smart as well as gorgeous. Natalia was less thrilled with the image of herself in the mirror, however.

"Look at Nat," Lola said. "She needs a makeover. *Cara*, do you ever consider wearing lipstick? Here. Take mine. You look white as a sheet."

"I can't wear that shade of red." Natalia pushed back the shiny tube.

"Don't be stubborn. Try it, at least." Lola swiveled the tube open as she rose from her chair and applied a swath to Natalia's lips. "There." She stood back to admire her quick work. "You look terrific. Doesn't she?"

"Not bad," Fionetta said, already mixing the chemicals for Mariel's touchup.

Mariel always encouraged Natalia to indulge herself with beauty treatments. "Maintenance" is how Mariel put it. She had been largely unsuccessful. Mariel treated herself to a salon visit once a month. There she got a manicure, a pedicure, a massage, and a dye job that kept her lustrous hair as shiny as it had been since her youth. But the salon was well beyond Natalia's budget, and even if it hadn't been, she had zero tolerance for marking time as a prisoner in so-called beauty parlors. So gray my hair will be, she mused, taking up the hand mirror and studying her unruly curls.

"Get these off me," Lola said, pointing to the foils covering her hair. "I'm done and I have to get going." She dug in her bag for her cell phone.

"Don't forget," Mariel said. "We're meeting in the usual place at seven on Natalia's birthday."

Fionetta removed the foils and brushed out Lola's long hair with a few deft strokes. "*Perfetto*," Lola said. "*Ciao. Ciao.*"

She kissed them each good-bye and clicked across to the door in her red heels.

"A force of nature, that girl," said Fionetta, scissors clicking as she started on Natalia.

Natalia nodded and pondered the mute warning delivered by her friend. As a child, she had fallen asleep to stories of Peppe "Long Nose" Misso and learned young about *pizzo*, the tax imposed on shopkeepers. When she stopped at Anatolia's candy store for her weekly chocolate, Enzo Spina was invariably there in the back. After witnessing him take a wad of bills from Anatolia, Natalia, with the innocence of a seven-year-old, asked "What's that for?"

"Children shouldn't be nosy," Enzo had said, tapping his large nose to illustrate.

"Why not?" Natalia asked.

"To protect the store," Anatolia said.

"From what?"

"From bad people," Enzo said, winking at Anatolia. "Now get over here and give us a kiss."

"No," Natalia said. She moved away.

"Do as he says," Anatolia said.

Natalia did. Enzo's beard was rough and scratchy and he smelled like cigarettes and wine. He must have kept his word about protecting Anatolia's store, though. She remained a fixture in the neighborhood for many years, often dragging her chair onto the sidewalk to hold court with the other widows. Her hair was lacquered black, well into her nineties. That she was low-level Camorra herself, and might have laundered money and sold tax-free cigarettes, didn't occur to Natalia until she was on the force.

As Fionetta finished the styling, Natalia's pager and phone both went off. Never a good sign. *Murder—Sorrento*, read the message.

The Friday traffic was heavy all the way out of the city. The sun was fierce, the car's air conditioning dicey at best. Natalia turned it off and rolled down the windows. Better hot air than none at all. A few Neapolitans were bathing in the fetid harbor. Many others were attempting to escape the unwelcome aromas wafting through Naples. Those lucky enough to possess a vehicle or rusty motorbike strapped on their luggage and set off. Traffic eased before she had to resort to the siren, much good as it would have done in moving her through the still-crowded streets.

The call had come in from the police in Sorrento. Neapolitan Carabinieri normally wouldn't be called to an investigation in Sorrento. But as a member of the RAS elite within the Carabinieri mandated to investigate anything involving the Camorra, she had been summoned. The victim was reported to be a Naples resident, and the murder had the earmarks of a criminal syndicate hit.

Reaching the outskirts of town, she thought she'd finally escape the stink of the Waste Management Crisis, as it was called by the politicians and press. But the outside shoulder of the road was strewn with garbage dumped by desperate Neapolitans. Outraged by the incompetence and corruption, they'd refused to recycle anything whatsoever and were separating nothing. Everything got tossed out together to bake on the roadways and streets. Could anarchy be far behind? She was some distance south of the city before the heaps of roadside garbage finally diminished.

As Natalia approached the intersection where the victim's van stood pushed across the road, traffic came to a stop. The road had no shoulder, so she maneuvered onto the painted median and stuck her siren on the hood of the unmarked Fiat. Blue light and siren screaming, she put her foot to the floor and reached the scene in minutes, grateful that no one on a motorcycle had had the same idea about getting around its four-wheeled neighbors.

The area was properly cordoned off, though the flares on the ground seemed redundant in the glare of the morning sun. Natalia flashed her ID as she walked to the white van that stood idle across several lanes. Its cab door was open and the driver sat upright, safety belts still in place. City police milled everywhere, clearing the way for an ambulance, containing gawkers that stood by the side of the road, directing traffic around the impediment, directing one another. Her "nemesis," Marshal dei Carabinieri Cervino, was chatting up the constabulary.

"I guess they broke *his* horns," she overheard him say. The two chuckled.

The dead driver was a bloody mess. On what was left of his head sat black devil's horns like those a child might wear on All Saints Night. His thick white hair was streaked with blood. She would know that pompadour anywhere. Angelo Tortorino. Proprietor of a popular gourmet shop and restaurant in the Fontanelle district. He was nearly unrecognizable, the single shot having taken out an eye and most of his mouth, which was stuffed with euros, a comment apparently on his fatal greed.

Natalia flashed on the man she'd seen lying dead in the street when she was eight. Her schoolmate's father, a shoe-maker who worked out of a tiny shop below their apartment. He had often treated the two of them to biscotti and hot chocolate in the winter, apricots and strawberries in spring. He'd missed a payment and mouthed off to the collector, the neighbors said. And then he was dead, like this.

According to scuttlebutt, which Natalia had been privy to, Tortorino had spoken against Gambini and the rotting garbage ruining his restaurant business, had even put up a picture of the mob boss wearing devil's horns.

Cervino dispatched officers to protect the immediate family. The immunity the Sicilian mafia reputedly had once granted family members and innocent civilians had never been accorded by the Camorra. If the offender was "in the wind," relatives were substituted: wives, mothers, cousins, even children. No one was exempted from the Camorra's wrath and vengeance. Not old girlfriends or distant cousins. Priests, policemen, prosecutors, investigating magistrates—all had been targets of Camorra assassins.

A Sorrento detective approached her, his ID clipped to his lapel.

"Tried to cart away his own garbage, from the looks of it. I guess he got desperate—but, Jesus, what was he thinking?"

"Yeah," Natalia said.

Neapolitans were an odd lot, living as they did at the edge of a volcano. When an eruption threatened, the city would activate its plan to evacuate the populace in a forty-eight-hour window. Police and firemen would be deployed and all roads would be made outgoing. Yet no one would leave town. The beltway and highways would remain empty, the citizens ensconced in their favorite cafés.

"The horns?" the detective said. "Driven into his head with a nail gun."

"You missed an important call-out, Sergeant," Natalia said, looking up from her notes at Pino.

"My bike had a flat. Sorry."

Natalia had given up on her campaign to insist that Pino wear his watch, which she had bought herself, from the Bangladeshi by the train station. Pino had worn it for one week, forgot it the next.

"Maybe," she said, "you need to think about giving up that bicycle of yours."

"Yes, Captain."

She held out the report she'd just typed. "Angelo Tortorino. Gunned down this morning, trying to haul away some of his garbage."

"Christ."

"Yeah. The man died for a load of garbage."

"Sorry to have missed the call-out, Captain."

"Apology accepted. But Pino, it really is time you joined this century, know what I mean?"

Pino took the report and began scanning it.

"Colonel Donati," she said, "has called a meeting in a few minutes to discuss this killing and the garbage crisis. A female resident of the Spanish Quarter is in the hospital. They suspect cholera. Likewise an elderly priest who took ill last night. He died on the way to the hospital."

They were the last to enter the conference room. Colonel Donati was already at the lectern.

"Tourism is being negatively affected. The mayor is pissed. She hates the publicity the garbage crisis is generating and would just as soon let the rival mob carters settle their problem as they always have—violently and privately. Except there's nowhere for the garbage to go, really. The landfills are full and officially closed, despite the insistence of the prime minister, who is carrying on about the unfinished incinerator project, but that's not happening either."

"Why kill Tortorino?" Marshal Cervino asked.

"Disrespect. An object lesson for everyone else. A week ago, he put up a picture of Gambini in his store showing him with devil's horns. A week later. . . ."

Cervino cleared his throat. "I hope he was already dead when the nails went in."

"The medical examiner hasn't said yet." Donati shook his head. "Just when things couldn't get worse, a child fell ill yesterday after eating buffalo mozzarella. Seems the accumulation of garbage is poisoning the water runoff, which is poisoning the water table, which is contaminating the local water itself, whose flavor gives our mozzarella that distinctive taste."

Pino said, "Yeah, *E. coli.* Who is challenging Gambini on the garbage removal?"

"The consensus guess is that Bianca Strozzi's group is ramping up, leasing and buying heavy hauling equipment. Since Gambini began expanding beyond Naples and looking abroad, his group's power base has dissipated a little at home, making Miss Strozzi more ambitious. And more aggressive. What is happening is a struggle between Camorra factions over the right to haul garbage. Never mind that it has nowhere to go at the moment. I suppose it's the principle of the thing."

"I don't think it is that alone," Natalia said. "I suspect that the trash collection is vital for another reason."

"That being?" Donati asked.

"I think Gambini has been using the trucks to camouflage the transport of major drug shipments. This trash-collection crisis has forced them to invent alternate methods and reduce the size of the quantities they can move at a time, probably considerably smaller than the shipments the massive garbage trucks cloaked. They want to hold on to their means of making big deliveries undetected."

All eyes turned to Natalia. "Gesù," Donati said. "That gives me pause."

"Sort of perfect," Cervino added. "Who is going to crawl through all that crap to search for illegal drugs? You may well be right, Captain." It was the first positive nod the marshal had ever given her.

Colonel Donati collected his papers. "Marshal Cervino will handle this murder investigation. We will keep you abreast of developments at further briefings."

~

Finally, work was over for the day. Pino arrived home and collapsed in his armchair. On the coffee table sat his bracelet made from the seeds of the tree beneath which Buddha sat and found enlightenment. Ordinary-looking brown seeds carved and strung on elastic. Sometimes Pino wore it, mostly not.

Pino had only been a practicing Buddhist for five years. He had left the Church when not yet an adolescent, soon after his mother died. And even if she had lived, he might have come to the same decision. He hated the Church's take on sin and damnation. Life on earth was enough of a challenge.

Impulsively he slipped the bracelet on. There was a knock on his door. It was close to ten P.M.—late for a visitor, and Pino's visitors were few and far between. Natalia? More likely Signora Lucci from upstairs, with a plate of food—or a new scheme to save his soul. Just in case it wasn't, he took along his pistol, holding it barrel-down behind his thigh.

"Yes?" He cracked the door open, expecting to see his neighbor. But it was the girl from the bakery—Tina. In a black lace skirt—the style they were all affecting—with a petticoat sticking out. And leggings, in spite of the heat. To top it off, she was wearing hiking boots. But her midriff was bare and smooth, her lips moist and red.

She laughed. "You look funny in pajamas."

Her hair was pinker than last time, when he'd seen her crying in the meditation room of the Zendo. Christ. He rubbed his beard. Barefoot, he was in cotton pajama bottoms with umbrellas printed on them. No shirt.

"What are you doing walking around so late?"

"I couldn't sleep. Can I come in?"

"How did you know where I lived?"

"Do you think I'd make a good detective?"

"I'm going to call a cab for you."

"Don't. Please. I'm eighteen. You're safe . . . sort of." She leaned into the doorway. "I have a problem."

"A police problem, or another problem of the heart?" he asked.

"The latter. And it's the same romantic problem as before."

"What?"

"You, Sergeant Loriano."

Pino sighed. "You are not an adult."

"Nor am I a child. I know what I'm doing." The pout was perfect: sullen and erotic.

"You *think* you know what you're doing. You are involved in a case I'm working on. I could lose my job."

"Shhhh. Nobody will know. Please?"

Pino led her through to the kitchen. He'd give her a drink of juice or water, he thought, then call a cab. Knowing all the while that he was lying to himself. You're a coward, he admonished himself. If anyone at the station could see this. If Natalia . . . Christ!

But Natalia had made it clear that she was not interested in him. And who could blame her? She could do better than a solitary, eccentric man, he a lowly sergeant, she a captain. His last girlfriend had accused him of being a monk. Some monk. Weaknesses of the flesh, Pino thought, and loneliness. Rationalizations, he knew, as he reached for the drinking glasses, and the girl pressed up against him, wrapping her soft arms around his back.

8

When Pino woke, it was daylight. His neighbor across the courtyard had already hung out his laundry. Everything he owned was either black or white. His clothing punctuated the faded pink walls. Pino's arm brushed a soft breast. Pink hair blossomed on his pillow. She'd draped one leg over his, and she was snoring. He couldn't resist looking at the child's tuft of hair covering her sex. He took in the magnificent body that had been his last night.

A dragonfly floated into the room. Gauzy wings. Tiny beads, like emeralds, along its back. Pino could hear the old woman in the apartment above, talking to her cat. No doubt she had already been to confession. For her, a day without its burdens, its suffering, didn't count.

Pino showered and returned wrapped in a towel. He found Tina awake.

"Come here, baby," she said.

He walked to the bed and kissed her.

She grabbed his shoulders, trying to pull him down.

"I have to get to work," he said.

"Can't you take a day off?"

"Not today."

"You know something odd? Really weird?"

"What?"

"Turrido."

"Who?"

"Turrido, the baker at El Nilo."

"What about him?" Pino pulled on his pants.

"I don't know. He's a loner. A little odd. Three days ago, he came to work dressed in black. Except for his apron. But nobody had died. It's not like he's married or anything. He's too strange." She laughed. "And a couple of times when I went into the kitchen, he was down on a knee, praying. I know he's religious, but . . . I think he knew the girl who was killed—Teresa Steiner."

"What?"

"See? Now I have your attention."

"Tina, this isn't a game. Why didn't you say something before, when we came around?"

"I didn't think it was anything. Then I remembered. About a month ago, I left a scarf in the bakery, and I went back for it late in the afternoon. Turrido was sitting at a table talking to a woman. He never sat down, so that was odd. I figured she was a relative or something. Her back was to me. But I could swear she had red hair. Wouldn't I make a good detective? We could work together."

Natalia thumbed through the files of open cases on her desk. The stack was growing. The oldest and thickest file was one she had just signed out: Vesuvio's Bakery, in which Turrido's mother had died. She and Pino spent an hour with it, then left in the unmarked Fiat. They drove through the Forcella district past the main railroad station, down the hill toward the bay. The city flattened as it progressed to the sea. Near the harbor, government buildings and boxy sixties hotels paralleled the strand. They followed a band of green parkland toward the seedier waterfront farther east. Finally arriving, Natalia got out and stretched. Freighters and cruise ships plied the harbor, emitting melancholy sounds of arrival and departure that carried across the water. She closed her eyes. For just a moment there was only wind and sea.

"Fuck," she said. Pino was surprised, as she rarely cursed.

Two little girls twirled umbrellas. One was blond, and the other dark-haired—"Snow White and Rose Red," as Natalia recalled from a childhood tale. They followed after as she and Pino walked.

"You're a police!" the youngest announced, pointing at Natalia.

"Not police, stupid. Carabinieri! Don't you know *any-thing*?" the older one said.

"We're national police. It's almost the same," Natalia said to the dark-haired one. Her name was embroidered on her jumper. She couldn't have been much older than three, and she looked like she was about to cry. "Anna, isn't it?"

"Yes." She smiled, dignity restored. A front tooth was missing.

Natalia and Pino found the address. Natalia went to the downstairs door alone, carrying a box. The kitten inside it, by some miracle, had fallen asleep. Natalia rang Turrido's bell. There was no intercom. If he didn't want to answer the door, what could she do? But he did—unshaven and disheveled.

"I went by Nilo. They said it was your day off."

The kitten stirred. "What's that?" Turrido said.

"I brought you something. Would you mind if I come up?"

"If you want," he said, letting her in.

They climbed the stairs without talking. When they got into Turrido's room, Natalia put the box down.

"I remembered how much you loved cats," Natalia said, opening the box. A tiny gray kitten jumped out and rubbed languidly against Turrido's legs.

"See? The kitten wants to stay with you. I brought some food for her," Natalia said. She took cans out of her bag. "Keep her for a week. If you don't want her, I'll take her back. Okay? For me?"

"Okay, I'll take the kitten. For now."

There were clothes strewn on the bed. Dirty dishes in the sink. And a rotting sack of garbage. The kitten nibbled on a dead potted plant.

"What happened to your plant?"

"I'm a good cook and baker, not a gardener."

"What shall we call the cat?"

"Purity."

The kitten ran right up to him. He picked her up and handed her to Natalia.

"Purity. Good. I brought some extra food. For Purity."

"Thanks." Turrido said. "Listen, I'm cooking a chicken. You ever have my chicken? You could stay? It's my mother's recipe. Delicious. There's more than enough."

"Turrido, maybe you shouldn't dwell so much on the past. Remember you told me that once?"

He didn't answer.

"Another time," she said, "I'd love to. But I'm on duty. We're in the middle of cases. Remember the Teresa Steiner murder I told you about? The girl who patronized your café?"

"Yes, yes."

"Perhaps you remember when she'd had a fight with her professor and went to El Nilo for coffee and your wonderful bread—for solace. Was she crying?"

Turrido nodded.

"Did you bring her her coffee?"

Turrido nodded again. "And bread."

Natalia could see it. He was a shy man. Not attractive to women. But perhaps attracted.

"Teresa was grateful," he said. "She was nice to me whenever she came in. She kissed me once, the way she would have kissed an uncle. I misunderstood at first. I thought. . . ." He gave a dejected wave. "I am very sorry she is gone. She cheered up my day."

A tear trailed down Turrido's cheek. Purity purred at his feet.

Natalia touched his arm. "Good-bye," she said, pulling the door tight behind her.

Pino was waiting outside. "Well?"

She shook her head slowly. "I don't think so, but I don't know. I don't know."

~

Colonel Donati motioned Natalia and Pino to the handsome wooden chairs that faced his desk. The military haircut was clipped tight at his neck, evidence of his daily trip to the barber. Over the years various people had urged Colonel Donati to modernize his office; he always refused, preferring the Spartan appearance.

"Do you mind?" Donati asked as he shook a cigarette out of a package. "I've fallen off the wagon, so to speak."

He opened the window behind his desk. In the past couple of years, gray had overtaken his thick black hair, and lines now eroded the once-youthful smoothness of his skin.

Once a year, between Christmas and the New Year, the colonel hosted a dinner for the detectives. Everyone drank too much and said things they probably didn't really mean to. Instead of bonuses, there were gifts. Thoughtful ones, probably selected by Elisabetta: Gucci scarves, leather belts, excellent bottles of wine. Last year, Pino had opened his small gift box and found a laughing Buddha.

"I had a call from Gambini's lawyer just now."

"Mmmm." Natalia pushed forward on her seat. "We believe Teresa Steiner was working for Gambini, collecting shrine money."

"Was Gambini involved with the girl?"

"There's no hard evidence of it," Pino said, "but they met socially before he employed her."

"And the other suspects?"

"Her thesis adviser, Professor Lattanza," Natalia said. "A young novice monk related to Gambini. Maybe a cook-and-baker at a café she frequented. Oh, I need you to sign off on a search request for the premises of Gina Falcone and a criminalist's search of Teresa Steiner's rented room."

Donati puffed out a circle of smoke. Natalia slid the search authorizations across to him to sign. The colonel scrawled his signature with a flourish.

"Gambini acts like a civilized man," he said. "He's not. Please remember, the Camorra is even bigger and older than our organization. The Carabinieri were born out of distrust—to make sure no one ministry would have all the military and police power. Our forefathers spread it out. Which is why we answer to the minister of the interior and the minister of the exterior and the minister of defense and whoever the hell else they can think of saddling us with. But the Camorra, it is not that—or even like a crime syndicate. It is like a second government. It has its internal rivalries too, but they are far more . . . final. Be careful."

"Yes, sir," Natalia said.

"Filthy habit," Donati crushed the half-smoked cigarette into a glass tray. "Keep me posted."

Natalia and Pino went back to their office. She sat down and opened the Vesuvio's Bakery file.

"Gambini didn't light the match, Natalia."

"Gambini never touches the match, the gun, the knife."

"Yes, that's why he's Boss Gambini. And why you'll never prove he was involved. Besides, it's not your job to fix everything that's gone wrong."

"What *is* my job, then?"

"The Vesuvio's arson death is in the past, Natalia. Turrido is alive. Teresa Steiner is newly dead."

"You're right." Natalia set aside the folder. Exhaustion was part of every investigation—both physical and emotional—and it was getting to her. "What is the point?" Natalia's voice surprised her. She shoved her notebook into her bag, hugged herself trying to get warm. "The Camorra are everywhere among us."

"That's the wrong question," Pino said.

"What is the right question, then?"

Pino took off his sports jacket, and hung it next to Natalia's. He was wearing his shoulder holster today. "I don't know what the right question is. That is complicated. There is not one question, obviously. But I do know that we have to find out who killed her."

"Right. We start with Dr. Francesca." And off they went to the morgue in the basement.

Natalia blinked at the unfriendly fluorescent light, and there was a smell she and Pino both hated— formaldehyde. It was lunch hour. Dr. Francesca Agari was alone in the lab, hunched over a microscope. She got up when they came in, long legs unfolding. She was wearing black stockings and a short black skirt, heels, and a white lab coat over a turquoise sweater. Natalia pulled a frumpy sweater out of her bag. It was missing buttons and there was a moth hole at the neck. Pino shivered, having forgotten his.

"Put this on, Sergeant." Dr. Francesca took an extra lab coat off a hook on the wall and handed it to him.

"*Grazie.*"

"My pleasure." A warm smile for him.

Pino, standing close to Dr. Francesca, picked up a scent of her perfume. As usual, Dr. Francesca's hair was sleek, with a range of tones from brown to gold. Pearl earrings adorned her ears. Natalia recognized the large teardrop design: Mariel had bought a pair in Milan. They were luscious and expensive. Fashion was a hedge against everything, a wonderful distraction. It made sense. Francesca's job was unpleasant, certainly, but on the positive side she ran her own show and dressed to kill.

Pino and Natalia had an open invitation to attend the autopsies themselves. But, except for the rare occasion when it was crucial to an investigation, they rarely witnessed the procedure. Better to have Francesca fill them in secondhand.

"As suspected," Francesca began, bringing them up to date on the autopsy of Teresa Steiner, "the knife went deep into the heart, severed major arteries. This caused Teresa Steiner's death. The bruises on her neck are quite severe, but strangulation did not kill her. Similarly, the frontal stab was almost an afterthought. The first and primary wound was in her back. From a right-handed assailant." Francesca demonstrated on Pino, holding him as if they were dancing. "Delivered from close in, as if in an embrace."

"Interesting," Pino said. He stepped back from Francesca, crossing his arms for warmth.

"There were fibers, but so small that we had to send them to the SCIS labs in Rome. I don't expect much to come of them, frankly."

Francesca's beeper went off. "Sorry." She snapped open her phone and conversed. "*Pronto. Sì. Sono Francesca.*" She was still listening as she said, "I have to go. Three men were just shot to death in their car, a block from the harbor. Broad daylight. They think it's in retaliation for attacks last week. Two bystanders were hit as well by the sprayed gunfire."

Her white coat was off and she was gone before they'd even shed their sweater and lab coat.

They spent the rest of the day typing forms and reports. Catching Giulio before he left for the day, Natalia asked him to find her an urban archeologist. It was early evening by the time Natalia and Pino left the office. A few colleagues, smoking outside, nodded at them as they walked by.

Natalia stretched her arms over her head. "Fancy a spin on my chariot? We could come back for your bike."

"*Perfetto*," Pino said, walking with her toward the Vespa.

"Pino!" a female voice called from across the street. A girl was waving her arms at them. Tight yellow pants, midriff showing. Her pink top matched her hair.

"Isn't that your friend?" Natalia said.

"I'll be right back." Pino jogged into the street, intercepting Tina as she headed into traffic, and led her back to the far corner.

Natalia wanted to look away but it was compelling. Her partner seemed to have gotten involved with a kid. The girl acted annoyed. They argued. Pino touched her shoulder. She pulled away from him and ran. He stood for a moment, helpless. "Sorry," he said as he sprinted back to Natalia. "A mess—sort of."

"It's your personal business."

"She's infatuated, that's all. I can handle it."

"Can *she*?" Natalia unlocked the motorbike and rolled it away from the building.

"It's ridiculous," he said. "She's just a kid."

"Sergeant Loriano, come on. Love is love."

"Captain Monte, you've made it clear that *you're* not available—to me, anyway."

It was only when the Vespa started climbing the hill that Pino put his arms around her waist. Near the top, Natalia pulled into a lookout sometimes used as a lovers' lane. She cut the engine. They got off the bike and walked to the railing. It was quiet. The harbor glittered, and a few ships. Venus pulsed lavender on the horizon.

"Beautiful, isn't it?" Natalia took a deep breath.

"I had my first kiss here," Pino said.

Natalia laughed. "You too?"

"Natalia."

"What?" Natalia moved away from her partner.

"Cold?" he asked, slipping off his jacket and offering it to her.

"No, I'm fine. Your coffee," she said, pouring him a cup from her thermos.

"To us," he said, raising the cup. "Naples's best."

"If you hadn't become Carabinieri, what would you have done?" she asked.

"Oh, I don't know. Poet, maybe. Wandering monk. Probably a bum."

"Such a pretty view," Natalia said. "A nice gift for a birthday."

"It's your birthday?"

"Afraid so."

"*Tanti auguri.* Many good wishes," he said as he kissed her.

"Natalia?" Pino touched Natalia's cheek.

"Don't," she said. He took his hand away. "For one thing, I am your boss. And even if we wanted to risk that, I think you are confused. The girl is living with you, no?"

Pino looked down. "No."

"Regardless, she is in love with you. Be careful."

"It's not the same as how I feel about you."

"I'm due at my friend's for our traditional girls' birthday evening."

She dropped Pino at his bike and drove to Mariel's building. Lola's grandmother lived on the floor below. On the pretext of visiting her *nonna*, Lola had attended all the birthday celebrations upstairs in Mariel's flat, including her own, all catered by Lola's grandmother. It was a thin deception, more for show than to really fool anyone. As everyone knew, the three of them had been friends since childhood.

Mariel lived in the Palazzo, the grand but run-down apartment building where she'd grown up. Her parents ran an art gallery. And Natalia's mother tended house and her father was a street cleaner for the Municipality of Napoli. Up at five A.M., he left the house by six. A year into adolescence, on a class trip to Galleria Umberto II, Natalia had been embarrassed by the man pushing the mop across the vast marble floors who had called her name. She had pretended not to hear.

Because the girls were such good friends, a dinner was arranged. Natalia could still see her father nervously squeezing oil into his thick rough hair. Her mother, in her blue serge church dress, was frumpy next to Mariel's mother, in high heels and a red cocktail dress cut low in the back. Food was served on gold-rimmed china, and there was a servant. Roses decorated the table. Natalia's mother chattered nervously. Mariel's parents tried to put her at ease. Her father's one comment about the evening, a comment he repeated over the years, was that there was not enough meat on Mariel's mother's bones.

Five years after their meal, Mariel's parents were killed on the Autobahn, driving to an art fair in Frankfurt. Mariel was seventeen. She insisted on staying in the apartment; her mother's sister came for a year. When Mariel could finally talk about her parents again, she said reading had saved her life. That and Natalia's parents, who treated her like a second daughter.

Now, immediately upon arriving at Mariel's, Natalia blurted out what had just happened with Pino on the hill above the harbor.

"It's an illusion, dear," Mariel said, pouring her friend a glass of wine. "You're not in love with Pino Loriano. Trust me."

"I hate that expression—'trust me.' It generally means the opposite."

"Sorry."

"No, *I'm* sorry. I'm being terrible."

"Don't apologize. You're under a lot of pressure. A girl is dead. Her killer is walking around. You have a difficult job. Impossible. Give yourself a break. Besides, maybe I'm wrong. After all, I haven't exactly been too successful in the men department."

Natalia shook her head. "That's because you don't want to be."

"Yes. Maybe."

"Here's to you. To us." Lola smiled as she and Mariel clinked Natalia's glass.

"To us."

Mariel handed over presents: a pair of black Capri pants, then an orange chiffon top with a plunging neckline.

"I can't wear this!" Natalia protested, holding up the top and laughing.

"You are thirty-five, not a hundred and five. Wear it! That's an order, Captain Monte! Oh, and this is from Lola."

"Lola?"

"Yes. Me."

It was a pair of gold earrings, nestled inside a plain black box. They were lavish—a cascade of delicate gold bits, studded with some kind of gemstones.

"Lola, what have you *done*?" Natalia said, holding one of the earrings up to her face. "What do you think?"

"Gorgeous," Mariel said. "Let me see those."

"Girlfriend," said Lola, "those are sapphires and pearls!"

Natalia gasped. "You're kidding!"

"So," Natalia said to Mariel, taking a sip of wine. "What's the latest with Stefano?"

"Stefano is married," Mariel said, with a dismissive wave.

"If he weren't."

"But he is."

"Don't be difficult."

"Okay. Yes. Maybe. In the next life, I'll date him—okay? And I'll spring for a new set of teeth."

"The next life. You sound like your *nonna*."

"I've been thinking about her today. Remember how she always said, 'Sometimes a thing seems like a piece of cake, but then you never know how long the cake has been sitting around'?"

"Yeah." Lola laughed.

"I don't think she was talking about cake, but remember her chocolate cake? We stopped in after school at least twice a week."

"Stop. You're making me hungry again."

"You're in luck. I bought a *torta al cioccolato* for you—for old times' sake."

"You sweetheart."

"Yes, well . . . I've been thinking about Nonna a lot lately, wondering if she was lonely in her last years."

"My Nonna loved you," said Natalia.

Lola's grandmother knocked on the ceiling to signal dinner, and the friends retired to the floor below to eat and enjoy one another further. The three rarely managed to get together any more. Nonna had outdone herself preparing Natalia's favorite: *branzino*, freshly grilled—garlic and parsley added, along with Parmigiano, pine nuts, and raisins.

Around midnight, Mariel stood up. "I'm tipsy. It's late. You'll take the rest of the cake with you. I'll call a cab."

"Not the whole cake. A piece," Natalia said. "And no cab. The walk will do me good."

"Then I'll walk with you," Lola said. She went into the kitchen and returned with a large bag.

"Cake and presents. Here."

"You're like my Nonna," Natalia said to Lola's nonna, "always trying to fatten me up." She took the bag. "*Ti ringrazio tanto.* But, Lola, you stay here. Otherwise we'll be walking each other back and forth until the sun comes up."

Mariel giggled. "What kind of Carabiniere is afraid to walk by herself at night?"

Natalia kissed her friends on each cheek and picked up another present, a thin blue cashmere scarf. She draped it around her neck. It set off her new earrings splendidly.

"*Bella,*" Lola said, admiring.

"Be careful," her grandmother said. "You have your big gun with you?"

"Yes, Mama, I have my gun." She kissed Nonna goodbye and thanked her for the delicious meal.

Natalia's heels echoed on the stairs and the street. Most people were home, preparing for bed or already deep in the land of dreams. She passed the Musici per il Momento music shop. The store had been in this same spot her entire life. During business hours, an aria from an opera scratched from a speaker by the door. Farther along, a bouquet of mimosa stood in a pitcher in front of a shrine. A fat candle burned beside it.

Natalia crossed at the intersection.

She could smell a cigarette burning—most likely a *donna* on her balcony, invisible in the dark, enjoying a smoke. Suddenly there were footsteps behind her. She looked around. There were only shadows. Panicky, she slipped her hand into the special compartment housing her 9-mm Beretta and took hold of the large grip. She had only fired her weapon once in the line of duty. A man moved out of the darkness. A crazy man, his hair wild.

"Hey, Beautiful!" he called.

When he got close, she recognized the first boy she'd ever kissed. His grin was as sweet as when she'd been fifteen and he eighteen, but a couple of his teeth had gone missing.

Gypsy blood, her mother had said when she discovered Natalia and Tomas together in Piazza Gaetano. Her mother's disapproval only made her want him more. Heavy petting followed. She let him touch her breasts. Shocking, the first inkling of real sexual desire.

"Tomas," she said, smiling.

Natalia stepped closer. He still had the deep-set eyes that, when they caught the light, appeared to be amber. Tonight they were merely dark, the circles under them more pronounced. Natalia must have spent a hundred hours looking into his eyes back then.

"So." He took her hands in his. His grip was firm. "I wondered what happened to you. I heard bits and pieces over the years. And my mother always asks about you. She hoped we'd get married." He laughed. "So did I."

"It is amazing to run into you. After all this time."

He let go of her hands. "You're in law enforcement. And you never married. Did I break your heart?"

"What about you, Tomas?" Natalia asked. "How did you make out?"

"Me? Pretty good. I pour concrete. Supervise it. There's a living in it. I got three kids. A wife. I married Concetta Milo."

Natalia recalled Concetta, a tough girl from Tomas's block. The third of ten children. Her mother cleaned houses. Her father turnstiled in and out of jail. At thirteen, Concetta had frosted her hair, put on short skirts, and came on to any man who looked her way. She could have done worse than Tomas.

"But you look good, Natalia, real good! You kept your

figure. My mother always liked you. Said you were too good for me. So . . . what are you doin' out so late?"

"Birthday dinner with my girlfriends. You remember Mariel. And Lola?"

"Your old gang. Yeah, yeah. Mariel the reader. And that's Lola who married Frankie, right?"

"Yes. We still see each other whenever we can."

"Must be complicated for you with Lola being . . . never mind," he stammered. "We should get together too, some time. A coffee. Dinner."

The moment deflated. She sensed a lame come-on coming on. Hopefully it would be another decade and a half before she ran into him again. We made our choices, she wanted to say, now we have to live with them.

"Yeah, sure," she said. "That would be nice. Great to see you, Tomas."

"You too," he said. "Look. . . ." He took her hands again.

"It's—ah—late. I better get going."

Natalia tried to take back her hands from his. He didn't let go.

"Tomas!" she said, pulling harder. "Cut it out."

The *donna* had gone from her balcony. They were alone in the dark street. A shadow moved toward them from the wall and grabbed her purse but didn't snatch it off her shoulder, just held it.

"Don't worry," Tomas said. "No one is going to hurt you."

The shadow man slipped something into the purse.

"What is this about, Tomas?" she said, trying to keep her voice from shaking.

"A donation to your favorite charity. A cruise. A car. Anything you want it to be, honey."

"*What?*"

"There's an envelope in your handbag with fifty thousand euros."

"Excuse me?"

"Work with me here and we don't have a problem. It's simple. You don't have to tire your pretty head. Okay?"

He was getting irritated. Natalia willed herself not to say anything.

"Remember where you come from, is all. You're one of us—like Lola and me—not them."

"You're with Gambini," she said. "Tomas—"

"Happy birthday."

Her hands came free and he vanished back into the dark from where he had come. A Camorra thug. Her mother was right. But what choice did Tomas really have, born in the slums of Naples? Where had the sweet boy gone with whom she'd lost her virginity? Would she have to meet more old friends clandestinely from now on, as she did Lola, because so many had gone over to illegality and were no longer proper acquaintances for an officer of the Carabinieri? What would she do if they called her on it?

Natalia located her gun and her wallet. There was the envelope. She took it out and opened it. Bills. Lots of them. Did Gambini truly think he could buy her? Had he succeeded with this gambit with any of her colleagues? She never heard it discussed, but she knew it happened. It was easy to imagine someone struggling financially, in debt. Coping with an ailing parent. A sick child. Carabinieri salaries weren't much.

She continued across the small deserted piazza into which Via Altri, her street, dead-ended. Hand on her gun, she opened the door to the courtyard. The windows above were dark. A couple of towels remained on the line. They twisted in the black night, illuminated by the moon.

Bypassing the elevator, she climbed the three flights. She was out of breath by the time she reached her landing. She slipped her key into the lock and opened her front door, then secured it behind her. Putting down her bags and purse, she took out her automatic and slipped out of her shoes. In the kitchen, she rummaged in the cabinet for an old bottle of scotch, opened it and poured out a shot, slugging it down. Then she stripped off her clothes and fell exhausted into bed, holding her Beretta to her breast like a doll.

How excited she had been to have her own apartment, and proud that day with Mariel and Tomas when they'd found it, rundown, like all flats in the old neighborhoods, but with marble floors in the kitchen and bathroom and decorative molding along the edges of the high ceiling. She'd enlisted Tomas to bring a ladder, and he had helped her plaster over the cracks and paint the rooms. Buttercup for the kitchen, ochre for the bedroom, a faint red in the living room, and the ceiling a periwinkle blue.

She'd inherited her parents' carved bed and a dresser. Mariel contributed the most elegant piece—a dusty-rose velvet couch of her grandmother's. Natalia remembered the place fondly, and the lazy afternoons in bed with Tomas. There had been no dramatic breakup, more like a slow drifting in different directions. One day he just stopped coming around.

Natalia hadn't purchased anything new for the house in years—she who once had fantasized hosting elegant dinner parties hadn't so much as a coaster to offer guests. Not that there were many. After a day at work, she barely managed to warm some pizza and eat it by herself from a tray.

Too wound up to sleep, she got up, slipped on a robe, and stepped out on the balcony. The night was warm and quiet. Windows were shuttered. Across the way, Mrs. Bruna's balcony was thick with potted plants she had carried out from her apartment in anticipation of rain. Her arthritis was more reliable than the weather reports. The perfume of honeysuckle and red lilies reached across to Natalia.

Down below, a lone parked car hugged the wall of the narrow street. Not a street where anyone parked their vehicle for the night. The tip of a cigarette flared in the windshield on the driver's side. Heart thudding, Natalia returned inside and found her cell phone. It was three-thirty in the morning when she punched in Pino's number.

"*Pronto.*" His voice was sleepy.

"Pino?"

"Natalia. What's wrong?"

"I just got hassled by one of Gambini's men on the way home and now there's someone sitting in a Fiat downstairs—watching."

"I'll be there in nine minutes." The phone went dead.

Natalia put on pajamas and the robe again, took up her pistol and cell phone, and headed downstairs. In the court-yard, she went to the smaller exterior door and opened it a crack. The passenger-side window was open on the Fiat: an elbow protruded. The odor of the garbage at street level was more than pungent. Anger was catching up to her fear and passing it. Natalia calmed herself and stepped out into the street, the Beretta in both hands, finger on the trigger. Safety off, barrel down, she walked slowly toward the car.

The cigarette flew out onto the cobblestones as she approached. Headlights snapped on. The engine surged as the Fiat backed away fast, turning around at the next intersection with an alley, and screeching off.

Natalia exhaled, re-engaged the safety, and walked back toward her house.

"Natalia!"

She turned toward Pino. "Whoever it was took off."

He holstered his weapon and embraced her. "You're okay?"

"Yes. A bit shaken, but yeah. How did you get here so fast?"

"Taxi."

"That's a first." *You must love me*, she wanted to tease, but thought better of it. "You told me Buddhists don't believe in taxis."

"Taxes. I said taxes."

They wandered slowly back toward the apartment house, her heart still racing, her breathing shallow. Upstairs, Natalia walked into the bathroom, splashed her face with water. Looking into the mirror, she was horrified; she tried to tame her wild curls. "No need to look like hell, *cara*," she said, hearing Lola's voice admonish her. Rummaging through the medicine cabinet's shelves, she found the untouched tube of glittery lip gloss, courtesy of Mariel, applied it, and returned to the living room.

"Why don't I stay for a while—just till you calm down."

Natalia flushed. "I don't know. . . ."

"Look," he said, "it's okay. Line of duty. I won't bite. Promise." He patted the bed.

"Okay," she said, yawning. "You win."

"Good."

He stretched out on the bed. She lay down next to him, resting her head on his chest.

"Better," he said, stroking her hair.

Natalia made a contented noise and said, "Yes." In seconds, she was asleep. Pino unwedged his 9-millimeter from his belt and slowly drifted off too.

9

Natalia stood on her balcony, trying to wake up. She barely remembered Pino slipping away at first light.

Blue flowers dotted the hills. It smelled like rain. She gathered up her things, checking her weapon before leaving for work. Shading her eyes, Natalia crossed the street downstairs and walked into a bright piazza. In spite of the heat, there were elderly men bowling small bocce balls down dirt lanes, strategizing between shots. A young girl in a headscarf stood next to a man with a face like a bulldog, both waiting for the light. A boy of four or five did wheelies on a tiny bike. His mother was too preoccupied with a new baby to tell him to stop.

Natalia's childbearing years were practically gone. She considered the baby. This perfect creature with impossible skin and opaque eyes.

A man bumped her. She almost pulled her weapon until she saw that he was listening to an iPod. "*Scusi,*" he said.

In the middle of the next block, a young man and woman were kissing, hands in one another's jean pockets.

Natalia stepped around them. Surely these young people were not burdened by the superstitions of their parents. Not the girl with bright aquamarine hair, or the boy with her, a score by Liszt under one arm. Did they ever think about blood oaths or the Camorra, the Mafia, the 'Ndrangheta, or the half-dozen other not-so-secret secret societies that catacombed their country?

Natalia got to the office early. She spent an hour cleaning and organizing her desk as she tried to push away the events of the previous evening and the realization that she had a full-blown crush on her partner. How shocking that her first love had gone over to the enemy and was lost to her, even in memory.

To distract herself, she dumped three bottles of nail polish, a compact, and two lipsticks into the trash. There was a perfume bottle, a fancy brand, a gift, courtesy of Mariel, when Natalia joined the force. The lid had started to corrode. Most of the perfume must have evaporated over the years it had been in her drawer. She picked it up, managed to open the lid. Then she tipped the bottle over, dabbing the last few drops onto her wrist. She brought it to her nose and inhaled a trace of verbena.

She put Vivaldi on her CD player. The album was a gift from her last serious boyfriend, Giorgio, a violinist. Had it been three years? They'd parted amicably, and every few months there was a message from him—from Prague or London.

She'd been thirteen when she was exposed to the beauty of Vivaldi—the same year her mother allowed her to go to the Luchettis' street festival. Guillermo Luchetti owned the neighborhood bar. Definitely a Camorra man. As a good Catholic, he wanted to minimize his time in purgatory, so every year he threw a huge party to right the balance. How excited she was, the first time she went with Lola. Mariel was so jealous when she found out. They'd eaten an early dinner and started out as the sun was setting. Night took over Naples. Fireworks went off as loud as bombs. The noise scared all the cats off the streets.

Natalia and Lola joined the crowds and marched with them. On one float in a glass coffin, Jesus was laid out. On another a brass band played. People danced, even though the music was mournful. Father Ponti walked through, smiling and shaking hands. Luchetti hosted the dignitaries, including Signor Gambini. Women held up their babies for the monsignor to kiss. Natalia stayed for hours.

"Captain, someone is waiting to see you," Giulio informed Natalia, standing at her door, interrupting her reverie. "A woman."

Giulio had been eating pistachios. Natalia could smell them. "Who is it?" she asked.

"A Signora Ruttola," he said, wiping salt off his lips. "Says she has information about the Teresa Steiner case."

"Thanks."

Lattanza's wife was sitting on a chair in the reception area, wearing a lovely white dress that drew the envious eyes of two female carabinieri who were passing by. But her perfect look was marred by her face, streaked with mascara.

She dabbed her eyes as Natalia approached. "I had to talk to you."

"Come."

The two women walked back to Natalia's office. Natalia pulled out a chair for Signora Ruttola and closed the blinds on her window before sitting down at her desk.

"What is it?"

"Marco," she sobbed. "I was away at a design conference in Milan and came home a day early. Thought I'd play wife for once—make a nice dinner, wear a negligee. Couples get busy and forget to take time for one another. I'm sure you know about that."

Natalia nodded, though she couldn't imagine parading around in a transparent negligee for Marco Lattanza.

"I walked in on him—them. The bastard didn't even have the decency to go to a hotel."

She straightened before continuing: "He wasn't home the night the girl was killed—Teresa Steiner. I lied. I'm tired of the lies. He promised me he had nothing to do with her murder. We've been together a long time; we have a daughter." Black beads streamed down her cheeks.

"You are willing to sign a statement?" Natalia asked.

"Yes," Marissa Ruttola said.

"We'll need to bring him in for further questioning. Maybe hold him on suspicion. We have witnesses who overheard him threaten the girl. You may want to take your daughter away from the apartment. It probably won't be until tomorrow. Are you sure you can act 'normal' until we can pick him up?"

"Absolutely."

After Marissa read the statement on videotape and signed, Natalia called Pino on his cell phone and informed Colonel Donati's secretary. It was then that she saw the call slip for a phone call she'd missed. *Hope you liked the earrings. Lola,* the note said. The PLEASE CALL box was checked. Lola had never called Natalia's office before.

Pino finally appeared. He had news as well.

"The criminalists' search of Teresa Steiner's rented room turned up a journal hidden in the hollow brass bedpost."

"Fabulous."

"There's more. The search of the bone cleaner's apartment turned up this—Kiyoshi number 7, the special chef's knife missing from the monastery kitchen."

He held up both in their clear plastic evidence bags, happy as a kid bringing home goldfish.

Natalia clapped her hands. "Bingo and bingo."

Pino waited in the car in the unloading area while Natalia went into the railroad terminal by herself. She crossed the cavernous waiting hall and reached the public toilets. There was a line, as usual. The woman at the head of the line smelled like she hadn't bathed in a while. The woman directly in front of Natalia was elegant—white capri pants and a bright Gucci blouse. The line proceeded inside.

Two prostitutes were doing laundry in a sink. One of the women washing her underwear had black stringy hair. Her sundress showed a bony frame and sores along her arm. The other woman, heftier, wore tight pants and a halter top. The woman in front of Natalia clutched her bags and made the sign of the cross as she realized that the large woman was, in fact, a man.

"Can you tell me where I might find Father Pacelli?" Natalia asked.

"Sure. Try Track 22, at the far end."

Exiting the bathroom, Natalia proceeded to Binario 22, the track farthest from the waiting room. Carabiniere Cesare beamed as Natalia approached. He appeared as happy as ever.

"Captain."

"Carabiniere. Good day. Would you know where the priest is who works with the prostitutes?"

"The Jesuit. Sure." He pointed her in the direction of a large door.

She passed the waiting room, separated from the main hall by a guard and a barrier. One could only enter with a ticket. A godsend for women traveling alone.

Natalia was aware that she no longer collected wolf whistles and stares from men, the way she had when she was younger. This made her grateful on the one hand, but aware on the other that she was aging. Young girls took it for granted, their smooth skin and easy smiles making the path of daily life in many ways smoother. Teresa Steiner had been at the height of her powers—physically and intellectually. Her killer could very well be someone who had misinterpreted her friendliness for something else. And when he was scorned. . . .

And what about Lattanza the serial seducer? He'd had plenty of opportunities. And probably plenty of young girls. But maybe this time he wanted to keep the relationship, and she was ready to move on to younger men. His ego wouldn't accept it. Maybe Lattanza was feeling the loss of power—sexual and otherwise. He didn't mean to, things got out of hand. Maybe, maybe, maybe. Pino didn't like Lattanza for the killer, but Pino did not have a history with him, had not seen him get angry.

She pushed through the door to Track 22 where an empty train stood idle, and there Pacelli was, sitting on a plastic crate, head bent close to a prostitute seated on another, listening intently to her. Two monks handed out coffee and bread with cheese slices crudely layered on top. It took a moment for her to realize that Pacelli wasn't deep in a two-way conversation with the whore: rather, he was hearing her confession. In the eighteenth century, the Jesuits had preached to prostitutes, offered them a decent place to live in exchange for their faith, and founded a hospital for syphilitics in Naples. "Angels of Peace," the fallen women called the Jesuits.

The streetwalker crossed herself and rose to her feet. Pacelli resumed his duties distributing refreshments.

"Monsignor," Natalia called out.

"Captain." Pacelli waved her over as he extended a cup of coffee to the last girl in line. She appeared to be forty.

"We're looking for Benito."

"You tried his room at the monastery?"

"Yes. Not there. His clothes either."

"He may have gone to his parents'. He was saying something about that the other day."

"Thanks. We'll try him there."

"May I ask why you want him?"

"We've come up with some incriminating evidence and need to speak to him."

Pacelli looked pained. "He didn't harm that girl. He couldn't have."

"He was in love with her," she countered.

"Obviously. But violent toward her? Not possible." He pursed his lips, troubled by the conversation. "Yes, he was infatuated. We may be in holy orders, but we are human too."

"My point exactly," she said. "Monk or not, he is a man."

"Please be kind to him when you catch up."

"I will do my best, Monsignor."

"I'll pray for you both."

"You take confessions, Monsignor."

"Of course. I'm a priest."

"The girl who was killed. Did she ever come to you privately? After all, she visited your church many times, according to Benito. She was a lapsed Catholic. When she visited Benito—a perfect opportunity to reconnect with the Church."

"Why do you ask?"

"She may have told you something that could help us find her killer."

"I'm sorry. I didn't know her."

"No? Such a small parish. . . ."

"Nevertheless. . . ."

"What about Benito? Did he come to you? Did he confess to you that he'd killed the girl?"

"You know I can't divulge the contents of confession."

"Monsignor!" A tall woman with huge jiggly breasts walked swiftly toward them. Her underwear was visible through her flimsy yellow dress.

But up close, she was another man, with a man's build, moustache shadowed above pink lips.

"Ida, give me a minute, okay?"

"It's important." She scowled at Natalia, snapped open a compact and applied more powder.

"No rest for the weary, I'm afraid," Pacelli said. "I'm sorry I don't have more time. But please, don't be a stranger. Any way I can be of help."

"Thank you."

"Can I speak frankly?"

"Of course."

"You have a difficult job, Officer Monte, very difficult. You see many things no one should ever lay their eyes on. If you ever feel the need of solace, please . . . you know where to find me. After ten P.M., you can ring the bell, and someone will come—myself, or one of the brothers. We all need help. Even priests. The strength of a higher power. Or even a human ear. A comforting hand." He touched her shoulder.

"Thank you, Monsignor."

They were standing so close to one another that she could see the copper freckles on the bridge of his nose, and his lovely green eyes. A handsome man, Natalia realized as an announcement came over the loudspeaker and a train pulled into the opposite track.

No "*Scusi*" from the woman with an enormous suitcase, purple lipstick, and anxious look as she bashed into her. A young man hurried behind. He tossed his cigarette and rushed with her for the train.

~

It was Natalia's decision to start with Benito's parents. Pino was happy to find himself Natalia's passenger in a department Alfa Romeo, zooming past the large ugly buildings that ringed the old city. Before they set out, she phoned Lola and left a brief message on the answering machine without identifying herself.

They stopped for lunch at a dingy *trattoria* near Cosenza. They were the only customers. The *padrone* cooked their meal—surprisingly good *risotto ai funghi*. Now he was sitting at a table, drinking a glass of wine. A large black fly buzzed around their table.

"A walk?" Natalia suggested.

The *padrone* was busy with paperwork as they passed. On the street, a dog howled. For a second, the clouds blew apart. There were some run-down buildings. A face at a window checked them out. It was too chilly to dally. In a few minutes they were on a country road. There was a long wall beautifully composed of ancient smooth stones, with vineyards on the hillsides. Then a gate. Neglected, the wood had rotted, the gate fallen open.

"Look." Natalia picked up something off the ground. "Lemons." She handed one to Pino. "There's a grove back there." She pointed to a few trees.

"*Then rain falls, wearying the earth, the winter tedium weighs on the roofs, the light grows miserly, bitter the soul. When one day through a half-shut gate, among the leafage of a court the yellows of the lemon blaze and the heart's ice melts and songs pour into the breast from golden trumpets of solarity.*"

"That's beautiful," Natalia said.

"Montale, 'The Lemon Trees.'"

They got back in the car. When they arrived at the farmhouse, the kitchen door was open.

"Benito?" His mother grabbed the cross on a gold chain around her neck. Jesus's eyes were diamonds. "He's okay?"

"Can we come in, Signora Gambini?" Natalia flipped open her identification card.

"Pasquale!" she called, as she directed them to a couple of chairs. "My husband."

When he didn't come, she walked into the other room. Natalia stood up and followed her.

The curtains were homemade. The walls hadn't been

painted in a long time. There was one small bookcase with more empty shelves than books. The couch was shabby, but the chair Pasquale was sitting in must have been expensive—it had a feature that allowed it to swivel and tilt.

"Get up!" She pounded him on the arm. "Carabinieri."

Pasquale sat up, rubbing a hand over his beard. Then he stood, making sure his fly was zipped. A large dog followed him toward the kitchen. When it saw the visitors, it barked. "Shush." Pasquale swatted the dog on the nose.

"Have you heard from Benito recently?" Natalia asked.

"What's this about?" Pasquale asked, looking at his wife like it was her fault.

"Did Benito ever talk to you about a girl?" Natalia said.

"Benito is a man of the church." The father was fully awake now. "He's about to take holy orders."

"Not quite," Pino corrected him.

"Benito is a good boy."

"A girl was murdered inside his church last week," Natalia said.

"Oh, my God!" The wife clutched her rosary.

"This had nothing to do with my son," Pasquale said.

"We hope not. But he knew her."

"No!" The mother said. She picked up a dishcloth and put it back down.

"Sit down," Natalia said, guiding her into a chair.

Pasquale stared out the window.

"When was the last time you spoke with your son?"

"Benito calls us every week," his mother said, "usually Monday. He's busy on Sundays. He called us yesterday."

"Do you know where he called from?" Pino asked.

"No. He said he wanted to come for a visit. Usually he comes only once a year—around Christmas time. I asked him, was something wrong. He said he missed us, that's all."

"Aldo Gambini is your brother, isn't he?"

"Aldo?" Pasquale raised his head. "Yes."

"We know. We've been talking to Gina Falcone. She discovered the body."

"We grew up together."

"Yes," Pino said. "We don't want to upset you further, but we think Aldo may have had something to do with the murder."

"Aldo is no good."

"You don't have a relationship with your brother?"

"No."

"What about your son?" Pino said.

"Did he have a relationship with his uncle?" asked Natalia. The old man shook his head. "No—nothing."

"The TV dish and your rosary," Pino said. "Expensive, no?"

"Benito." Pasquale said. "He saved. From his work before he was a *monachello*. We don't like handouts."

His wife fingered the beads of the rosary.

"We want to help your son," Natalia said. "If you hear from him again, call us right away." Natalia put her card on the arm of Pasquale's chair.

Driving the Alfa back to Naples, Pino turned to her for a moment. "You have that look," Pino said. "Thinking about Professor Lattanza again—right?"

"I don't know, it's so convoluted. It would be like him to construct a labyrinth that only he understands. He must have resented Teresa Steiner from the moment she showed him her research."

"That's a big stretch, isn't it, from jealousy to murder?"

"Jealousy as a motive for murder is right at the top of the motives list, no?"

"Romantic jealousy, maybe. But professional?" He signaled a lane change and eased into the fast lane.

"This could be both."

"Teresa Steiner is hardly an innocent in this. She got involved with a novice monk, for Christ's sake. The nephew of a mobster. Maybe with the mobster too."

"And she certainly did with an egomaniacal professor who lusted after her and her thesis. She was a tremendously smart girl, but devious as well and not too discriminating about men. And as a result, she's in the morgue. You think her soul deserves an 'F' for fucking them all, or a merciful passing 'D' for dead? What, are we judging her *right* to live based on *how* she lived?"

Pino shook his head. They didn't speak for some moments.

He said, "Would Lattanza even have been *able* to carry her body down into those crypts?"

"He's always prided himself on keeping fit."

"We don't know for sure if Teresa and Benito were involved, do we?"

"We don't?" She laughed. "We do, Pino. We do. They weren't just friends."

"You think it's Professor Lattanza who killed her?"

"I think Marco Lattanza. Yes."

Pino said: "But if it's someone else and we're not paying attention. . . . Teresa Steiner could have easily fallen afoul of Gambini. She was killed near his nephew's church, probably with a weapon from his nephew's monastery kitchen. From what we are hearing about her, she could have easily found it fun to sneak into the monastery for a tryst with him."

"Benito was in love with the girl," Natalia said as she lowered her sun visor. "Gambini has a soft spot for his nephew, whom she jilted to have an affair with Lattanza. Maybe she bedded Gambini too."

"I'm just pointing out," Pino said, and paused. "Look. You may be right about Professor Lattanza, but your antagonism for him—"

"Listen, Sergeant Loriano. I'm responsible for the investigation. It's *my* ass on the line!"

"By rank, you are my superior. But we're a team, no?"

They fell into a sullen silence.

"Hey," he said. He squeezed her shoulder. "Listen, I didn't mean to upset you."

"No, you're right. I'm too close to this."

"You're being hard on yourself."

"No. I'm not. This is important. I'll do better." She looked at him. "Friends?"

"Foolish question, Captain Monte. Foolish questions don't deserve answers."

She checked her mobile for messages: no callback from Lola.

Pino said, "You think we should worry about the car that's tailing us?"

Natalia glanced up at the mirror. "Undoubtedly Gambini's minders."

"I think that's a safe assumption."

"If Gambini's responsible for Teresa Steiner's murder, I worry that we won't be able to tie him to it. And at the same time I worry that we will, and that we'll have to arrest him and run the gauntlet of Camorra vengeance."

Pino smirked. "What is it the Americans call that—*lose-lose?*"

"Did you hear the rumor around the station that Colonel Donati is contemplating retirement?"

"I wouldn't be surprised," he said. "The Colonel becomes eligible at the end of the year. A major Camorra arrest would be a fine cap to his record. He'd get a commendation from the prime minister, a handsome sendoff to commemorate his faithful service. He'd go off into the sunset, and we'd get hung out there like a bag of laundry."

"Is the car still following us?"

Pino checked the mirror. "Yeah. Yeah, the silver Wrangler. Two back."

"Listen. Tomorrow—"

"Yes?"

"Be in uniform. We need to confront the man himself."

10

Pino removed the black uniform from the cleaner's plastic coverings and prepared it for use, polishing the brim of his hat, his belt, and his shoes until they shined, polishing his buttons, brushing the epaulettes and reddish insignia chevrons that designated his non-commissioned officer's rank of sergeant: *vice brigadiere dei Carabinieri*. Natalia was undoubtedly doing the same. Done, Pino turned to his pistol and cleaned the weapon, then loaded extra magazines for it. They were going into the heartland of the enemy. They needed to impress. They wouldn't have much protection beyond their deportment. Half past eight, Natalia rang the downstairs bell and he went down. She was at the wheel of a blue official patrol car, with CARABINIERI in large letters running above a red horizontal stripe along the length of it. A blue bubble light sat on top. Her jacket was on a hanger in the back. He added his hat to hers on the back seat and slid in next to her. She sped off before he was even belted in.

Natalia drove fast with the window down. Three kilometers out of town, the countryside grew lovely. Mist burned off the fields, filled with orange poppies. Horses lifted their heads to watch them passing. Pino recognized the trees. Walnut. There must have been fifty walnut trees. They proceeded a few more miles at a fast pace, until Natalia suddenly slowed the car and pulled off the road. Luckily, there was no traffic. Without speaking, they got out of the car and walked under a row of sheltering oaks encased in vines, flanking a large field of uniformly placed walnut trees that had started to blossom. Dried shells were scattered on the ground.

"Like my grandparents' farm," Pino said.

Every Neapolitan knew that traditionally the nuts had to be picked on San Giovanni Battista's Day, when they were still green. Their dark brown liquor was extracted and made into an after-dinner drink, a heavily spiced, almost bitter digestive. Natalia had never cared for the drink, but she loved nothing better than a fresh walnut and picked up a whole nut and handed it to Pino. He took her hand and brought it to his cheek.

"We'd better go," Natalia said, palm against his face.

"It would be nice to spend the day here. It's a shame we have to go."

They drove on as if in a time machine, rolling backward five centuries to a feudal period when the barons and *signorotti*, the princes, ruled, issuing directives and laws. The *guappi*, the senior Camorristi, had supplanted this aristocracy in its authority and entitlement.

Though built on the bones of the poor, the Camorra was extremely class-conscious. The top mobsters dressed well, mixed with polite society, and banked their millions in Switzerland, in Liechtenstein, and on Gibraltar. They bought politicians and preyed on shopkeepers, selling them counterfeit goods to retail. They smuggled tax-free contraband cigarettes, fixed soccer playoffs, and dealt arms, and drugs.

Camorra life revolved around the oligarchs like Gambini. He was no less a feudal lord. A dictator with total power. No Italian government had challenged the Camorra or the other mafia brotherhoods since Mussolini.

Natalia and Pino were very much on their own. Unprotected. If the two of them met an untimely death, the public would express outrage. The media would speculate, the government investigate and make its customary self-righteous noises. For a while.

"There are two Heckler and Koch assault rifles in the trunk," Pino said, "if you feel the need of more firepower than our pistols."

"No, I don't think we are going to defeat Mr. Gambini today by force of arms."

In thirty minutes more, they arrived on the outskirts of the village where Gambini made his home. The plazas were filled with idling youth and gnarled old men taking their ease beneath boxwood trees and maples. They rode through and onto the grounds of Gambini's estate on the far side, passing black Hummers stationed by the roadside in orchards and olive groves.

The driveway to the door was more than two miles long. More men languished along the way, picking wild raspberries, shotguns slung on their shoulders. No doubt even more heavily armed men were lingering nearby. Given the level of security, she thought there must be trouble in gangland. Since Gambini had begun expanding abroad, neighboring clans had grown more ambitious at home. Bianca Strozzi's crew was rumored to be especially envious of Gambini's hold on the trash-hauling contracts with the city.

Natalia and Pino finally reached the main house and a cobblestone courtyard in front, with yellow primroses and large plants potted in bleached yellow planters. Time and the sun had bleached the front doors too. Only a few fragments suggested the original blue. The pair donned their jackets and hats and marched in step toward the front entrance of the baroque mansion. The side of the house was engulfed in bougainvillea. Natalia nodded at Pino as they arrived at the partially open door.

"Carabinieri!" he announced as he pushed one side of the walnut door all the way open. It scraped across the stone floor. An old man approached, and they told him they were there to speak with Signor Gambini. The old retainer showed them past armed guards lounging in a long vaulted corridor that led to a large hall all the way in the back of the mansion off the garden, where four men sat around a table. They were ordinary-looking country gentlemen in casual clothes. The air stank of cigars. They were playing cards.

Sitting with his back to them was Gambini. She had seen him from afar all her life but had never dared engage him in conversation. She and Pino marched closer, uniforms immaculate, leather boots and belts creaking in the silence. They came to a stop beside him. He was freshly shaved and wearing a gray Armani T-shirt, white trousers, and velvet Paciotti slippers embroidered with a crest. With his plump pink cheeks and crinkly blue eyes, Aldo Gambini could have passed for a sweet, prosperous grandfather or Father Christmas on holiday.

Gambini was married and also supported several girl-friends and the one serious mistress Lola had mentioned. Unlike a good many contemporaries, he was not content with just the summer palace. He had a villa on the isle of Procida and a yacht in the marina there, though both were largely unused of late. He also had his family's apartment in his old slum neighborhood in Naples, and a lush villa on the water and a new office suite in the chic Chiaia district. The bulk of his time, he was in the city, commanding the defense against the recent challenge to his businesses.

"You're late," Gambini said. "You must have stopped along the way." Natalia and Pino circled the table to face him. They had deliberately come unannounced.

"I didn't know you read cards, too," she said.

A scar ran from his cheek down his neck. "Yeah. I tell fortunes as well sometimes." He got up. "Let me get a look at you. I've heard things about the lady cop," he said, scanning Natalia up and down. "Impressive. We share the same clothing designer. Coffee?" he offered.

"No, thank you," Pino said.

"I'm Captain Monte," she said. "And this is Sergeant Loriano."

"What can we do for you, signora?" he asked.

"We need to speak. Privately."

With the slightest gesture, he cleared the room, his men retreating into the confines of the large house. Natalia swallowed. Despite the high ceiling, the vast room was hot from the day's heat, and stuffy. She was also nervous and tried to stem her anxiety. Where did she get the idea that a visit from them could intimidate the likes of Zazu Gambini? Natalia removed a photograph of Teresa Steiner from an envelope and dropped it on the table in front of him. He looked at it for a moment.

"Pretty girl," he said. "Luca's photo in the paper didn't do her justice."

"We heard she was doing some work for you at the shrines in Naples."

"A lot of people work for me maintaining the shrines. Hundreds. Maybe a thousand," he said.

"Yeah. It must be hard to keep track," Pino said.

"This one is dead," Natalia said. "Murdered below one of your shrines."

Gambini shrugged. "People die. Whaddya gonna do?"

"Have you talked to your nephew lately?" Natalia said.

"Which one?"

"Your nephew Benito, who lives with the Capuchin monks. Have you spoken with him recently, in the last day or two?"

"My nephew is a holy person. A novice monk. I am fond of him, but we are separated by age and interests and don't communicate much. Besides, I've been traveling."

Natalia referred to her notebook. "Yes. Nine countries in eleven months: the U.S., Brazil, Peru, Colombia, Switzerland, Yugoslavia, Germany twice, England, the south of France."

"I travel for business. What of it?"

"Drug business."

"Pharmaceuticals. And cruise ships and art galleries, among other ventures." Gambini tapped the ends of his fingers together.

"Yes." Natalia turned a page. "You have quite a portfolio." She read down the list: "Spring water bottling, shoe manufacturing, meatpacking, earth moving, cement. Travel agencies, restaurants, movie theaters, farms, apartment complexes, service companies, clothing factories, wineries, a sugar refinery, travel agency, professional soccer team, iron foundry, a private school—and your very own bank, and a half interest in another in Monaco. Yes?"

"Mmmm. My financial advisers are always urging me to diversify. But investing responsibly is a real challenge. There are so many charlatans in the financial world."

"You mean diversify into prostitution, usury, gambling, smuggling, drugs, extortion, protection—?"

"Lies, Captain. Allegations by jealous rivals."

"Were you and the deceased girl involved—romantically, I mean?"

"I am a married man, Captain."

"Are you saying you weren't involved with her, or that your wife was unaware of it?"

Gambini laughed. "You *are* a fresh one. No, I wasn't intimate with the young lady. I met her by accident and hired her to do some work for me in Naples. She said she was German, in Italy studying, and wanted to study the shrines. She said she wanted to experience them personally. Also to examine our whole organization from a sociological perspective, with the idea of reporting how we interacted with the Church and the federal government in carrying out our operations, our fiduciary duties with respect to the group's income, its further dispersal to parties in the government, dependents of deceased members and those currently detained by law enforcement, reinvestments locally of our profits, investments internationally. Et cetera, et cetera."

Pino and Natalia were dumbfounded hearing this. Pino said, "She wanted permission to study your. . . ?"

"Business interests. Yes." He ticked them off on his fingers. "The cleaning services, the casinos, rubbish collection, construction companies, credit unions, import-export. . . . She intended to do a graduate paper for the University, maybe write a book, and wanted my blessing and cooperation." He laughed. "Outrageous, eh?"

"How did you respond?" Natalia said.

"I said I admired her gumption and could arrange something for her about the shrines. But the rest"—he swept the air with the back of a hand—"would be inadvisable, her interest unwelcome."

"You put her to work collecting from the shrines," Natalia said.

"Yeah. As sanctioned by Church representatives. Perfectly legal."

"And she was reliable in her work and satisfactory?" Pino said.

"Not completely, but enough." He seemed momentarily wistful. "She should've been a boy."

"Was Signora Gambini aware of her . . . employment?" Natalia asked.

"No, nor of anyone else's."

"Is the signora available for a brief interview?"

Gambini colored. "You would not want to approach my wife or question her . . . about anything."

"That is not your decision to make."

"It would be unwise to contact my wife, Captain," he said. "She has no part in our dealings, yours and mine, and there is no need for her to be interrogated or exposed."

"We are officers of the Republic," Natalia said. "The Law says we may. You can't be threatening us?"

"Heaven forbid," Gambini exclaimed, all innocence. "You have a law degree from the Officers College in Rome. Bravo. But you are *Napoletani*—both of you. You know how we are."

She pulled out the envelope of cash pushed on her in the night by her first beau and tossed it on the table in front of Gambini.

"What's this?" Gambini darkened.

"A Valentine I received the other night. Fifty thousand euros. Maybe Signora Gambini has charitable interests." Natalia put on her hat. "We'll be in touch," she said as she walked to the door. Sergeant Loriano followed.

They strode down the long corridor again and out the front. Outside, the gravel crunched underfoot. A curtain flickered in the caretaker's house next to Gambini's garage and stables. Pino's hand went to his holstered weapon.

"Christ!" Natalia said to her partner as they got into the car. "Bad idea, this."

"Maybe not. I liked your move with the bribe money. Why would he try that if he wasn't involved?"

"Yeah. He reminds me of a viper." Natalia wiped a patch of sweat from her lip. "Calm when you come across it, but ready to spring the next instant."

"Well, you unsettled him, anyway."

"How could you tell? He's as cool as they come."

She put the key in the ignition and snapped her seatbelt on. Pino rolled down his window.

"Your seatbelt," Natalia said.

"What?" Pino seemed confused.

"Fasten your seatbelt," Natalia said.

"Yes, Mama." Pino smiled and obeyed.

"That's 'Big Mama' to you."

The day was nearly used up, and the last shrine that Teresa Steiner had collected from was on the route back. Natalia and Pino decided to check it out, since they had the safety of their uniforms and the shrine was deep in a Camorra neighborhood. By the time they reached the *piazza* outside the Metro station, the sun was dipping toward the sea. The uncollected garbage seemed even higher in this part of town.

Natalia and Pino entered the small park. It smelled of urine, and the benches were broken. At a folding table, four men played cards. Below, on Cavour, orange buses spewed black smoke. Natalia took a drink from the water bottle she carried. Three large bony dogs appeared, gobbled chunks of sausage, then drank, splashing water onto the pavement.

"You want some?" she handed the bottle to Pino.

Several elderly men sat around a concrete table. Off to the side, another old-timer was smashing a chair against the ground with impressive vigor. Broken legs and splinters of wood surrounded him.

Approaching the group, Pino said, "Gentlemen, we have some photographs we'd like you to look at." The men put down their cards. The chair-smasher abandoned his pile of wood and joined them.

"Is this shrine around here?" Natalia held up one of Teresa's photos of it.

"Ask him," the chair-smasher gestured with his chin.

Natalia and Pino hadn't noticed the man sitting apart

from the others. He was dressed like a *boulevardier*—pressed
trousers and long-sleeved white shirt, albeit frayed and the
pants stained. His sandals were held together with tape.

"Are you students?" one of the card players asked Natalia.

The chair-smasher laughed. "Students! What are you, an
idiot? *Vaffanculo.* Fuck off." He spat. Pino and Natalia recognized two of the men. Once they had been mules for the
Provenzanos, questioned numerous times at headquarters
and even held a night or two in jail.

"Don't mind him," the dignified loner said. "It's over
there, past Via Cimitile. You can't miss it."

Natalia next held out a picture of Teresa. "Maybe you've
seen her around here?"

The chair-smasher pushed his face forward to get a
better look. "Sure! That girl was here. A few times. Took
our photograph. So what?"

"She's dead," Pino said, trying to get a reading from
their expressions.

"Was she alone when she was here?" Natalia asked,
wiping her forehead.

"There was a priest," the chair-smasher said. "I remember, because to see a priest with a pretty girl. . . ." He winked
and kissed his pinched fingers.

She and Pino thanked the group and continued on. A
short distance farther, they came upon the shrine. Paint
was flaking off it. A can with a spray of cheap white carna-
tions, neatly arranged, rested at its foot. Natalia and Pino
walked up to the niche. A plaster limb hung lashed to the
outside; a bunch of half-dead wildflowers lay on the ground
in front of it. Inside the frame of the shrine was a photograph of a priest with a white moustache. He too was
fading, courtesy of time.

The glass on the box was fogged with grime. Two figures
were barely visible—the Madonna and Child. Natalia
stepped closer and peered inside. Framing Mary were the

long horns of a cow and a solar disk. The figures were actually an ancient bas-relief. Crudely done but recognizable—
Isis, the Egyptians' Queen of Heaven, and her son, who was
also her reincarnated husband. A virgin birth, Natalia
recalled. The sculpted figures predated Christianity, having
somehow survived in this recess of wall left from Roman
times, when the Empire's legions had them up as a favored
deity.

Natalia bent down to get a better look. Teresa, Teresa,
she thought. You were on to something.

"Looking for tomorrow?" came a female voice.

The woman couldn't have been more than fifty. Plump,
her hair dyed blue-black. Red pants and a yellow shirt.
Lime-colored sandals. A few yards behind her stood a few
young mothers, curious about the intruders. Their tod-
dlers wandered the cobblestones. Growing up here, they
didn't even have the luxury of school beyond the earliest
grades. A girl became a woman as soon as she sprouted
breasts and could lactate. Few toiled at labors, other than
the hard work of raising large broods and keeping house.

"Go home," the woman said to the mothers, who immediately disappeared.

"They call me the mayor around here. No insult
intended. I'm telling you friendly," the woman said. "Carabinieri or not, outsiders aren't welcome here. Like that
bitch who was taking out of our pockets." She tapped her
chest. "I'm in charge of collections, or was until she showed
up. Mister G sent her to collect even though we'd been
doing it for years. It was ours until she came. Why he
wanted to use that Bosch harlot, we couldn't figure.
Unless . . . you know." She made an obscene gesture.

Abruptly, she pulled her shopping bags into a doorway
and closed the door behind her. A scrawny cat sprinted out
just as it shut. That Aldo Gambini had an arrangement with
the local churches for fairs and the shrine collection boxes

was common knowledge. If the authorities interfered with the shrines, there would be civil unrest. The churches got a monthly stipend and nobody said anything, certainly not the penitents who dropped coins and stuffed their hard-earned bills into the wooden boxes. As long as someone was listening to their prayers. . . .

Another voice. "Please, Signora." Natalia couldn't tell at first where it was coming from.

"Please, I'm hungry."

Finally she saw bony fingers wiggling out of a basement window. The face must have been eighty. Natalia stooped by the window and dug in her shoulder bag for a couple of euros. For wine, most likely.

The bullets struck suddenly. One pocked the wall above the shrine, another kicked loose some mortar close to Natalia. A grandmother, pinning socks on a line in front of her building, fell and shrieked: "I'm gonna die! I'm gonna die!"

Natalia and Pino pulled their Berettas. She crouched, pistol raised. She scanned rooftops and windows for the shooter. No faces at the windows. Balconies empty. It was quiet. A baby cried. Slowly they retreated from the alley, walking out backward, weapons still pointed back at the houses.

"Are you okay?" Pino said, and offered her a handker-chief.

"I've felt better." Natalia accepted it and wiped her sweaty face. "Thanks."

"It was for your arm."

She looked at one, then the other. Her right forearm was bleeding, the sleeve torn. Pino folded back the sleeve.

"It's nothing," she said. "I guess a shard kicked off a façade and struck me."

The handkerchief was soaked red. "I'm taking you to the hospital."

"Absolutely not, Sergeant."

"Let's stop at my place, then," Pino suggested. "It's not far."

Natalia, shaken, nodded. An obese man in a sleeveless undershirt peeped out a window and yanked the shutters closed.

When they reached the street outside, life seemed to be normal. Younger children straggled home from school, people went about their business. If they'd heard the gunshots, there was no indication.

Pino and Natalia returned to their car and drove to his apartment house. Natalia recognized the building. It had once been elegant, but now it was worn down. The outer door was unlocked. Pino went in first and held out his hand to help Natalia over the ledge of the small door mounted in the larger one.

It was quiet in the courtyard. Most of his neighbors were at work, older kids still at their school desks struggling over sums and dates of events past.

"*Giorno*, Lilia," Pino said to the woman scrubbing the stairs.

"*Giorno, tenent*." She stopped for a moment, scrub brush in hand, watching as they passed by.

"Excuse the mess," Pino said, unlocking his front door. He went in first. He picked up a stack of papers from the couch and put them on the floor. An empty wine glass sat forlorn on the coffee table. It didn't seem changed from the time Natalia had been here years ago.

Pino unlatched the shutters and the doors to the balcony. Afternoon light flowed into the room. Natalia looked around. The high ceilings made it seem larger than it was. Aside from the couch, a chair, and one lamp, there was no furniture. Books were lined up on the floor along one wall. A small Buddha glowed. There was a lavender cushion on the floor in front of it. Must be where Pino meditated. Natalia identified the smell of incense.

"A mess?" she said. "Not compared to my place."

There were no photos or mementos. She slumped onto his couch.

"Something to drink?" Pino asked. "I have flat water in bottles, and I have wine."

"Water," Natalia answered. "A little wine, and I might not be in control of myself."

"Would that be so bad?" Pino asked.

"Yes."

"There's something I wanted to tell you."

"That's okay," Natalia said.

"No. I want to."

"Okay. What?"

"It's over with Tina."

"Oh. I'm sorry."

"Don't be. Natalia—"

"I'm dying of thirst."

"Okay. I'll be right back."

Natalia sat on the couch and leaned her head against the cushions. She closed her eyes, falling immediately into sleep. A few moments later, Pino touched her arm, holding out the water.

"I fell asleep? I can't believe it."

"Drink," Pino said, sitting next to her, as he handed her the glass of boutique spring water. "This has electrolytes and vitamins. You'll feel better."

Neither spoke for a moment. Then Pino pulled his chair up to her and reached for her hand.

"What are you thinking?" he said.

"I'm thinking, what's the point?" She pulled her hand away and took a drink. "What are we and the police clearing—three percent of the violent felonies? I'm thinking the Camorra owns this town. They own us. One goes and two spring up. You know it. And I know it. We're the bravest. The toughest, the best. We have a silver medallion on our hats and we take home a few extra euros to prove we're formidable.

"But to the Camorra, we're no more threatening than dust. No one can back us or really protect us, Pino. Not Colonel Donati, not the mayor, not even the president of the republic. No one. If Gambini killed Teresa Steiner and we proved it, he'd make sure we didn't survive here. They'd have to ship us to some former colony to live under assumed names. We're like sacrificial lambs, Pino. We could have been killed back there. Added to some plaque and promptly forgotten." She took a sip of water and lay back. "Aren't you ever afraid?"

"Every day. But we can't turn away from reality—neither its beauty nor its dangers. Or so Buddha teaches us."

"What about putting yourself in harm's way? What does he say about that?"

"I don't see that we really have a choice," Pino said. "You and I have both been offered postings in Rome, at better salaries and with less dangerous responsibilities. Neither of us has left." Taking Natalia's hand again, he lifted it to his lips to kiss it. "Stay the night."

Natalia got up and walked to the balcony, heart beating fast. She tried to think.

The front of Pino's building faced Piazzetta Materdei, which boasted one tree and a collection of pigeons. There were broken cobblestones and one bench complete with the requisite widows. Today there were two of them parked with their shopping, to rest their feet and gossip.

"How long have you lived here?" Natalia asked. Pino stepped out on the balcony behind her.

"This apartment belonged to a childhood friend of my Uncle Ricci. A sweet, funny man. Beppe, we called him. Beppe never recovered from his wife's death. He stopped going out. Started to collect newspapers. It was like a maze in here. Luckily there wasn't a fire. Uncle Ricci visited him every week. Brought him food when he didn't shop for himself. Ten years ago, Beppe died. He willed the apartment to Uncle Ricci. When I finished the sergeants' course in Modena and was assigned to Naples, my uncle offered it to me. Five rooms. A palace. I was thrilled. It took weeks to clear it out. I wallpapered a room with the rarer editions of the newspapers."

"Your Uncle Ricci sounds like a great guy."

"He is. Natalia, listen to me—we can't know the future. We can't see it. There is only now. We are here today. That's all there is."

Pino drew her back into the apartment. He'd laid out a first aid kit. She sat while he tended to her wound. It wasn't too bad, just bloody. It had clotted. He cleaned the wound, disinfected it, and applied a gauze pad, taping it in place. As he gathered up the swabs and debris, Natalia leaned forward and kissed him, first lightly, then with ardor.

"May I?" Pino asked, kissing her throat as he unbuttoned her blouse.

"Let me." Natalia lifted her shirt over her head and dropped it to the floor. She unhooked her bra and slipped it off.

"Beautiful," Pino whispered, openly staring at her nakedness. "Two roses."

He kissed her breasts and her hard nipples. He took off his shirt. She ran her hands over his chest. She could feel his heart pounding. His skin was starkly darker than hers. He touched her cheek as they kissed again.

"Wait," she said, "wait."

"What?"

"I smell like a crime scene."

"Yeah, erotic."

She pushed him back and headed for the bathroom.

"There are towels in the cupboard behind the door. Cover your wound. Keep it dry. Look for plastic bags there, in a basket."

Pino's bathroom was ancient but immaculate. Figured. There was no tub, only a shower with a giant showerhead the size of a sunflower. Natalia laid out towels on the porcelain sink, crackled with age, and sat to pee. A mascara stick poked out of the hedge of toothbrushes upright in a cup. Tina's, no doubt. Natalia flushed and the room practically shook with the rush of water into the bowl. She nearly laughed as she started the shower.

She wrapped her injured forearm in plastic and tucked the edges in. The water was quickly hot and she stepped in, reveling in the warmth that soothed her back muscles and arms as it cascaded along her body from head to foot.

Pino's soap smelled lemony, like him. She lathered and washed, basking in the sensations, then reluctantly turned off the stream. Swaddled in a large towel, she returned to Pino.

"Your turn."

Pino advanced into the steamy bathroom. Natalia dried her hair as she walked the living room, snooping. Aside from books and the basics, there wasn't much. On the small table near the windows were some sheets of paper held down by a plain rock. She lifted it and read the unfinished poem beneath.

> *After the roses—rosehips (after the flesh, the bone)*
> *Silver-lidded morning after sleep.*
> *Rain, the worm in its sheath.*
> *Beyond summer's green.*
> *A ruby-tinted leaf.*

"White Fields," he'd titled it. A policeman-poet. Her junior officer, her subordinate, about to be her lover. It can't be a good idea. Good or not, it was too late. Pino was coming back, towel around his waist. She replaced the rock and looked at him.

Pino said, "I've wanted this for a long time." He embraced her, slipping a hand under her breast—the other reached down to touch her. Natalia was already moist. Desire in charge.

He guided her into the bedroom, to the mattress on the floor. A small Buddha witnessed them. An offering of an orange and rose blossom occupied a small bowl next to it. Pino laid her down and nuzzled her.

"Shall I turn off the bedside light?" he asked.

"No. We are adults and this needs to be premeditated. If we're to break the rules, we should do it with full knowledge."

"Don't go away," he said, and went to a small chest of drawers, coming back with a foil packet. Kneeling next to her, he tore it open. She plucked it out and unrolled the sheath onto his penis.

In a moment, he was inside her. No preamble, no foreplay. Natalia wrapped her legs around him as he thrusted gently. Soon they were slowly rocking back and forth, staring into each other's eyes, abandoning themselves to the pleasure, letting it take them. Mouths open, they kissed. She groaned as he kissed her collarbone, her shoulder. Soon the pulsing was unbearable and claimed them.

They made love until they were sore and their flesh oversensitive.

"Don't touch me," Natalia gasped, laughing, when Pino threatened her again. She turned away and he slid up behind her, an arm around her waist. Cupped together, they drifted toward sleep.

"Silver-lidded morning after sleep," she said, kissing him.

"You've been reading my poetry. Spying."

"That's an unfortunate and imprecise term."

"What would you call it, if not snooping?"

"Investigating." She kissed him. "It's my job."

11

No matter how heavy the rain, people ventured out into the day, holding umbrellas or newspapers over their heads. Motorcycles and scooters splashed pedestrians and sped away.

Swallows took refuge under the eaves and in bell towers. Children in school were a bit more bored than usual, hypnotized by the water sheeting down the panes. The markets opened, with tarps and plastic roofs rigged over the goods. Sidewalk café tables leaned, folded-up and stacked, under opened awnings. Occasionally a waiter would come out to push with a broom at the bulge of water collecting overhead. Just before they went downstairs, the rain eased.

Outside, Natalia unlocked her Vespa motorbike. Cream and purple, not a speck of dirt on it.

"Want a ride?" she asked.

Pino shook his head, but she insisted. Natalia honked the horn as they accelerated and bumped off the slight curb, into traffic. At the office, she signed out the journal discovered by the forensics squad in the hollow of Teresa

Steiner's brass bedstead. The cover was a peacock-feather design. On the first page, written neatly in red ink below her name: PERSONAL. Natalia turned the page: *Reality is a social construct.*

Pure Lattanza.

"*How a mountain is regarded is of no importance to the mountain.*"—Kierkegaard. Interpreted by L: *Nature is indifferent.*

She must have been impressed with herself when her professor showed such interest. Innocence and hope. Lattanza preys on both. Once, Natalia had been as naïve as Teresa. She quotes him again:

If an immigrant is viewed as unwanted, dirty, poor by the society he or she enters, they will forever be affected by that view.

True, Natalia thought. If only Lattanza were as enlightened in his personal affairs as in his observations about the world. It was common knowledge around the University that he came on to at least one student every semester. But he'd never actually fallen for any of them before.

L. and I went to Procida. L. surprised me with a ferry ride. I didn't know where we were going. There were tiny islands where goats came right down to the water to watch us pass. I stayed on deck the whole way. I felt so free, refreshed. L. arranged for us to stay at a pensione on the side of the island away from the dock. Less chance for someone to see us. It was run by a very religious woman. Kind of like a nun. L. got separate rooms, but I'm sure she knew what was going on. Jesus was everywhere. Over the beds. On the wall by the staircase. Outside the front door—the message being that when you enter here, you enter his realm, and when you leave, you are thrown back into the dangerous world.

"*Paradise,*" *I told her, when she showed me my room on the roof. It had a view of lemon groves and the sea.*

"*Paradise is not here on earth,*" *she answered, angrily slapping some sheets on the bed. When L. and I were having coffee the first morning on a patio near these magnificent blue flowers, she watched us with suspicion. Pippo brought us fresh bread and honey. Lovely man. He doubles as the gardener. After breakfast he gave us a tour of the rose garden. We met his cat, Michou, a huge caramel girl. Then he took us to the shed in back where he slaughters rabbits.*

"*Gross!*" *I said. I couldn't stop myself.*

"*Such a city girl,*" *L. said, smiling at Pippo. Men! And who is he to talk? He won't go to the beach because he doesn't want sand on his feet. Won't even swim in the sea, because of the salt. Our sojourn didn't work out as planned. We had a fight. And I met someone.*

Yes, Lattanza might well have fallen in love. Ironically, perhaps for the first time. Did she grow tired of him once he was captivated? Did his pedagogy begin to bore her? Did she find someone else? Gambini, Benito. . . ?

There was a widow across the road. Every night she came out at dusk to tend her lemon trees. Such a peaceful life. The donna is still a young woman, attractive in a way. But such a sad face. Regal posture, and lustrous hair, but she keeps it in check in a tight bun. She lives alone there with two elderly aunts. One is sprightly and manages the kitchen. The other is an invalid. In the mornings the donna took her around the perimeter of the garden. They moved slowly, the aunt with her metal walker, the donna guiding her. Such devotion. Such a pious life. But deadly boring.

Natalia turned the page. There was no more about the trip. Then this:

Roman Myth—note to self—There is a shrine to Isis in Naples! In 19 CE, Tiberius crucified the priestess of Isis and exiled her followers to Sardinia.

(about P.—what can I say? The fruits of transgression. Sin. Pure thrill. Maybe another article? I'll have to use a fake name.)

A thrill? Natalia thought. Sleeping with another woman's man? Whatever happened to feminism? Sisterhood? Or does the "P" refer to Benito? The thrill of sleeping with a clergyman. Every Catholic girl's secret fantasy. She read on:

Magical thinking in Naples increased after the cholera epidemic in 1884. Disease came from the Far East, through Provence, and back to Naples with infected migrant workers. Conditions were ripe for an epidemic. Polluted drinking water. No regulation. Fields crisscrossed with waterways where animal feces were dumped. Produce rinsed in the same water and brought to market. Tens of thousands died in a matter of weeks. The Church suggested the illness was retribution for sin. The desperate chipped away the plaster from the street shrines that had been covered over since unification to make Italy appear more modern and dignified. People offered up votive candles, flowers, whatever coins they could, desperate for salvation. They pleaded for their saints to intercede.

When I showed my notes to L., he laughed. Said, "Save your pretty head for better things." But he doesn't know what I know. He invited me to a conference in Paris. He's talking about leaving his wife. What a fool.

So Lattanza had lied when he said his relationship with Teresa Steiner was over. Natalia closed the journal and swapped it for the dead girl's bulging file. She dug out xeroxes of primary source material on the Egyptian goddess Isis. An ancient text: *Athanasius Kircher.* "Collegio Romano" was superimposed on the page at a corner.

Corporal Giulio came in, bringing her the name of an urban archeologist at the University she had requested. He also announced a phone call for her.

"Hello," she said into the receiver.

"Good morning, Captain."

"Who is this?"

"Benito."

"Benito Gambini, you are a suspect in a murder case. We need to speak with you."

"What about?"

"We found the knife that was missing from the monastery kitchen. We believe it was used to kill Teresa."

"You should talk to her Professor Lattanza. He threatened her. After she split with him."

"Tell me again about the night Teresa was killed. The truth."

"I was sleeping. I heard someone screaming. I got up and ran out to the alley in my pajamas. Others came. They said there was blood on the ground. A lot of blood. Gina Falcone came by. She told me to go back to the monastery, which I did. Later, I heard who it was who'd been murdered. I haven't been able to sleep a night through since."

"Does anyone have a grudge against you?"

"Against *me?* No."

"Were you and Teresa lovers?"

"She was my friend."

Meaning yes, but he was unable to say it. Hesitant. Aggressive in a muted way. Dependent on others' protection in a world he didn't really want to deal with. Teresa's friendship must have meant a lot to him. A brash shield. Had he fallen in love with her? If she ended it, had it made him desperate enough to commit murder?

"I'm not coming in to be questioned or detained," Benito said. There was a long empty pause. "I loved her," he announced and hung up.

"I know," Natalia said into the dead phone.

Teresa Steiner and the little *monachello.* Had they gotten involved with drugs? Had they gotten greedy and taken more than their agreed-upon commission from the donation-box collections? Had she gotten too nosy about Camorra business? Had Brother Benito stabbed her as he held her, and taken her life?

"Damn."

A note was slid under the door. Creamy white envelope. Creamy white stationery, gold-bordered. Looked like a fancy invitation. Natalia sat on the edge of her desk and read it.

N.
It's been a while. Lunch soon, okay?
Do watch your back.
That German girl is trouble.
Be in touch.
L.

Pino arrived but avoided eye contact, as if somehow that would reveal to everyone what they had experienced last night. Natalia smiled to herself and went back to her reading. At noon she slipped out for some air, too sated to eat, too distracted to talk to anyone.

"Natalia Monte!"

A rattan awning shaded the outdoor tables at the café on the corner. Where it was torn, the sun oozed through onto Professor Marco Lattanza. Still handsome, but now he looked ratty around the edges. Unshaved. Wearing a shirt that clashed with his pants. Knowing that he was going to be picked up on suspicion of murder and questioned further, Natalia felt a surge of power.

Lattanza stood up. "What luck. Will you join me?" he asked, smiling. But his lips quivered. Desperate, alone, contriving this "chance" meeting. She almost felt sorry for him.

"If not lunch, a drink then?" he persisted.

"No, thank you," Natalia said. "I'm really not supposed to talk to you, given my history with you. We wouldn't want to bias the ongoing investigation of your role in Miss Steiner's death."

"Please." He snapped his fingers for the waiter to bring another chair. "I'm delighted at this coincidence. I wanted to talk to you anyway. I was going to ring you up at home. I thought we might behave like two adults and renew our friendship. We were that once—friends and colleagues—weren't we?" His voice was unnaturally soft, pleading.

When she didn't answer, he took out a letter from his

inside pocket. "I thought you might be amused by this," he said, voice full of bravado and resentment. He passed it to her like an amusement, a self-abasement she was party to. His hands were shaking. "I received this yesterday."

She recognized the address logo. It was from the Academy of Sociology in Rome. Natalia unfolded it all the way open. They were still using the thin elegant parchment they'd used when she was a student. *We are sorry we must rescind our offer for presentation of your latest work at our spring conference. . . . Regretfully. . . .* She couldn't make out the scrawled signature of the director.

"That's too bad," she said, handing the letter back that had been presented to her like evidence of pain exacted and paid. Debts fulfilled.

"That's all you have to say? What are you all trying to do to me? I'm not going to have my best work ruined by this situation, understand?"

"What are you going to do—kill me? Like Teresa Steiner?"

"Natalia, I'm pleading with you."

"Your wife came in and signed a statement yesterday. She says you weren't home the night Teresa Steiner was murdered."

He brushed his hand through his hair. "We should be friends. Christ, Natalia, when are you going to get over it?"

"You haven't changed. You seduced Teresa. Then she turned you down."

"Wrong."

"You had your customary tryst but she got to you. Then she turned away and you found yourself conquered and cast off instead of in command of her affections and career. Speaking of which, we've asked around. Your own career is stalled—seriously. Enough to jeopardize your position at the University. They are considering early retirement for you."

"That's ridiculous."

"Last month you presented a paper at the art historians' convention in Lyons: *Feminist Iconography—Shrines and the Rebel Church*. Not unlike Teresa Steiner's thesis. If you recall, I wanted to do a similar project. You told me it was ridiculous, but feminist theory is more the rage now, yes? Do you borrow from your students regularly?"

"I could bring suit against you for slander. I'm not joking about suing if you people force me to. But I don't wish to do battle with you, Natalia."

"You bedded Teresa Steiner. Then you tried to steal her work. But she didn't go away quietly like I did. She fought back. Broke up with you. Confronted you and threatened to expose you."

"Look, I made a mistake with you and I've regretted it deeply all these years. I'm sorry, and I would like to make it up to you. Can't you forgive? You were lovely as a young student. I succumbed. I desired you and you wouldn't respond. I wasn't used to being spurned. Natalia, you're still so lovely."

"And you're still a prick."

"Why are you so hostile? Are you jealous of my relationship with Teresa? Haven't you ever been in love?"

Natalia's beeper went off.

He raked his hair again. "Look, Natalia." He gestured toward his table. "I just—"

"If you address me, it's Captain Monte. And if you approach me privately again, I will have you charged."

"Get out of my sight."

"What, no kiss, no cuddle, Professor?" Natalia said. "Catch you later."

She walked away.

Now you know what it feels like to have the rug pulled out from under you, she thought. Guilty or innocent, the suspicion alone would finish his university appointment. There was not a speck of mercy in her, and it felt good. Only Pino's arresting him for murder would have felt better.

Once a month, to balance his sense of obligation to his long-deceased parents, Pino dropped by to visit Uncle Ricci, his father's brother. His uncle's three dogs started barking ferociously, even before Pino touched the bell. A couple of generations of canines had come and gone since Pino was a boy, each generation equally indulged.

Antonio Ricci had lived in the same palazzo since Pino was a child. Nothing had changed in the apartment in all that time. The shabby brown couch was still shabby, with perhaps a little more stuffing sticking out. Pino took his usual seat, the blue lounge chair, its fabric worn and soft. As always, the first thing Uncle Ricci did, after greeting his nephew, was to take one *biscotto* from the box that Pino had brought and divide it among the three current dogs. Then he limped into the kitchen to get their coffee. As a child, he'd had polio and lived for two years in the Children's Hospital. Pino thought this was what had made his uncle more contemplative than most people. Pino had always felt close to him. Among Pino's Catholic relatives, he alone seemed to understand his nephew's devotion to Buddhism.

"How's the coffee?" his uncle said, interrupting the reverie.

"Good." Pino smiled. "Good."

"You seem happily distracted."

"Yes?"

"Like a man in love."

"Maybe so, Uncle. Maybe so."

Aunt Annunziata had been widowed young, and Uncle Ricci never married. Pino always harbored the secret wish that they would get married to each other. When Pino's mother died, and again a couple of years later when his father passed on, Zia Annunziata washed the bodies with alcohol and put them in pajamas while Uncle Ricci covered the mirrors to protect them from evil spirits. Although he wasn't comfortable with these rituals, Pino nonetheless lighted the candelabras and put them around the death-bed of first his mother and, a few years later, of his father. His uncle kissed the corpse, as did Pino. Afterward, Zia Annunziata swept the house to rid it of death. The proprieties and customs were all observed. Months later, when they opened his father's coffin for the second burial, the bones were dried and unbroken, the way they should be. There was no soul demanding its life back.

Pino had been fifteen when a special courthouse was built outside Palermo to try members of the mob. The televised trials captivated all of Italy. Pino went to Uncle Ricci's to watch them on the television. It was better than a movie. Three hundred mobsters in cages. They screamed obscenities and threatened witnesses, pulling fingers across their own throats to illustrate their ill intent. One man, already long imprisoned, testified in a stylish blue suit.

The heroes were the Palermo investigating magistrates, who managed to gain convictions for over three hundred Camorristi. Within minutes of his return home from Rome, the lead prosecuting magistrate and his beautiful new bride were blown to pieces on the airport road, along with their police escorts. The funeral was televised too. A widow of a bodyguard addressed the crowds. She was a beauty, with black ringlets, no more than twenty-five. Grief gave her the bent aspect of an old woman. Yet she spoke coura-geously, pleaded with the mob. She called Palermo a "city of blood" and pleaded for reform. She begged and wept, exclaiming, "You won't ever change!" She seemed on the verge of collapsing.

Thousands grieved with her, standing in the rain. They overflowed the piazza, their colorful umbrellas like flowers on the dark afternoon. Slowly the widow gathered courage, and she called for a new day when citizens would no longer be terrorized by the mob. It was at that moment that Pino declared he wanted to be a Carabinieri. Uncle Ricci smiled and patted him on the head.

"Are you crazy? They will be running things long after you and I are no more than a pile of bones."

The second magistrate was killed soon after.

Years later, Pino had been sworn in. Annunziata and Uncle Ricci were there to witness it. At lunch after the ceremony, Uncle Ricci ordered a bottle of champagne, and Annunziata presented her nephew with an amulet, a special one, to protect him from the Camorra.

Now Pino said: "Uncle Tonio, make me a promise."

"What, Pino?"

"If anything goes wrong for me in the next few weeks, I want you to leave Naples. Go visit your lady friend in Milan. Go on vacation. Just do it immediately, the moment you hear. Don't wait, don't pack. Grab the first train to wherever it's going. When you get to another city, fly where you wish."

Antonio looked concerned. "Is there anything I can do?"

"No, just get away—quick. Be safe. I couldn't bear it if I brought you trouble."

12

Vesuvius released a plume of black smoke, a squid shooting ink into the blue. Ferries arrived and embarked, the blast of their horns vigorous, then melancholy. The sound floated out, finished. The seagulls were oblivious. A few circled overhead, pale kites drifting on the thermal currents. Most were stationed inland, fattening up on the garbage piled everywhere.

For two weeks the garbage had lain in the streets uncollected. Each morning the street sweepers attempted to clear paths so people could get out to school or work, do their shopping and chores. But by dark the paths would be blocked again with bottles and cans and festering refuse in boxes, crates, burlap, plastic, cardboard. Mounds of it, high as walls, clogging cramped alleys and wide thoroughfares, large piazzas and compact *piazzettas*. The flowing ridges of garbage overwhelmed Naples, slowly decomposing into a magma of rot, a putrid sewage threatening to bury the city alive.

Priests had taken to setting burning incense by church doors and alongside pews to try to mask the smells, to no avail. Although the World Health Organization had sent shipments of surgical masks, nobody wore them, the Neapolitans instead preferring to feign indifference. But the garbage crisis was reaching critical mass. Cases of cholera had started to appear, as well as hepatitis C. The government was threatening to send in troops to deal with it, if the private carting companies wouldn't. There were five of them. Four were Camorra firms run by *teste di legno*, straw men who fronted for the syndicate. None were touching the refuse until it had somewhere to go. The trash lay abandoned. Anyone who attempted to have it carted away by private means would be punished. The object lesson of the dead restaurateur who had attempted it hadn't been lost on anyone. In the wide median of the Via dei Tribunali, under the free-standing medieval arches, rotting fruits and vegetables, carcasses of fish, and meat scraps lay next to fresh goods on sale.

Natalia could hardly believe what she was seeing. A shriveled woman exited her building, clutching a brown pocketbook and a tiny sack of trash. She placed it beside the stinking hill that nearly blocked her street. As she walked on, a neighbor heaved a bag from her window. It fell on the heap and burst open, scattering peels and diapers. The old woman ignored it but cursed the Camorra out loud.

Gypsies, hired to set fire to the wastes, used whatever flammables were at hand—gasoline, kerosene, lighter fluid, diesel fuel, packing materials, cardboard. . . . The air was filled with toxins. Naples looked like something out of Dante. The collusion of organized crime and political powers had failed and made the illicit collaboration oddly public and exposed.

Natalia walked through the ancient heart of her city, twenty-eight centuries old, and through what had been, at the time of Nero, an Egyptian neighborhood. At the corner of the Piazzetta Nilo, she passed the reclining statue of the bearded god Nile. *'O cuorpo 'e napule*, read the inscription. O body of Naples.

In spite of the trash bags piled up, the bookstalls were open, locals and tourists browsing. A distracted woman slapped her noisy little boy as she nibbled on sugarcoated almonds. Natalia had a weakness for these candies, sold in their flimsy paper cones.

Virginia Woolf greeted Natalia with a wide cat yawn as she opened the door to Mariel's bookshop. The caramel-colored giant rubbed against her legs and leaped up on the sales counter to stroll across quite regally. Mariel had found Virginia W. abandoned when she took over the space. Her parents' death had left her well off. She used her inheritance to open the bookstore.

The shop was plain: bookcases and fluorescent lights. The black-and-white terrazzo floor was the one touch of elegance—that, and Mariel herself. Mariel came out of the back office. "I didn't hear you come in."

Mariel's hair was in a fashionable bun, white cashmere sweater perfect, black cotton skirt, fat pearls. Natalia could still see the girl in her, stretched out on the chaise longue, reading. Mariel stepped to the door and locked it, slipping the CLOSED sign into place, then led Natalia back into the shop to a small sitting area. Lola was there, and a younger woman in yellow T-shirt and pants and gold high heels decorated with sequins. Bianca Strozzi, the queen of the contraband cigarette business in Naples. Natalia hid her surprise. Lola and her husband Frankie had been in Gambini's camp forever.

Bianca Strozzi employed thousands, bringing in untaxed cigarettes by truck convoy from Puglia, cigarettes she bought in huge quantities directly from people working with the major cigarette companies. She didn't trust banks and was rumored to lease storerooms stuffed floor to ceiling with U.S. dollars. Widowed young, she had stepped into her husband's role in the Camorra and did what had come naturally to her as the daughter of a Camorra family who had grown up in Naples's criminal subculture: she took over. Not unusual in the contraband cigarette trade. It was mostly populated by women buying, hauling, storing, selling tax-free "blondes," as the haulers called them.

"I've heard a lot about you," said Bianca, taking the risk of extending her hand.

Natalia couldn't slight her friend's new friend, who had herself run a considerable risk arranging this meeting. She shook Bianca's offered hand.

"Mutual."

"I'll get right down to it," said Bianca. "We've leased the equipment, ships, and overseas landfill. We want to cut a deal with the mayor. Come Monday, we want to start hauling garbage."

"The mayor will be delighted to hear it," Natalia said. "The companies that hold the contract now have obviously abrogated their responsibilities and failed to perform. You'll probably get a medal from the prime minister."

And a bullet from Gambini.

"Here's what we hope to get, too: police protection."

Natalia could imagine the violence this might unleash on the city.

"It's not unprecedented," Bianca hastily added.

"No, I know, I know. You want your drivers and rigs escorted. The Army might even be here by then. I'll certainly pass this to my superiors. It's reasonable, I suppose."

Costly too, because it will certainly set off hostilities between Strozzi's camp and Gambini's. But the city was desperate to rid itself of the garbage and would undoubtedly embrace the possibility despite the inevitable clash.

Bianca nodded. Natalia didn't state the obvious: Bianca Strozzi was challenging the prevailing order, shaking the tree. The dispute would be bloody.

"Why don't you negotiate this directly with the mayor?"

"I don't trust politicians—or men. They're all for sale. Four hundred a week for a street cop. Four thousand a month for a connected cop's information. A hundred twenty thousand American dollars and a man's gold bracelet buys a court decision. Gambini's even bought the Neapolitan Communists. Lola says you deliver and that you're not for sale. Is that true?"

"So far, nobody's come up with my price." She smiled.

"I like you," Bianca said. "I appreciate your help. Let me know if I can ever return the favor."

With that, Bianca collected her handbag and pressed a speed-dial number on her mobile phone. As she strolled to the door, a four-door car pulled up and a thin woman stepped out carrying a raincoat with something rigid underneath it. Bianca slipped into the back seat. The thin woman closed the door and let herself into the front passenger seat. The car glided away.

"Have you heard?" Lola said. "Gambini is running for a seat in Parliament."

"Perfect. His *galoppini* will certainly get out the right voters. As long as he holds his seat, he'll have immunity from prosecution. And he won't be lonely. There must be two dozen convicted legislators already there, and more than twice that number appealing verdicts or running out the statute of limitations on some infraction."

"Or awaiting a pardon from a judge they've gotten to. Yeah, Gambini enjoys a good gimmick."

"Speaking of which," said Natalia, "what the hell are you doing with Bianca Strozzi? Your husband has worked for Gambini since he was a kid. Zazu isn't going to take this challenge from Strozzi lightly, or anyone who sides with her."

"Things aren't so good between us and Gambini."

It had to be serious for Lola to risk Gambini's wrath. And

Gambini's hold had to be slipping, for Frankie and her to even think of switching their allegiance.

Natalia nodded. "Let's hope he doesn't see Bianca coming at him."

Back at her office, she startled Colonel Donati with Bianca Strozzi's proposal. He would pass it on to the prefecture and mayor immediately, he said, and added: "They just brought in your friend for an interview, by the way."

"Friend?"

"The esteemed Professor Lattanza. Cervino and his partner have him in the Fish Bowl."

Natalia climbed the flight of stairs up to the third floor and checked with the desk clerk to see what room they were in, then proceeded to the adjoining observation room. She pushed back the curtain on the one-way mirror. The grilling was already under way. There he was, Lattanza in all his glory, wearing a custom-made lavender shirt with hand-stitched cuffs and discreet monogram, hair freshly cut. Relaxed. She couldn't bear to hear his dissembling and left the audio switch off.

Marco Lattanza pushed aside a lock of thinning hair with a studied gesture. The index finger came to the side of his forehead, indicative of deep thought, an attentive and courteous concentration on whatever point the two carabinieri were making. He shot his cuffs, fingers checking the gold cufflinks as he constructed his compelling narrative, explaining, man to man, why he'd lied about his whereabouts on the night Teresa Steiner died. He leaned in, fingers pinched together, then waved his open hand in emphasis, eyebrows momentarily arched as he decried the vindictiveness of his wife on discovering his infidelities with a young mistress.

Lattanza turned coy, playful, and outlined the shape of a woman with both hands. He laughed. The younger detective smiled. Marshal Cervino sat stony-faced. Lattanza looked down at his hands, contrite, and nodded rapidly. The hands flew up and out. What was a man to do?

Teresa Steiner pursued him, her professor. He did the only polite thing an Italian male could. But the relationship soon grew burdensome and so he ended it. Why would he have killed someone so young and lovely?

Lattanza looked confident and controlled. But the tiniest bit forced, his animation the slightest bit excessive. Marshal Cervino had sensed it too. Lattanza suddenly fell silent and still, a puppet with its strings cut. Interview over. Cervino began the interrogation.

Natalia and Pino climbed Via San Mattia, en route to lunch in the Spanish Quarter. It was the toughest section in the city, but still she couldn't resist it. They diverted into a small inclined street. The alley twisted, a dark ribbon with a slice of sky above. Most alleys here were augmented intermittently with stone steps to aid in the steep ascent up toward the Vomero hill district on the ridge, some eight hundred feet above. A widow in black knelt, scrubbing the stone beneath a local shrine, clearing a small rectangle amid the grime. The stone was worn smooth with centuries of scrubbing. A blizzard of signs hung over the street, announcing the nature of the services offered within the shops that lined both sides.

Pino and Natalia discussed their second suspect as they climbed.

"Where would a blind monk hide?" Natalia asked.

Three boys kicked a ball across the expanse of the Piazza Dante. They were using garbage bags as goalposts.

"What is he doing for money?" she asked.

"His fellow monks would supply him with some."

"No doubt. Or Father Pacelli. But where would he hide out? I can't see him checking into a hotel."

"Me either," said Pino. "Maybe a hiding space under the church?"

"In the crypts? Too awful to contemplate."

"But for him, hiding in the dark would be perfect. He'd actually have the advantage."

"How would he eat? Maintain himself?" She shook her head. "No. He's up here with us somewhere."

"Where wouldn't we think of looking for him?" Pino asked.

"In the monastery?"

"We've already tried that. No. Where would he not stand out? Go unnoticed?"

"Someplace with other blind people. A hospital?"

"Or in an assistance program for the blind. Maybe a special residence."

Turning into a street running parallel to the hill, they came to a small plaza. Just a few tables were set up outdoors, as far from the mounds of garbage bags as possible. A cook spun a wheel of dough in the window of a pizzeria. The odor of garlic pervaded all, stronger even than the sickly sweet smell of refuse.

Two beautiful Nigerian men passed, their smiles startling. A woman rushed past, screaming. A French tourist, her expensive bag now on the arm of a youth who was racing away. Her husband made a show of concern for her well-being to avoid giving chase. She slapped at his hands, screaming and pointing in the direction the purse-snatcher had gone. Big Doro's aunt stood on her balcony above them. He must have been nearby: he was the *camorrista* who ran the immigrants who thieved in the quarter. Rumor had it there was a monthly quota on pick-pocketed wallets and snatched handbags that the police would tolerate, the price of admission for slumming tourists.

No one had a bank account here, no credit cards, and only the children ate decently. The residents all looked sinewy and gaunt. Half the men under thirty were unemployed, and three quarters of the women.

Two Bangladeshi trailed them for a block. At first Natalia worried about their designs on Pino and her, then realized they were just more undocumented stateless souls trawling for casual labor: a floor needing sweeping, a display window requiring washing. Failing that, they might grab up an unattended handbag. Natalia clutched hers closer, momentarily concerned not to lose her weapon to a cutpurse too naïve to recognize the special bag carried by plainclothes policewomen and female Carabinieri.

"Where's my money?" a woman yelled at her companion. A drug addict, judging from the sunken cheeks and the sores on her lips. The sequins on her T-shirt flashed. She had on fashionably torn black jeans and leopardskin boots. An alley filled with Chinese women, sweatshop workers taking a rare break. The dozen streets of the quarter were a grid laid out in military precision, perpendicularly crossed by another eighteen, most no more than a dozen feet wide. They were too narrow even for sidewalks and were paved with large, flat stones. Five hundred years earlier, Spanish invaders had built the district to quarter their troops. The six-story buildings dated back centuries and looked their age. Repairs layered repairs.

Natalia and Pino reached their favorite *trattoria* and greeted their regular waiter. He was happy to have customers for an early lunch. The place was empty. He gestured toward their usual table, a step into the open-sided restaurant near the cash register. Neapolitans passed by, shopping bags and briefcases in hand, heading toward the tram

station and the funicular car that would winch them from
the cramped and weathered alleys of the quarter up the
steep incline to the wide boulevards and tree-lined residential streets atop the ridge.

There was shouting in the street outside.

"Now what?" Natalia exclaimed. "Go ahead and order.
I'll be right back."

A crowd stood gathered at the top of the street, watching
several dogs snarling at one another, fighting over rotted
meat they'd extricated from a ripped garbage bag. The
yelping dogs were sinewy but muscular, tough as the streets
they inhabited. The latest scourge to befall the city—feral
dogs. Packs of them came down from God knows where in
large numbers to feast on the garbage.

The wild dogs were too mangy to appear pedigreed, but
the aspects of German shepherd, bulldog, terrier, and
Doberman were present. Running in a pack, they roamed
where they pleased, baring their teeth at any creatures foolish enough to interfere with their scrounging. They turned
their attention to a small woman clutching her shopping
and her baby.

"I can't get into my house," she cried. "They'll bite."

She was a gypsy, scarf tied around her head. The lead
dog growled, eyeing a packet of meat poking out of the top
of her bag. Natalia approached the woman steadily. She
reached into the bag and tossed the meat. As most of the
pack ran off, Natalia escorted the woman into her house.
Then she put in a call to the dog-catchers. They were hor-
ribly overtaxed, but she got through after a dozen rings.
Her lucky day. An animal-control van was nearby on a call
in the quarter and would come over.

"That didn't help my appetite," Natalia said, rejoining
Pino, who was already enjoying their pizza.

"I took the liberty of ordering wine," he said. "May I?"

"Please."

He poured, and she immediately took a sip. "That's definitely nicer than wild dogs."

"Or garbage," he said. "The paper this morning said thirty-nine landfills are completely overloaded and not accepting any more from Naples."

"The public is coming unhinged. A mob of irate citizens attacked the police station in Pianura last night, set buses ablaze, broke windows."

"When is Bianca going to defy Gambini and unleash her trash collectors?"

"God. Soon, I hope. Colonel Donati's wife is agitating for them to move. She can't stand it any more, he said."

Pino sighed. "Why are we talking about this at lunch?"

"What should we be talking about?"

"Us. Last night. Its greater cosmic meaning."

"Last night was wonderful," she said.

"You think people can tell?"

Natalia took ravenous bites of pizza. "If you keep fondling my knee, I think they might come to suspect."

"Sorry. I can't help it."

"Look. Last night was great. I told you already."

"But?" he said.

"Do I have to fill in the blanks? We work together. Today is today."

"What's that—a Zen koan? I'm not familiar with it."

"Pino, please. If we become a couple, we can't remain partners."

"We *are* a couple, Natalia. As of midnight last night."

Natalia sighed. "I don't know, Pino. We have to keep it a secret, but you know as well as I, there aren't any secrets at the station. Somebody will find out and tell everyone else. I'm worried too that our feelings could jeopardize our lives out here on the street, never mind our careers."

"What *about* our careers?" Now he looked a little grim too.

"The regulations. Sergeant fraternizing with a superior officer. Superior officer fraternizing with her subordinate. They would make us choose. One of us would go. I don't want it to be you. And it won't be me. I can't abandon another career and start over. I don't want to."

"I don't want you to. You've worked too hard, have too much invested."

"And you?"

"Yeah, me too." Reality began to sink in. "But you should know. I'm not giving you up."

The guards and groundskeepers were finishing lunch when Natalia reached the Orto Botanico. They were discussing last night's football game and ignored her as she walked through the iron gates and climbed the stairs. After the fumes of the city, the green crown of trees was a relief.

The garden had been a favorite of hers when she was a child, her parents' destination after church and on her father's one day off. Every Sunday, if the weather allowed, they'd stop home after mass to change. Her mother packed up the salami sandwiches prepared the night before, along with a jug of lemonade, and they'd set off. Sometimes Mariel or Lola would come too.

Natalia's father could name all the birds chattering round them as they picnicked—kestrels, wrens, robins. At home he had books with photographs and names of hundreds of species and records of their songs. One year, Natalia's mother saved up and bought him a splendid pair of binoculars.

Natalia sat on the bench in front of the greenhouse where she and Lola had agreed to meet. Giant purple and red blossoms hung off of thick green stems. A bright yellow bird flew over her head. Below the chestnut trees, a gardener trimmed hedges. Otherwise, it was the birds, and distant traffic.

A butterfly landed at her feet. Black-and-orange wings paddled open and shut. A brief life, but nearly perfect. Odd that Lola wasn't here yet. Appearances aside, she had always been the more punctual. As Natalia took out her phone to call, she heard the explosion. Hundreds of birds rippled out of the trees.

So much for peace and quiet. She'd catch up with Lola later. She dropped her cell phone into her purse and sprinted toward where the sound had come from.

Sirens grew louder.

Three blocks away, the car was black and twisted. Local police were already there. Natalia flashed her badge and pushed through the crowd. A woman sat at the curb, screaming, her face bloody, blouse and stockings spattered with blood. Lola.

Natalia crouched, took a handkerchief from her bag, and wiped Lola's forehead.

"Frankie," Lola said, sobbing hysterically. "Nico, my poor baby. Nico."

"Sssh. There's no pain, Lol. They're gone, Lola. They're gone."

"It's my fault. He shouldn't have gone with Frankie. It's my fault."

"No, Lola. No."

Natalia pulled Lola closer and rocked her like a child, blocking her sight of the car and the thick black gasoline smoke curling skyward.

13

The police guard at the door waved Natalia into Lola's room. Her beautiful hair was jagged, partly cut away to get at the cuts in her scalp. She was sitting up, her eyes closed. Natalia walked to the bed and touched her arm. Lola opened her eyes. Dead eyes, Natalia thought.

"They got Frankie and Nico."

"I know," Natalia said, touching her cheek.

"I have to tell you—"

"You don't have to do that now."

"No. I do."

"He can kill you and your two younger ones. We won't be able to guard you three all the time. Lola, your kids are down to one parent."

"I know, I know. The damn girl."

"Teresa Steiner?"

"Yes. We worked together, she and I, for the last six months. Frankie was as much of a prima donna as she and quickly got sick of her. But Gambini seemed so taken with this girl Teresa, and was determined to bring her in.

Frankie flapped around and said he wanted to quit the organization. He couldn't, of course. It would be betrayal. So I took over working with her."

"On the shrines?"

Lola nodded. "I knew all about the shrines—my uncle ran the collections years ago. Gambini thought we'd make a good team. He had big plans for her. The shrines were nothing. He wanted her moving heroin for him. No easing into it, maybe starting her in hashish or kobret. No, he just drops her on us—boom. She had plans as well and wanted to know everything about us. How everything worked, what everyone did. Made us all leery of her."

"Gambini had her running part of the drug operation?"

"I know—odd. I'd keep track of the shipments coming in and Teresa would move them out—to our local people operating open-air markets and to distributors in Germany. She was perfect, Gambini said. Spoke Italian and German fluently, of course, and easily traveled back and forth. Who would suspect a beautiful young girl—an honors student on her way to becoming a professor?"

"Did she want to be a professor?"

"She wanted everything, sure. Except for this problem with her adviser."

"Lattanza?"

"Yeah. Said he was a devious shit. Just scum. He was, but she had led him on too. He threatened to ruin her academic career if she didn't take him back. She still wouldn't come around and he threatened her, the fool. He had no idea who she was associating with. Teresa laughed about him. Said the University was worse than the mob."

"Was she afraid of Lattanza?"

"Not even a little. She said he didn't have the balls to hurt her."

"Did Gambini know about her relationship with Lattanza?"

"He knew. Lattanza was lucky Gambini didn't dip him in a boiling fondue. Teresa wouldn't have it. She liked his wife too much."

"Did Gambini know she was sleeping with his nephew Benito?"

Lola sat up. "He knew. Didn't seem bothered. Gambini figured since she was doing research on the shrines already, it was a perfect setup. She said she needed to see them up close and operating. And needed some money for her mother's medical treatment—a lie. Gambini laughed and laughed when we told him and acted like he was proud of her con. He said her mother had cancer, but had died from it when Teresa was in her last undergraduate year. You knew that too, right?"

"From the beginning. Go on. But don't tire yourself out, okay?"

"No. It helps to talk. Teresa wanted us to take a bigger cut than Gambini had authorized. To hold out on him. Totally nuts. Suicidal. As if Gambini wouldn't find out. She was willfully naïve. She thought she had him wrapped around her little finger. Funny thing is, she did. We thought he was gonna drop her in the Mediterranean. Instead, she came back from a holiday wearing a spectacular necklace he'd bought her. Rubies and pearls. We'd never seen him behave like that. Then she sort of hit on Frankie and scared him to death. That was the last straw for him."

"Was he jealous of her?"

"I suppose. He'd always been Gambini's boy. His future wasn't so shiny once she came along. When she came on to him, he got worried about what Gambini would think or do."

Lola reached for her water. Natalia handed her the glass.

"Thanks." Lola took it, hand trembling. "Teresa boasted about everything. The necklace she said was worth a quarter of a million. Said we'd be able to buy our own jewels soon enough. She had the names of the German narco contacts. They'd told her they'd be delighted to do business with us. I told her she was crazy. She wanted to know everything about the Camorra. About the Camorra women, how they'd come to power. Teresa called us the 'new feminists.' She said this was our chance, our opportunity. We'd make a killing."

"Easy, Lola." Natalia took the glass and tipped it gently to Lola's mouth.

"Thanks. The girl was an idiot. I told her she'd get both of us killed. When I said I wouldn't go along, she said she'd go it alone. She made fun—teased me. Such a fool."

"Gambini too, from the sound of it."

"There was something going on there. When he took her to Frankfurt, he told her everything about our legit business interests there and introduced her to the biggest drug dealers we service. He was planning to put her in it big time. Zazu Gambini invested in Teresa Steiner like no one else, emotionally and otherwise. And she disrespected him. It was a 'no-brainer,' as Mariel would say. It was certain he would kill her. He'd have to, given what she was doing. There was no stopping her. I was going to say something, warn him maybe, so it wouldn't come back to bite me. Frankie said no, keep away. He was trying to slide away himself and go out on his own. I didn't listen to him."

"You told Gambini what she was up to?"

"I didn't have a choice. I couldn't be seen to side with her. Can you imagine—belittling Gambini?" Tears spilled from Lola. "My baby!"

She sobbed convulsively. A nursing nun in traditional habit rushed in and poured her a cup of water and handed her a small yellow pill. Lola swallowed. The sister motioned for Natalia to follow her. As the nun's dark habit swept away, Natalia was reminded of school, when she and Lola were both still girls. It felt like a million years ago. Just outside the door, she ran into Mariel, who kissed both her cheeks as they embraced.

"She's just taken a sedative," Natalia said.

"Ah, not the right moment to visit. You have time for a coffee?"

The friends left together and retired to a café nearby. The University wasn't far, and the place was crowded. They grabbed the last outdoor table.

"Looks like tourist season has begun," Mariel said. A troop of red-faced Germans in sun hats marched past, guidebooks in hand, cameras suspended chest-high. The customers on the dark patio were mostly locals and university kids. The tourists were like colorful tropical birds attracted to the shiny chrome in the cafés ringing the upscale piazzas.

"How is she?" Mariel said.

"Not good."

"Poor baby."

They ordered espresso from a young waiter with dark wavy hair. "And how is your young swain?" Mariel asked.

"Determined."

"Excellent. Then all you have to do is maintain your energy and keep up with your young beau."

"Listen, Em," Natalia said, rifling through her bag, "while I have you here. . . ." She extracted the photocopies of primary source material Teresa Steiner had acquired in her research. "What can you tell me about this?"

Mariel took out reading glasses and examined the oversized sheets.

"You need an antiquarian book dealer for this. Ah, *Athanasius Kircher*. Medieval text. Copied from the original at the Collegio Romano—you know, the palace built by Ignazio of Loyola, the soldier who founded the Jesuits."

"Anything else?"

"I don't think the library is open to civilians. Someone

had to intercede for her to get this: her professor, or someone in the order."

"A Jesuit?"

"Yes."

Natalia continued: "Teresa Steiner evidently was looking
for evidence to support her idea that all the Black Madonnas venerated by the faithful were inspired by depictions of
Isis. Likewise the Madonna and Infant Christ seemed
inspired by Isis holding her infant in the same pose."

"Aren't there several Black Madonnas in Italy? Hey,
remember when we were fifteen, we went to Montolvo to
see one and the priest wouldn't let me because I had on a
halter top and short skirt?"

"Yes." Natalia stabbed the air with a finger for emphasis.
"And that old crone took pity on you and lent you her
shawl. And a hanky to wear on your head."

"Damn *paparazzi*," a man shouted behind them. "Get the
hell out of my face or I'll break yours."

Both women turned. A seated man swiped at a photographer crouched close by, grabbed his camera by the lens
and toppled him backward onto his buttocks. Chairs
scraped as patrons got up from their tables and helped the
elderly man up. It was Luca, the photographer who special-
ized in crime and the Camorra. He had pestered them for
years, catching them unawares, sometimes unconscious,
passed out in clubs, often dead in the streets—executed.
Three cameras hung from his neck.

"Take another shot and it will be your last," the patron
shouted. Natalia recognized him from a photo array of
Camorristi recently taken arriving at the airport. This one
was in the cement business in Albania, home undoubtedly for a vacation from his overseas assignment for his
organization.

"Come on, Luca," she said, helping him to his feet.
"Come sit with me and Mariel."

"Captain, thank you."

Natalia turned to the seated mobster. "I hope you enjoyed your lunch."

"What the fuck are you talking about? We haven't *had* our lunch."

"Thank you for your patronage." She pushed back her jacket, revealing her 9-millimeter automatic.

"Who are you?"

"Captain Monte. Carabiniere." She waved away the waiter approaching with their drink order. "Have a nice afternoon."

The Camorra man rose up, looming over her. "We'll meet again, *Captain.*"

"I'll count the minutes."

The man stalked off with his friend, and Natalia joined Luca and Mariel at their table.

"Thank you for saving me and my cameras," Luca said, worriedly clicking through the photos.

"Digital camera," Mariel said.

"Has to be, these days," Luca said, "to get the photos into the paper. It's all digital. No more darkrooms and chemicals. Everything's electronic."

Natalia sat next to him. "How long ago did you take these?"

"These? Of Zazu? More than a month."

"Let me see the previous one."

The shot was of Aldo Gambini and Teresa Steiner. There were several. One in a café—Gambini leaning over, whispering something to her—or kissing her; it was hard to tell.

"They let you take this?" she said.

"No way. Five hundred millimeter lens. I was miles away. There are a couple more."

He flitted through the next series—Gambini and Teresa Steiner violently arguing.

"Is there a market for candid photos of Camorra celebrities?"

"Not much for the live ones," Luca said. "Most maga-zines don't dare run them, unless it's a public event they're attending or if it's with an obituary or crime story. Besides not wanting their faces flashed around, the hoods think I'm bad luck."

Luca forwarded through another half-dozen. More shots of Gambini in the company of Teresa Steiner, taken at dif-ferent times. Natalia took her time examining each.

More Gambini lies about how often he'd seen her. Clearly they hadn't met just twice. Nor were they such casual acquaintances. Never had she seen the look in Aldo Gambini's eyes that Luca had captured in some of the photos. Warmth. Did uncle and nephew vie for the girl?

"I need copies," she said.

Luca nodded. "Thought you might say that."

Luca departed, followed by Mariel. Natalia checked her watch and waited for Pino. One table over was a lithe young black man. Could be a dancer. Tidy dreadlocks hung down his back. He turned and she caught his lovely smile in pro-file. Milk-chocolate skin. His companion was also young. Plump and blond, dressed in cheerful blue. A creamy com-plexion. They were laughing, leaning into one another, speaking French, maps and guidebooks among their cups of espresso and café au lait.

Students rushed in and out, as if they were all on impor-tant missions, as she had once, when the world was hers for the taking. The same dour *barista* was behind the cappuc-cino machine, making the coffee. So much time had passed since she'd met here with her professor to discuss her thesis.

Ah, well, but revenge is sweet, she thought, stirring an extra spoonful of sugar into her cup. Professor Lattanza, Marshal Cervino had informed her, was relocating to a leased room in a middle-class section, quite a comedown from his previous digs. Also, an impressive number of graduates had suddenly brought complaints against him to senior faculty for things he had done and threatened them with when they were students.

Pino appeared at the curb. She left payment and wended her way through the youngsters. They would just make the appointment Giulio had arranged with the urban archeologist.

—

Dr. Michael Heller was Dutch, blue-eyed, tall, too handsome to look scholarly. In a photo above the desk in his tiny departmental office, an Italian beauty held two children.

"What if he didn't carry her down through the church?" Natalia said. "There's just no trace evidence that he did."

Heller nodded. "Another entry. Why not? Naples is undermined with quarries the ancient Greeks excavated for the volcanic building-rock the city sits on. And the empty Roman cisterns, dug before Christ, to serve as underground reservoirs. Huge things. Some were fitted out with bathrooms and beds during World War II. Bomb shelters. And there are mortuary crypts beneath the temples and churches, of course. Also caves used as catacombs. Subway tunnels are down there, too." He raised a finger. "Give me a moment."

Heller returned with an oversized volume. "Your church—Il Purgatorio," he said, laying open the pages that traced the crypts.

"Are there any passages radiating away from the crypts?" Pino asked.

"Hard to say," Heller replied, peering at the crude schematic. "These plans are unfortunately incomplete. Close by, you can see these passages excavated in the volcanic rock, but they don't appear to connect with the crypts. Not that that means anything. Only a third of all the labyrinths have been explored and recorded. There are huge caverns, some tunnels so narrow you have to crawl through and hope you can even turn around in if you have to back up. It would be worth your while to go look. Just don't get lost down there. The excavations under the city go on for hundreds of miles—two thirds of them, like I said, uncharted. There are an awful lot of urban legends of people going down there and not coming back out."

Heller spent another twenty minutes explaining to them some procedures they might use to avoid getting lost, and then he lent them some equipment.

"It sounds complicated," Natalia said, starting to feel claustrophobic.

"It is. You know what? I haven't been down in a while. Perhaps I could accompany you?"

The church was empty. It took them a few moments to find the discreet door to the tunnel leading down to the burial vaults, and then they were on the way, descending. Natalia didn't relish the prospect of confined spaces. When she was fifteen, her class had gone on a lengthy tour of Naples's underworld. In the dank air of the narrowest tunnel, her light had gone out. The memory remained fresh all these years later.

Thankfully, Dr. Heller led the way, his light breaking the darkness in front of them. The whole mortuary area consisted of six rooms. Niches carved into the walls were empty.

"They once held individual bodies in upright fetal positions," Heller explained, "while they putrefied. Those rounded cavities held up their heads."

They searched each room methodically. Pino's light revealed graffiti faintly chalked on a wall.

"Enlightened vandals," he said and read: "*Such wast thou / Who art now / But buried dust and rusted skeletons.*"

Natalia sneezed.

"The great Leopardi," said Pino. "Giacomo Leopardi."

"It's amazing what these ancient structures have with-stood," Natalia said. "Volcanic eruptions, earthquakes."

"Yes." Heller pointed at the white mortar holding together the large stones that made up one foundation wall. "They used mostly lime, sometimes mixed with a little linseed oil. It turned out to be perfect because it remained flexible even when subjected to seismic shocks."

Heller preceded them into the adjoining rooms and pointed out where they should look for passages. Pino found one, but it led downward and no one was keen to follow it.

"Check the corners carefully," Heller said. "They some-times used optical illusions to camouflage."

In a corner of the fourth chamber, Pino discovered that the walls didn't meet. Instead, there was a nearly invisible lateral passageway. It was narrow but passable, and they inched along sideways. High on the wall, Heller planted a self-contained light to mark their way. The passage wid-ened and started to ascend at an angle. They came to a low arch and stopped. Neither Pino nor Natalia was doing well in the close subterranean environment.

"Any chance of this coming down on us any time soon?"

"I don't think so," Heller said, "or I wouldn't have been so quick to volunteer. The subsoil is not a problem. The tufa stone is light and durable."

"And this arch? It looks repaired."

"It has been. Decayed building stones have been cut out and new ones substituted." Heller touched the pair. "*Pin-nare*, it was called. They did a good job: raked and repaired the lime mortar and mortised the blocks."

They followed it for forty feet and came to another low opening. No arch this time, just natural stone. On the wall above it was a smudged handprint. Natalia thought it was blood. Pino planted more lights and they pressed on, duck-ing through into a small chamber. They advanced bent over, the ceiling too low for them to stand normally. There were no more worked stones, just sheer tunneled rock.

"How old do you think this shaft is?" Natalia asked.

"Heaps," Heller panted, sweat dripping off his chin. "Five hundred years? Two thousand? It's like a hive under the city. Has been like that since before the Romans, before Christ."

They stopped to gulp some water and then pressed on. Carabinieri were tested for claustrophobia. Natalia assured herself that hers wasn't bad, but she grew less convinced the farther they went. The idea of having to retrace their steps through what they'd come through seemed inconceivable, and she blocked it from her mind.

The tunnel ascended slowly. They resumed their climb. More bloodstains, this time on crude steps cut into limestone. Natalia counted twenty up to a ledge. There, they found themselves standing upright in a small square space.

"Mason's marks on rock," Heller said, touching the wall. "Building stones."

His light fell on a heavy wooden slab standing upright in the wall. There was no passageway going farther. Unholstering their weapons, Natalia and Pino lashed the flashlights to their belts and pushed. The slab was hinged. A door. It resisted, then creaked open ever so slowly.

Natalia and Pino drew their guns and stepped, blinking, into the light: it was the interior walkway of a courtyard. A heavy-set monk turned and gasped at the new arrivals. His hood fell away. "Christ have mercy," he said.

Pino and Natalia holstered their weapons and grabbed him by the elbows before he could topple. Judging by his garb, a Capuchin. It was Benito's monastery.

"I'm Captain Monte of the Carabinieri," Natalia said. "We didn't mean to startle you."

The monk pressed a hand to his face, as though still uncertain as to the reality of his visitors. "No one uses that door. It's been sealed for years."

"Have you seen Brother Benito?" Pino asked. "Today? Maybe yesterday?"

The monk shook his head.

Heller examined the door. "It opened easily enough," he said. "Someone's used it recently."

⁓

Natalia and Pino returned to the station, dirty and exhausted. Natalia collapsed in her desk chair and slipped off her walking shoes. Giulio brought her water and an aspirin unbidden. She hadn't the energy even to thank him. Half an hour later, Father Pacelli arrived, as summoned. He was wearing street clothes and looking like a distinguished author or a professor in his turtleneck and corduroy jacket. A graceful man, she realized again. She and Pino questioned him in an interview room, tape running.

"Thank you for coming so promptly, Father," said Natalia.

"Not at all. How can I help?"

"We have a question to put to you about a book. Among the late Teresa Steiner's academic notes, we found photocopies of some pages of a rare volume apparently copied at the Collegio Romano."

"*Athanasius Kircher*, yes. I arranged for her privileges there so she could have access."

"Did you accompany her to Rome?"

"I was required to be there, yes—to vouch for her. We took the local train in the morning. Around ten, as I recall. I introduced her to the chief librarian and left to visit some brothers at Santa Maria Maggiore and returned to Naples by train in the early evening."

"You lied to me when I spoke with you at the *Termini*. Why? You told me you didn't know her, hadn't met her."

"I did it for your sake, really. Not to waste your time. It wasn't—isn't—pertinent to your investigation."

"That isn't up to you to decide. Where did Ms. Steiner go after your research mission?"

"I don't know."

"Was that the last time you saw her?"

"No."

Natalia glanced at Pino and waited to hear more.

"You seem hesitant, Father," she said.

"I *am* hesitant."

"Why so?"

"I heard her confession several times. But that is as much as I am comfortable confiding."

"Because of your vows? Of course. I understand the silence imposed on you as her confessor."

"That's very considerate. I appreciate it."

"Were you aware of the tunnel connecting the crypt under the church to the cloister in the monastery?"

"Not before you revealed it so dramatically. Though the abbot says he knew of its existence. And a couple of the brothers who are the order's gardeners. You might want to discuss it with him."

"How did you come to intervene for Teresa Steiner at the library in Rome?"

"Benito. He asked me, as a favor. I'd seen her a few times with him, and in the confessional. She also sought me out once to thank me for my help, and promised me a copy of her thesis."

"Have you seen or heard from him lately?"

"Seen? No."

"Spoken to. . . ?"

He pursed his lips and nodded. "Yes."

"Did he happen to tell you where he was?"

"No. But he did say he was innocent of this crime." Father Pacelli looked at them both in turn. "He is, you know."

"Are you speaking definitively, as his confessor?" said Natalia. "Or hopefully?"

"I wouldn't even be permitted to respond to that if I had heard his confessions. But no. The abbot is his confessor and spiritual adviser. I say it as his friend. Benito is not capable of killing Teresa Steiner or anyone else."

The disbelief was evident on Pino's face. Natalia thanked Father Pacelli for agreeing to be interviewed and saw him to the door. It closed after him. She turned back to her partner.

"You think he's withholding something—a man of the cloth, a priest?"

"A sin of omission perhaps. Yes. I can't say any more." Pino assumed his most arch and sarcastic manner, imitating the elegant deportment of Father Pacelli. "Privileged information."

14

Lola was asleep. Natalia waved at the guard on duty and tiptoed in. She went to the bedside table and removed the dead mimosas from the vase, replacing them with anemones. Lola opened her eyes.

"Hello, sweetheart." Natalia kissed her friend on the forehead.

"I was dreaming," Lola said, looking gaunt and anxious.

"I interrupted. Sorry."

"No, I'm glad you're here. It wasn't a good dream anyway." Natalia smoothed the sheet.

"They washed my hair."

"I noticed. It looks nice."

"Kind of blah, don't you think? But I can't do it." Lola held up her hands, swaddled in bandages. "I need Fionetta's magic touch."

"Or mine," Mariel said from the door.

"Hey," Lola said. "Just like mornings at the salon."

Natalia massaged Lola's shoulder. "Let it out, Lol. Let it out."

"I need to get ready."

Mariel set about trying to make her presentable. Half an hour later, Lola looked almost normal. Her two friends held up a mirror. They were just about ready when Bianca Strozzi entered like a corporate executive in a dark gray pantsuit and lighter blouse, her blond hair highlighted with streaks of white. Her two female companions were likewise attired.

The police guard who had slipped in behind Strozzi was nervous when she tried to dismiss him.

"I'm supposed to stay," he said.

"We'll protect her," Bianca assured him. "Go have a cigarette."

Natalia inclined her head toward the door. The officer said, "Ten minutes," and departed, saying, "A sector car is already downstairs, waiting to escort yours."

Bianca Strozzi and her two henchwomen were there to accompany Lola too. The meaning of the gesture was not lost on Natalia. Lola had joined the Strozzi group and was in open opposition to Gambini and his clan. All three women, Natalia could tell, were discreetly armed—as was she.

Mariel finished fussing with Lola's hair and makeup and helped her into the coat she would wear over her black dress. Then they added a hat and veil. The five of them escorted Lola to the elevators and down to the front of the hospital. A black Wrangler and two limousines awaited, each with a driver and a duo of Bianca Strozzi's women inside. Bianca saw them all into the center limo and climbed in after, sitting backwards to face the three old friends. The convoy traveled down the steep hill into Old Naples toward the Church of Christ the King. When they arrived, Strozzi's ladies stepped out to take up positions on the sidewalk and check those gathered outside, then signal their boss, who assisted Lola. She was still groggy from her injuries and leaned against Bianca as they walked.

A stormy night had deposited a carpet of pink petals on the walk outside. Mourners embraced Lola, and tears flowed, streaking cheeks with mascara—faces from the neighborhood that Natalia had not seen in years. Beseeching gestures animated the women. The men, in dark suits, stood stoic and silent. Anthony Turrido the baker looked awkward and stiff in an obviously borrowed suit jacket and mismatched pants.

Natalia summoned Lola inside. Eyes turned as she and Mariel helped Lola down the long center aisle, trailed by Bianca and the two bodyguards. The three of them took seats in the front pew, Bianca and her people immediately behind them. The caskets were closed, flanked with great bursts of flowers in huge vases, some stalks the height of small trees. Nico's coffin was a fraction of the size of his father's.

Mourners passed in a steady stream and stopped by Lola to express their condolences: somber men and weeping women, some accompanied by children who were uncharacteristically quiet and still amidst the roiling emotions they sensed all around. Half the old neighborhood had turned out: gents with hair gelled, ladies with permanents, teenage daughters teetering on five-inch heels, self-conscious boys in their fathers' oversized shirts and ties, and half a dozen widows who lived on their monthly Camorra stipends: a thousand euros or more, depending on their man's status, and token staples for the fridge. No one from Gambini's crew, though Frankie had spent most of his life in Zazu's organization.

Then, suddenly, Tomas. Bianca crossed her arms, casually brought her hand closer to her weapon. Lola accepted Tomas's hand and listened to his words. He kissed her on both cheeks and passed on.

The funeral mass was long. At the end, Lola was wrung out, but there was no escaping the trip to the cemetery itself. Roses and gladiolas covered the coffins. On the way, the cortege rolled by the bent figure of Gina Falcone as she trudged toward the graveyard, pushing her empty cart in front of her. Bianca, on the jump seat, bent toward Lola, whose head rested against the window.

"He will pay," she said. "I guarantee it."

No one had to ask who she meant.

Colonel Donati stood with arms crossed before the small group of colleagues in his office. "Bianca Strozzi's trucks are rolling, hauling away the garbage. A container ship of the stuff is on the high seas already, bound for God knows where. And huge fifty-truck convoys are hauling the bilge to Hamburg and two of the closed landfills the Army has reopened by force."

"As long as it's away from Naples," said Pino.

"Exactly," Donati said. "We have thirty-seven landfills entirely full up and chained shut, just two temporarily reopened. God knows how Rome will resolve the crisis finally, since the Camorra won't stand for incinerators being built. The farmers are desperate to get the toxic stuff away from their sacred soil, and the restaurateurs and shopkeepers are anxious to dispose of their mountains of garbage finally and get their patrons back. People just hate this situation and are livid with the government. Only the gangs of gypsy boys are regretful. They've been getting fifty euros per trash fire and pelting the firemen with garbage when they try to put them out. The citizens have had it and are joining in."

"Do you think Gambini will move against Strozzi?"

"He will undoubtedly make his displeasure known."

Natalia arrived late. "Sorry, sir."

"No, no," said Donati. "We were just chatting." He

ushered them over to his desk. "This is what I wanted to convey to you," he said, and passed across a single sheet with an address. "A tip from one of Cervino's informants as to the whereabouts of the missing monk."

Pino, seeing the address, sat up: the Scampia quarter. Natalia recalled the grim story told to all new recruits of a doctor who'd ignored the plague to visit a sick child in the Borgo Loreto slum. "He's come to kill us!" a crowd had screamed. Armed with sticks and stones, they went after him and would have killed him if a street sweeper hadn't run for the Carabinieri, twenty-five of whom arrived on foot and horseback to rescue him.

"We'll have to thank the marshal," she said.

Donati sensed no irony in her voice, or chose not to acknowledge it. "The prime minister has ordered troops put on alert in the South Central Military Region in case they have to be brought in. That's all," he said, dismissing them with a wave.

After they left, Pino said, "Jesus. Scampia. That's the worst slum area there is. Totally Camorra territory. You think this is serious information, or Cervino just having his fun?"

"Doesn't really matter," Natalia said. "We've got to check it out."

"Really. Where are we going to get the tanks to go in there? The police won't go near it. Whenever they have to, they mount major commando operations to do it. Battering rams, body armor, helmets, assault rifles."

Corporal Giulio appeared, bearing both a hand-delivered envelope for Natalia and the motorcycle courier's clipboard. She signed for it and tore open a strip along one edge that freed the contents.

"Important?" Pino said.

"It seems I'm being sued by the esteemed Professore Marco Lattanza."

Pino and Natalia changed into their work uniforms: black epaulet-shirts with red piping at the collar, sleeves rolled up; black fatigue trousers that looked like cargo pants; wine-red berets with the silver badges bearing the Carabinieri insignia: antique flaming grenades and the stylized initials of the king who had created their first company. Embroidered over the right shirt pocket and bordered in red was the word CARABINIERI. A badge over the other pocket announced rank.

Pino signed out two hand-held radios and a 12-gauge Franchi SPAS-15. Natalia took an AR-70 assault rifle and extra magazines in a shoulder pouch. As they left the station, Cervino appeared alongside, similarly dressed and armed.

"Mind if I join you, Captain?"

"Not at all, Marshal Cervino. We could use the company."

Together they got into the unmarked Alfa Romeo: Pino behind the wheel, Natalia beside him. Cervino, in back, strapped on his bulletproof vest. The headed due north on Via Toledo, what was once the old Roman road.

Scampia's forty-five thousand residents lived in poverty. Three fifths of the young males were unemployed, and nearly all the women. It had been like that since the sixties, when Scampia's first public housing towers had been erected: twenty-story slums.

On the way, Pino and Natalia decided not to wear bulletproof vests so as to signal less of an expectation of trouble. The shoulder of the road all the way there was piled high with garbage bags and litter of every description. The stench increased with the temperature.

The three carabinieri arrived and rolled toward their destination. The towers were surrounded by sun-baked dirt lots. There was no landscaping between the high-rise buildings, and there were no commercial businesses in sight: no stores, no cafés, no plazas with lovely fountains. No trees either. Instead, a garbage-strewn desert of abandoned cars and furniture and toys and crutches surrounded the structures. The skeletons of three elevator cars were out front, too, being used like huts by some early-bird dealers.

Natalia said, "This looks like deserted derelict housing. Except there are lights in windows and people going in and out. I expected a bustling drug market."

Cervino cocked his weapon. "Too early. It won't really crank up until the afternoon, but it'll go on late into the night. In another hour or two, this will all be an open-air bazaar for pills, cocaine, marijuana, hashish, heroin, kobret, glue."

The car jolted through potholes.

"Dealers' apartments are fitted out with heavy metal front doors," Cervino said. "So are the main entryways. There are armed sentries on the roofs and in the halls."

The alarm was sounded, a shout between the lookouts: "Maria, Maria."

"Why are they shouting 'Maria'?" asked Pino.

"Slang for 'cops,'" Cervino answered, staring up at the balconies. "You don't have to worry about the lookouts. The *vedette* aren't armed."

Locals rushed back into the buildings, and reinforced doors clanged shut. Windows were shuttered with steel.

"At least they haven't put up any roadblock checkpoints," Pino said.

"They will," said Cervino. "We need to be quick."

Pino pulled off the main road onto a rutted single lane that led in. Natalia could see tomatoes growing in pots on the balconies. And men with binoculars flanking them.

"They're very interested in us already," Cervino said.

A man on the fourth floor flipped open his cell phone and spoke into it. In the next moment, he hurled a string of firecrackers down onto the asphalt below. They popped madly. It was the signal to withdraw. The narco traffickers and the few shaky customers edged toward the building, along with some young moms pushing strollers.

"Great," Pino said. "What do you want us to do?"

"Proceed," Natalia said. "Benito is supposed to be in Tower Building D, on the left."

As they got out, Pino tossed Natalia her flak vest and slipped into his. She didn't argue, just put it on.

More steel doors slammed shut.

"The place is impregnable," Cervino said.

A woman emerged from the tower with three children. She'd put on a jacket over pajamas, and must have been trying to get her children safely to school. Her long black braid was halfway down her back. How, Natalia wondered, did she manage to survive here? The kids, all girls, were neatly dressed. The mother smiled at the three carabinieri, while the two oldest girls just stared. The youngest gave Natalia the finger.

The three walked on, weapons cradled: Natalia with her shotgun, Cervino and Pino each with assault rifles. No use. The building was locked down like a prison.

"This is impossible," Natalia said, eyes fixed on the armed men overhead. "The three of us aren't going to storm the place. We're not even going to get in the lobby."

Pino nodded. "If he was here, he's been moved to another flat by now or been spirited away out the back."

"If he's in there at all," Natalia said, "they'll move him again the moment we withdraw."

Glass shattered. The three turned toward the sound. A small band of young kids was gleefully smashing out the windows of their unmarked car and making off with whatever they could manage to strip away in a hurry.

"Hey!" Cervino shouted and jogged toward them. The youngsters scattered like bugs.

Luckily the engine started. They drove back to the station slowly, without talking.

While Cervino rushed off for an "important" meeting, Natalia and Pino returned the weapons to the armorer.

"Now what?" Pino said.

Natalia flipped through her notes. "We did hypothesize the possibility of his hiding out in that blind persons' residence. Do you want to try that?"

"Why not? At least the nuns won't point guns at us or break our windows."

⁓

The Sisters of Charity ran the mission house for the blind. Most wore street clothes, but all shared the same beatific, well-scrubbed look.

The mission house was a modern, four-story structure on a leafy street in the hilltop Vomero section that overlooks Old Naples. In the distance, Vesuvius coughed out a thin white cloud of smoke. Freighters and ferryboats put out to sea. A hawk glided by on the thermal currents.

The gates were rusty. A caretaker swept leaves in the courtyard. On a bench sat a nun in full habit, chatting with several old people. Standing at their approach, she identified herself as Sister Carolina.

Natalia showed her a picture of Benito. "We're looking for a young man who may have come here recently, looking for shelter."

"Yes," said Sister Carolina. "I recognize him."

"You're sure?"

"Yes, yes. Very polite, soft-spoken. We don't see many young people. Not any newcomers at all, really. These days, the young non-sighted or sight-impaired go elsewhere for training. They get jobs, lead normal lives. Our residents— well, a few can read some Braille, make potholders, that kind of thing, but not enough to manage out in the world. The young man you are inquiring about came to us on Tuesday."

"Is he here now?" said Pino.

"I'm afraid not. Unlike most of our residents, he had some funds and paid for a week. He left early, though, after only a few days."

"Did you know he is a monk?" Natalia asked.

"He didn't mention it, but I had the feeling he was a religious, too, like us. A monk and a priest visited him."

"Did he give a reason for cutting his stay short?"

"Not precisely. But two ladies came for him. They said they were relatives." Sister Carolina hid a smile with her hand. "He seemed surprised. Actually, I don't think he knew them at all. But he went along. I worried a little that he didn't realize who they were."

"How do you mean?"

"They were terribly nice but scantily attired, heavily made up. You know, low-cut tops, miniskirts."

"Fallen women?"

"I hesitate to say, but I suspected it, yes. Prostitutes. He couldn't see, of course. They made an incongruous trio."

Natalia and Pino thanked the sister and departed. On the street, they pondered their options.

Natalia asked, "How many brothels does Gambini run in Naples?"

"Five."

A man was selling flowers from the back of a truck. The partners didn't speak until they were out of his hearing, walking along Via Cinarosa.

"We need to find out which one he's hiding in. We won't get the manpower to simultaneously raid all five."

"Right," Pino agreed. "And if we raid just one Gambini brothel and it's the wrong one, he'll get instantly moved."

"Damn."

"Who might know, or find out for us?"

15

An enormous glass ceiling soared in the century-old Galleria Umberto mall. The shops were beyond Natalia's budget, and it had been here that her father toiled long hours mopping the black-and-white tiled floor.

Lost in sentiment, she didn't see Lola until her friend whistled to get her attention. Lola had commandeered a prime table and three chairs. One was piled with shopping bags from Ferragamo and Armani, among others. Balm for the grieving mother and new widow. Each purchased garment, Lola told her, was black. "To match the circles around my eyes," she said. She was wearing a beautiful gray headscarf knotted on the side. The ends brushed her pale cheek. "Haven't been out since the funeral."

"No more police guard?" Natalia scanned the hall.

"No. But you're here. Also one of Bianca's gun molls."

"Where?"

"Six tables to your right. The brunette in subdued Chinese red and espadrilles, trying to pass for a tourist. And, hey, I've got a spiffy new Glock. In my handbag."

"Christ, Lola. What are you doing with a Glock?"

"Accessorizing. You've got a 9-millimeter, why shouldn't I? What every girl needs: a manicure, a pedicure, a Glock. Look what I bought."

Lola pulled out a wad of tissue from a Versace bag and unveiled a black silk jacket. "Gorgeous, isn't it? The buttons are the darkest red garnets. I've decided: no more trash, no more designer copies. I'm going for the classical classy look—heartbreak and despair."

"It's beautiful," Natalia said.

"Mmm. Matches my mood."

"Black and expensive?"

Lola folded the garment and returned it to its bag. "That too, but no. *Sanguinoso.*"

"Bloodthirsty?" Natalia fixed her friend. "Don't do anything impetuous, Lola. Think of your two children."

"I do, and I think of my third boy too. He comes to me in my dreams, all black and burning. It's my fault he's dead."

"Lola, you can't assume the blame for others' actions."

Lola snapped her fingers and a waiter appeared. She ordered coffee for them both and checked out the other patrons as she lighted a thin black lady's cigarette. "What's so important that you have to ask me?"

"The prime suspect in Teresa Steiner's murder. We haven't located him as yet."

"The blind monk? Gambini's nephew?"

"Right. Might you know if he's hiding somewhere in Naples?"

"You think Gambini is helping him hide?"

"Very possibly. Blood is blood."

"Too bad it wasn't your old professor. Yeah, I might know someone who might know."

The waiter hovered a few feet away. Lola glanced over. "He's a little too interested in our conversation, wouldn't you say?"

"I think you have an admirer, is all. He can't take his eyes off you."

"Must be the grief. It's like pregnancy. Makes you shine like a moonbeam. He's cute. Looks a little like Frankie at that age."

"He looks like a thug."

"Exactly." Lola dialed a number on her red-lacquered cell phone. "Give me a minute," she said, rising from her seat. Hand over her other ear, she conversed with someone, then returned to the table. The call had taken seconds. "You're right. He's at Cavelli's. In a room on the second floor."

"Gambini's brothel on the waterfront?"

"Right. Via Cortese."

"You don't waste time," Natalia said.

"My time's running out too fast to waste it. There are things that need doing."

"I appreciate your help."

"And I yours, *cara mia.* I couldn't have survived this without you and Mariel."

Natalia said, "This is more trouble for you if Gambini finds out you tipped me."

"It's trouble for *you* if your bosses find out you've been hanging out with an undesirable like me." Lola stubbed out her cigarette. "He can't do anything more vindictive than he's done already. The kids and grandma are gone. Hidden. He won't be able to trace them."

⁓

Natalia and Pino walked into Cavelli's Bar. A second unit was blocking the back door used by patrons for discreet exits. The bartender was unpacking a carton of liquor, arranging amber and green bottles on the mirrored shelves. Higher up hung a black-and-white photo of a girl in a string bikini. Next to her, a faded reproduction of Giotto's *Madonna and Child.*

"*Fratelli Bianchi,*" he said in a loud voice. The White Brotherhood. What the nether dwellers call militarized police, usually out of earshot. The bartender made it a public announcement more than a greeting. Not that anyone was in the place yet.

A banquette hugged one wall. Three tables occupied the middle. The jukebox pulsed with the Mario D'Esposito Ensemble. An ordinary bar. Only the *conoscenti* knew about the rooms upstairs.

Brothels had operated in Naples for centuries. Only once, during the AIDS epidemic in the 1980s, had they been closed down by the authorities. The women had been tested for the disease. Those in good health had been issued condoms and lectured, regular inspections instituted. Underage females had been sent home. Since then, the vice arm of the Carabinieri had grown preoccupied with white slavery and other Camorra business and paid little attention to the sex trade. Customers were likewise lax, paying a bit more to forgo condoms and sometimes for rough coupling. Johns and prostitutes were occasionally found floating in the bay.

"You here for the pickpocket?" the bartender asked. The lone customer at the bar was snoring. "Sounds like a woodpecker, don't he? I keep warning him to keep his hands in his pockets, but—" The bartender gestured widely. "Hey," he called to the man. "Dummy."

"Don't bother," Natalia said. "He's not our concern today." She pointed upward. "We'd like to take a look upstairs. Please step out from behind the bar."

Cheeks puffed like a blowfish, he came out from the well. Natalia hoped he hadn't already set off any warning alarm and wanted him away from it. Corporal Giulio had followed them in. Pino pointed the bartender to the nearest table.

"Sit. Corporal, watch him."

Natalia and Pino proceeded into the kitchen. Boxes of liquor were stacked all around. It was cramped, illuminated only by a fluorescent strip nailed to the wall. A folding table doubled as a counter next to the stove, at which a man in torn jeans and white undershirt stirred a pot of stew meat, his cigarette ash poised to fall in at any moment.

"*Giorno*," Pino said. The man said nothing.

The door leading upstairs was painted red. Natalia opened it and Pino led the way up. Air freshener saturated the passage, not quite masking the odor of mold. The stairs were carpeted, the walls overlaid with gold brocade paper, peeling and smoke-stained. At the top, a foyer led to a large, well-appointed bar with black leather booths along one wall. At the end of the bar sat the madam, a Nigerian by the look of her. She was doing her books, writing up orders to restock the bar. If she was surprised by the appearance of carabinieri in the place, she didn't show it.

"You early," she said.

"We're looking for a young man—blind."

On the wall by the corridor was a photo-array of women in various poses, and their room numbers and nationalities: Ukrainian, Albanian, Russian, Brazilian, Nigerian.

Natalia and Pino proceeded down the hallway. Natalia eased open the first door. Inside, two girls in Mickey Mouse pajama bottoms and T-shirts slept on a king-size bed. In the mess atop the dressing table were a set of handcuffs and lace thongs. The girls woke. The ash blonde sat up. The dark one too. She was skinnier and younger, her eyebrows shaved. A diamond piercing glittered in her nose.

"How old are you girls?" Pino asked. He pulled open a drawer in the vanity table.

"Fuck you," the blonde said.

"Look," Natalia said, "if you ever want help getting out of this. . . ." She placed two cards on the bed. "We can arrange a place for you in a halfway house."

"And pay our bills?" the blonde said. "Cook our food? Tuck us in?"

The second room was empty of girls or customers. A mirrored ceiling reflected back the satin quilt on the double bed. A basket of masks sat on the floor next to it.

The third door was a bathroom. They heard male voices behind the fourth door. Natalia pushed it open with her drawn weapon. Benito Gambini sat on the bed, Father Pacelli in a chair next to him wearing his clerical collar and a purple ceremonial stole, bible open, their heads bowed.

Benito stirred. "Who is it?"

"Don't worry, my son," Pacelli said, reaching out for him. "It's the Carabinieri."

"Benito Gambini," Pino said, "we are placing you under arrest on suspicion of murder."

"Please. Benito Gambini is an innocent man."

How does he know that? Natalia wondered. And why was he protecting Benito so fiercely? Were he and Benito lovers? An hour or two of passion stolen from their grim lives? The distance from devoted acolyte to fervent lover was no more a distance than from chin to mouth. Or was she getting carried away? The priest seemed so certain about Benito's innocence. How could he be?

"I've sinned," Benito said, "but I've not killed."

Pino ordered Benito to stand and handcuffed him in front. Natalia didn't object to the breach of regulations.

"What about him?" Pino said, meaning Pacelli.

"Would you accompany us, Father?" Natalia asked. "We have some questions for you too."

"Of course," Pacelli said, and he preceded them out into the corridor and down into the bar.

Outside, Natalia directed Corporal Giulio and the

backup unit to transport Pacelli, while she and Pino took Benito. Back at the station, Pacelli and Benito Gambini were placed in separate interview rooms and left to stew. Word spread quickly of the arrest and the priest's detention. The observation rooms filled with a steady stream of carabinieri wanting to see the blind killer-monk and the cleric nabbed in a brothel in his priestly uniform.

Cervino volunteered to wear the monk down for Natalia and Pino, to be the unfamiliar face, the unsympathetic stranger pressing and probing. Natalia accepted, and Cervino had the young man tearing up and shaking in minutes, mostly by invoking his victim. She and Pino stepped next door to observe Pacelli. No one else was there watching the priest through the backside of the mirror. Pacelli, eyes closed, was meditating.

"Should we question the Jesuit together?" Pino asked.

"No. One-on-one. Let me go first."

Natalia slipped into the room. She didn't bother with the tape recorder so she wouldn't have to officially announce that the questioning had begun and possibly inhibit him.

"Sorry for the interruption."

"You have your job to do."

"Some questions."

"Please."

"How did you know Benito was at the brothel?"

"I heard it from the ladies at the train station. Ida, actually. So I went to the brothel a few days ago to see what help I might render. I found him, of course, and tried to comfort him. Benito was still distraught at Teresa's death, at being accused, hunted. I calmed him and assured him that no one would think him guilty of hurting her."

"You are that convinced of his innocence?"

"Yes."

"You went to see him again today."

"He asked me to come every day, and I did. Until you found us."

"Admirable loyalty."

Pacelli shifted in his chair. "I am his priest."

"That's all?"

"What are you implying?"

Natalia waited, sensing something she was uncertain of.

"What will you do with Benito?" Father Pacelli asked finally.

"Charge him formally. Try him. Most likely imprison him."

"That won't be necessary," Pacelli said. "He's innocent."

"You keep saying that with such conviction. Forgive me, Monsignor, but how the hell can you say that so confidently?"

"He's suffered enough. Castigated for being Gambini's nephew. Losing his sight."

"Nonetheless. . . . The evidence may be circumstantial, but there's a goodly amount of it."

"Benito is simple. A country boy. The girl's death, the tableaux—its reference to deep history, the pagan history, if you will—well beyond his abilities. The killer is not some naïf, as I'm sure you've figured. The use of the ex-voto, for instance."

Natalia sat up. The ex-voto was not public information. Nor were the other details of the tableaux. Natalia had scooped up the small silver heart before even Father Cirillo had noticed it.

"How did you know about the ex-voto?"

"I can't remember—probably Gina Falcone."

"No. She was out of there before she could identify anything but the dead girl."

"Sinners burning in hell," Father Pacelli muttered.

"What?"

"So dramatic, the tiny figures and the flames."

"The street shrine outside San Severo," Natalia said. "You have the key to San Severo, don't you, Monsignor? It was you Lattanza saw with Teresa Steiner. For once he was telling the truth. You murdered Teresa Steiner, and you were willing to let an innocent man stand in for your punishment."

"I have tried to convince you of Benito's innocence all along. You wouldn't believe me." Pacelli raised his head. "Sins of the flesh," he said quietly. "For fifty years I did not give in to temptation. And then I did."

Natalia pulled the control panel closer and pressed the button to begin recording. She cited the date and time, identified herself for the tape, and further noted Father Pacelli's presence.

Pacelli held up a hand in surrender. "I was intimate with the girl, Teresa Steiner. We transgressed in my room, once in the chapel at her insistence. She came to me originally for confession. But it was a false confession. She offered herself instead. Ironic, isn't it? The Jesuits were the first to hear confessions of women. They were to take place in churches, well-lighted spaces. Even so, Father Francis Xavier heard the confession of a female in 1537, and soon after she was found to be pregnant.

"For Teresa it was a thrill. The thrill of the illicit. For me it was something different. We went to Rome together, to the Jesuit library. I fell in love. I told her I would leave the monastery, the Church, to marry her. She was amused at first, pleased, I think, with her conquest. But it was all a game for her. Still, I didn't give up." He turned away for a moment, then continued.

"After Rome she refused me. Said Gambini wouldn't like it. She taunted me with the pearls he'd given her. Can you understand?—to have paradise and then have it taken away?"

"What happened the night she died?"

"I was in the communal kitchen when she turned up. She'd come to see Benito about something, or so she claimed, though she knew he would have retired already, following the monks' hours. I was the only one who might be awake. I pleaded with her to reconsider. She cursed me. She stormed out. I . . . followed her into the street. I still had the kitchen knife in my hand."

"You stabbed her."

"I lost control. May God forgive me."

"What happened then?"

"She screamed once. The blood poured out. A fountain of red. I like to believe she lost consciousness. I held her. 'At the hour of our death,' I whispered. She died in my arms."

They sat for a long moment. Someone knocked on the mirror. Not Pino. He'd never do that. She ignored the signal.

"You carried her back inside," she said.

"Yes. Yes, I knew about the tunnel to the crypt. A gardener had told me. I carried her down to the ossuarium and recited the last rites over her body." He looked straight into Natalia's eyes. "We were lovers, Teresa and I," he said, almost proudly. "Benito hurt no one. I am the guilty one."

16

Army units accompanied Bianca Strozzi's trucks as they removed the trash from the city's streets and plazas, from the sides of the highways leading out of town, and hauled the fetid refuse away. Far away. Hamburg, Sicily, China, wherever. Natalia never wanted to see another garbage bag in her life and volunteered this information to Pino as they cruised along the waterfront, backing up the soldiers following Strozzi's rolling armada. The garbage piles were shrinking away, the tide of garbage was going out.

Natalia leaned against the headrest and closed her eyes. Yesterday the phone had rung off the hook following their arrest of Teresa Steiner's murderer. The mayor had called, the prime minister's office. There was talk of a commendation. She and Pino had retreated to her bed for the night, hiding out from the world. They feasted on cold pasta and a chocolate cake from Dapolito's Bakery. They indulged themselves with food and love and slept peacefully, phone disconnected. The instant it was reconnected in the morning, it went off again and didn't stop. So she was happy to have escaped from it to her duty hours and the day's mindless chore of shadowing the Army guarding Strozzi's drivers and equipment.

The morning's paper lay discarded on the back seat, its front-page headline screaming KILLER PRIEST CRACKS UNDER INTERROGATION. Somehow Luca had managed shots of them leaving the brothel, Father Pacelli in black suit and collar, Benito Gambini in cuffs, but by midmorning the monk had been dropped from the later editions that plastered the news kiosks along their patrol route.

Life was going on semi-normally. They passed a *trattoria* where waiters were setting up tables. Crisp white cloths, napkins and silverware. Natalia, hungry, imagined a freshly grilled *branzino,* her favorite fish, glistening with olive oil.

"What is going on over there?" Pino asked.

A truck was parked across the road, backing the traffic up. Horns blared. Drivers got out to see what was happening. Pinto too. Natalia pushed her door open and stepped out.

The truck's cab door was open. No driver in sight. "There," Pino said, pointing to the driver slumped against a light post across the street. They were walking toward him when the truck exploded, strewing garbage everywhere: paper, peels, cans, vegetables, coffee grinds, the bodies of rats foraging seconds earlier. Windows imploded and shattered in the building behind them. More blasts followed, echoing across the city.

"Where was the Army escort?" the colonel demanded.

"Stopped for a break," Natalia answered.

"Break. I'd like to break. . . ." Donati tapped his desk blotter nervously. "Meanwhile, reports are coming in of addicts overdosing all over town, nodding off in public toilets and abandoned buildings and not waking up, passing out at their desks, at lunch, in the middle of treating patients. So far, there are nine of them. Each one dead."

"Testers?"

"No. These weren't coke whores and junkies test-driving the first shipments to see if they were properly cut and wouldn't kill you. These are mostly middle-class consumers who cashed in. Francesca ran a quick analysis of their heroin. It's been cut with the usual—benzocaine—but laced with strychnine. All the heroin is from Gambini distributors. All poisoned."

Natalia pushed back her hair. "Payback for the truck bombings. We should get a warning out to addicts."

"Dr. Francesca's called a press conference for one o'clock. What I want you to do is get word out on the streets immediately. And I want Gambini to withdraw his . . . product." Donati rapped the desktop. "Be fast."

They needed to split up to speed things up. Pino went off to see the duty officer to have the news communicated to the carabinieri on patrol and spread the word through the battalion. Natalia set out to persuade Gambini to stop killing his customers.

It wasn't far. The Via Chiaia ran northwest from downtown, parallel to the shoreline of the bay, fronted by a beautiful strip of parkland. In the distance, six kilometers east, brooded Vesuvius.

Huge plate-glass display windows of exclusive shops filled medieval arches made of Roman quarry stones. Versace, Cartier, Rubinacci. Gentlemen shopped at Marinella and Eddy Monetti's while their ladies rested their expensive selves at posh sidewalk cafés and gossiped. Once upon a time, the Chiaia district had housed a ruling Spanish elite in baroque mansions overlooking the water. Its dilapidated villas and stately art-nouveau apartment houses were in a state of perpetual restoration. The lavish palazzos again sheltered the *dolce vita–nouveau riche* crowd once referred to by the press as jet-setters, the beautiful people, Eurotrash—esteemed subjects all, of the Kingdom of Naples. The idle rich had been joined by the professional classes: doctors, dentists, lawyers, and the Camorra chieftain Aldo Gambini, enjoying the fruits of *la mala vita.*

In among the restored façades of their gentrified domiciles and offices were slummy residences of the poor. Their kids played in the streets, beneath endless lines of drying laundry strung across the narrow lanes and blind alleys, and skateboarded along the well-maintained streets. Bent old women trudged past the cafés, carrying groceries home, grimy youngsters in tow. A woman openly sold tax-free contraband cigarettes and lottery tickets at the corner, and two African peddlers offered knockoffs of designer handbags and watches. A young man sold gelato beneath a cheerful red-and-white-striped awning. It was a fashionable area reclaiming its past splendor, made all the more popular by its views of the water.

Aldo Gambini had recently relocated to Chiaia from the old Forcella neighborhood that had given rise to him and from which he seemed to be withdrawing, piece by piece. The modern four-story building was a far cry from the bare offices in the abandoned button factory behind the railroad station and the seedy social club next door. The new offices were on the top floor, with a view of the water. The male receptionist didn't look like much of a typist. Neither did the male secretary who came out to take her to their boss.

The décor in the office suite was ultra-modern: gray and black drapes, furniture, and rugs, with one spot of contrasting color: a bright red-lacquered vase holding stalks of dried opium poppies. Gambini appeared in matching gray suit and black shirt, with a deep-red silk tie. Tan and fit, he directed her to a gray couch and sat down in the charcoal armchair alongside. He crossed his legs. His shoes, expensive, had been recently shined.

"I've come to warn you, Mr. Gambini. We have a new health crisis, and we need your help." She explained about the dead junkies and the poisoned dope.

"Sabotaged, no doubt, but what has this to do with me?"

"Given your wide range of contacts and knowledge of the city, we were hoping you might reach out to whoever is in a position to have these recreational drugs removed from the market and have the entire supply tested."

"I see. Of course, I will make every attempt."

"There is also the matter of the attacks on the trucks hauling away the piled-up garbage."

Gambini nodded nobly. "I heard about that, on the news."

"Do you suppose there is any way to negotiate a cessation of the hostilities that brought this about?"

"I couldn't say definitively. But offhand I'd say . . . no."

"Unfortunate."

"Is there more I can help you with?" he said.

"We've made an arrest in the Steiner murder case and released your nephew from custody."

"I was pleased to learn of his vindication."

"The matter is closed, but I keep wondering about some aspects concerning the victim." Natalia took out an envelope of Luca's telephoto snapshots of Gambini and Teresa Steiner enjoying themselves on the town. She passed them over to him.

"Why are you giving me these?"

"I didn't think you'd want them seen by others and possibly made public at some point. Or misconstrued."

"Misconstrued?"

"And I thought you might want them as mementos."

"When did you figure it out?"

"That she was your daughter? You weren't entirely forthcoming about how often you'd seen her in Naples, and it raised suspicions. We finally received the report from Berlin on your activities and movements there. Nothing in the German records linked you to her or her mother. But on nearly every trip to Germany, you visited Ulm, although you had no business interests there whatsoever. Ulm—where Teresa was raised and lived with her single parent. Ownership of the two German firms that paid for her care and education doesn't trace back to you either, but both proved to conduct considerable business with your shell companies. Or am I a victim of my own imaginings?"

Gambini closed his eyes, massaged them with his fingers, then said, "No, you're not wrong. I met her mother when she was seventeen. We were young. I was just married and unprepared to be so taken with her. And she with me. By the time I came to my senses, she was pregnant. I made arrangements, got her out of Naples, out of Italy. Married off to Herr Steiner to give the child a name. Then divorced. It was all through lawyers. Her mother and I—we didn't meet again."

"The visits to Ulm?"

"Anonymous. I only saw my daughter from afar. In the park. Coming out of school. Playing soccer. She played rough. Sliding into opponents, red hair flying."

"Did she know all along that you were her father?"

"No one knew. She didn't, until her mother confessed it on her deathbed. Soon afterward she showed up in Naples and approached me. I never had other children. With Teresa, I thought we might actually have a relationship. Instead of being appalled by my . . . work, she seemed excited by it. She wanted to know everything." He looked out onto the vista of the bay. "It was wonderful to have a daughter. At first."

"At first?"

"Before she got angry. Angry at my abandoning her, missing her childhood. Angry that I wouldn't publicly acknowledge her even now. She'd love me one moment, erupt the next—shouting, carrying on. I was generous with her. It didn't help. She tried things no one else would have dared. Skimmed the take from the shrines. Attempted sabotage of my business in Germany. Conspired and plotted with everyone she came in contact with. As if they wouldn't inform me. It was unbearable. And personally painful in the extreme."

Gambini took out a cigarette but didn't light it.

"To the point that now I find myself thinking maybe Father Pacelli did me a favor. Killing her." Gambini lit his cigarette. "She had to be killed, of course. But I couldn't face doing it."

"But Frankie and his young son—*that* you could face?"

Gambini inhaled deeply. "You looking to solve another murder? What's your interest in Frankie's death?"

"Safety—for his wife and her two children."

"Your oldest friend, right? Go on."

"I will keep the secret of your paternity if you guarantee they'll stay safe from you."

Gambini laughed. "Sure. You have my word," he said, and laughed again.

Natalia took out the negatives to the pictures on the coffee table. "I'm missing the joke."

"The joke is that I didn't have Frankie dealt with. We weren't on good terms at the moment, but not bad enough to. . . ."

"I'm . . . confused."

"And their kid," Gambini said, "he wasn't supposed to be there at all. They didn't see him. His head was below the window."

"What are you saying?"

"Your oldest and dearest, Lola, came to me when things were shakiest between me and Frankie. She had a proposition. She'd ingratiate herself with Strozzi's bunch and spy on them for me, if Frankie left the scene."

"Why would she?"

"You know too much for your own good, Captain Monte." The words came out with the smoke. "That's unhealthy in this town."

"Why are you telling me, then?"

"I didn't want you thinking ill of me." In one motion, Aldo Gambini rose. Elegant. His party's next nominee to the Chamber of Deputies.

"Good-bye, Captain Monte."

When she got back to the station, an elderly couple was waiting for her. Teresa Steiner's grandparents, come all the way from Palermo to take their granddaughter home. They'd come on the train, second-class. They were going back by plane—a private jet.

Natalia drove them over to see Dr. Francesca and view the body. She worried that the ordeal might be too much for the white-haired couple. They'd already buried their daughter, now their grandchild. But they came from a hard life. Not so much as a sniffle or tear when the curtain was drawn back in the viewing area. Teresa Steiner was beautiful; the morticians had done exemplary work for Mr. Gambini.

Afterward, they signed the requisite forms and sat waiting for the hearse.

Dr. Francesca stopped by and apologized for the delay in releasing the body. "But everything is in order now. We will provide a police escort to make sure you get to the airport without problems."

"Thank you." The elderly woman turned to Natalia as the doctor left. "We have a family plot." She twisted her wedding ring anxiously. "We will look after her."

A road accident stalled traffic and delayed Natalia's

return. When she finally reached her office, Pino was in her chair and on her phone, an extended finger signaling trouble. He signed off and replaced the receiver slowly, deep in thought and a little apprehensive.

"You saw Gambini earlier?" he asked.

"Yes, at his elegant new offices. But you knew that."

"Yes," Pino said.

"Why are you puzzled?"

"Surprised, really." He stood. "Gambini's *dead.*"

"Really? How? Who did it?"

"No suspects yet."

"At his office?"

"No, a park. You're going to love this. He was shot dead by a mobile. A fake four-shot cell phone. Antenna muzzle. Two .22 calibers fired close up. Hit right behind the ear."

"Professional."

"Very." Pino surrendered the desk chair and handed her a message slip. "They want statements from you, about your visit, your whereabouts at the time of the shooting. You know the drill."

"What are the bodyguards saying?"

"They weren't with him. He went there alone. A grounds-keeper said he saw a woman in black coming from the vicinity."

"Where did it happen?"

"On Capodimonte."

"A small grove behind the museum."

"Yes, exactly. How did you guess?"

Natalia made for the door.

"Where are you going, Natalia? You've got to be inter-viewed. Natalia!"

17

Natalia drove back to the old neighborhood and parked near the building where she used to live. On the sidewalk, a man prayed beneath a statue of Christ. Painted gold, it was nailed to the trunk of a magnificent tree whose shade Natalia had appreciated summers when she was a girl. Vandals had broken off one of the Savior's arms. As Natalia walked past, the supplicant stood up and kissed the plaster form.

She proceeded to the *palazzo* of Mariel and Lola's grandmother, where Lola was staying. The officers on duty downstairs, guarding her, said she'd been in all day. But there was no answer when Natalia rang the bell. When she finally telephoned, Nonna answered and told her to come right up. Lola was expecting her.

The ancient elevator clattered and groaned to the sixth floor, and Natalia got off. The hallway was still painted green—"like an avocado," Lola always teased her *nonna*. It was dim as ever.

Lola met her by the door, wearing Capri pants and a black top printed in gold.

"Kids still away?" Natalia said.

"Yeah." Lola led the way inside.

Nonna retired to her room. The two women sat at the dining table, where Lola had been filling a huge ashtray with half-smoked cigarettes.

"I hope you didn't leave any of those at the scene," Natalia said. "They'll take DNA evidence off them."

"I'm impressed. How'd you figure it out so fast?"

"I saw Gambini just this afternoon. Right before you lured him to the museum garden, the one you and I loved so much when we were kids."

"I left no trace. Not a fingerprint, footprint, nothing. In fact, I've been here all afternoon. Ask my bodyguards downstairs. Or Nonna."

". . . who was napping, as usual, after lunch, no?"

"No one saw me."

"A groundskeeper saw a woman in black . . . at a distance."

"All the widows in Naples wear black. That's half the city. So what?"

"Gambini told me almost everything. He said you were infiltrating Strozzi's organization to spy for him."

"Yeah, well. . . . Now I'm doubly glad I shut him up before he ruined the rest of my life."

"He told me you wanted Frankie dead, and he obliged. Why, Lol?"

Lola's face suddenly looked old, the wrinkles around her eyes more pronounced. Her eyes themselves seemed closed off, as if the windows to her soul had been transformed to mirrors. "When Frankie and I got married, I knew he might be killed. He'd chosen a dangerous business, after all. A Camorra widow . . . I was prepared. But to be cheated on with young girls? No way! Frankie swore he would be faithful. And he knew what would happen if he broke his promise—so help him God."

She dabbed at her mascara.

"And he *was* faithful, too. Until last year."

"How could you tell he wasn't?"

"The way he looked. Guilty. And then I found a lipstick in our car. Not my color. I begged him to end it. He promised. But he didn't. 'She's pregnant,' he told me. Can you imagine? That was just before the German turned up. Teresa Steiner. Frankie didn't like her—and he got in trouble with Gambini. Zazu threatened him with a ban of suspicion. We would have been silenced. No one allowed to speak to us until the suspicion was disproved. Teresa wanted me to go in with her. Crazy schemes. I feared for all of us."

"Go on."

"Frankie hid out with his girlfriend, left me and the kids alone, unprotected. He left me to deal with Teresa, with everything. I went to Gambini and said I could solve his problem with Bianca Strozzi by defecting to her mob if he would do me this one thing that would completely convince Bianca my break with the organization was final and irreversible."

"Bombing Frankie's car."

"Yeah. But the fools blew up Frankie and my Nico both."

Tears welled again. "They were sorry, Gambini said. They didn't see the boy."

Never could Natalia have imagined anything like this. How many dozens of times had she hung out with Lola here—sat on this shabby wine-and-white-striped couch, and in the bedroom where Lola had modeled her first bra for her and Mariel?

In this very room, Lola had confessed her first kiss, her first lover. At the large walnut table, the girls had eaten her grandmother's *biscotti* and fretted about their waistlines and complexions, about what their husbands would be like, what their lives would be. Never this.

"Eliminating Gambini, was that part of your scheme all along?"

Lola nodded. "Yes. I'd had it with him after he brought Teresa in. And I'd had it with Frankie too." She reached for Natalia's hand. "Now that's it's over . . . I don't know. I don't know what to do. I thought I would. I don't. I hope you're not thinking I'm going to confess like that besotted priest."

"Listen to me. If they find this out, they'll take you down and everyone connected to you—me, and Mariel—especially if they get wind that you used me as a go-between to broker a deal for Bianca Strozzi in her bookstore. They'll kill you with your kids in your arms. Then do the kids too. It *has* to remain a secret, Lol. You and I are the only two who will ever know."

"I swear it."

"Swear on your kids, Lola. No one else will ever hear from you what you did."

"I swear. You're not going to arrest me, are you, Nat?"

"You'll work for Strozzi. Run whatever for her. You'll raise the kids. You'll—"

"Nico was the cutest baby. My first. Remember the black curls? *Cara mia*, I'm afraid for my babies."

Natalia squeezed Lola's hand. "We'll figure it out. You'll all be okay. Mariel and I will help."

On the sideboard was a photograph, black and white, of the three of them in school uniforms and braids.

"Which birthday was it that we swore undying friendship?" Natalia asked.

"Mariel's eleventh," Lola said.

"No boy would ever come between us," Natalia recalled. "No man. We were in Piazza Dante. We treated ourselves to pizza. Then we exchanged lipstick. Not blood."

There were shouts from the street—people talking, kids fighting, the snatch of a song.

The air felt limp and damp. Natalia recognized the flowers Mariel had brought days ago. Peonies. They occupied
a vase in the center of the table. Their pink blossoms were
splayed open now, edged with rust. She inhaled their
perfume—rotten, yet sweet, the scent of her beloved city.

Continue reading for a preview from the next
Captain Natalia Monte investigation

A FEW DROPS OF BLOOD

Chapter 1

The moon was a ghost when the call came in. The caller said she wished to notify Captain Natalia Monte about two bodies. Routed from another Carabinieri station to hers on Via Casanova, the voice announced herself a countess and said that she didn't trust ordinary police.

Moments later Natalia Monte raced through the pre-dawn gray, siren blaring, flashing lights throwing blue and white bolts across buildings and intersections. She drove along Via Carducci, turned onto the Riviera di Chiaia, past its expensive shops and the aquarium, still run down since the Second World War when the hungry raided its tanks.

The Alfa Romeo zipped along the boulevard, palm trees arched overhead, the plazas dark, the Bay of Naples a blur to her left. On Via Petrarca she shot past a fountain she'd loved as a girl, with marble cherubs blowing trumpets. Finally she slowed and searched for the turn.

Natalia spotted the driveway of Palazzo Carraciulo and passed through its open gates, up a long curved drive lush with royal palms. So different from the cramped alleys of old Naples where she lived and worked. A hundred yards in, she pulled alongside a new police Ferrari parked in front of a grey stone mansion, its pristine façade incorporating sleek pediments discreetly illuminated. An ancient butler directed her to the garden. Natalia followed a stone path around the side of the building and flashed her identification at the Carabiniere guarding the scene.

The lush garden was beautifully wild with grasses and flowers. Several cats dozed on the edge of a patio. Honeysuckle and jasmine perfumed the air. A yellow butterfly on an orange lily slowly opened and folded its wings.

Natalia stepped onto the grass and walked toward the rose bushes that surrounded a life-sized horse cast in metal, the centerpiece of a dry fountain half filled with potted blooms—white roses. The sculpture was enormous. Two male figures sat astride the unbridled steed—one man pitched forward, his arms draped along the animal's neck. The second man leaned into him from behind. Neither was clothed.

Natalia stepped closer. Dark splotches marred the creamy petals of flowers encircling the fountain. Already there were flies. She circled the statue slowly, shining a light up at the two, just barely making out dark punctures that riddled their chests. Young men—shotgunned from the look of them. Blood dripped down their torsos and loins, along their legs and the flanks of the horse into the fountain's basin. Its iron scent mixed with the lush bouquet of the roses.

Suddenly she noticed the woman by the rhododendrons, motionless as the men. Silver hair framed her face and flowed past her slim shoulders. She wore a white silk kimono printed with orange and purple cranes. Cranes symbolized long life, Pino, Natalia's ex, had told her once in an intimate moment. The woman's eyes were a startling shade of lavender.

Natalia held up her Carabinieri identification. "Captain Monte. As you requested."

"Contessa Antonella Maria Cavazza," she said and extended her hand, the tiny fingers like a child's. "Thank you for coming."

Natalia took the delicate, age-splotched hand.

"You found them?"

"Yes, I made the unhappy discovery."

"Do you know the victims?"

"The second man in back. Vincente Lattaruzzo. He's a senior curator at the Museo Archeologico."

"When did you find them?"

"Just before seven. I'm an early riser. Unless it's raining, I take my coffee here in the garden."

"Did you see or hear anything during the night or early this morning?"

"Hear? No. My bedroom is in the wing over there." Antonella Cavazza pointed to the far end of the building. "When I have trouble sleeping—which is often these days—I wander the house. But the windows are all double glazed and sealed for the air-conditioning. So, no. I didn't hear a disturbance."

"How do you know the victim?"

"I'm on the board of the museum. Once a year I host a dinner party. Senior staff are invited. I first met him there— last Christmas, I believe. And he had occasion to address the board at times. Terribly likeable."

The medical examiner, Dr. Francesca Agari, arrived, followed by the forensic photographer draped with equipment. He proceeded immediately to the dead men and began taking still pictures and videotaping the crime scene. A groundskeeper brought a ladder, and the photographer mounted it to get closer to the dead equestrians.

"Captain Monte," Dr. Agari said, acknowledging Natalia

as she came forward, then, "Nell." She kissed the countess on each cheek. "How terrible for you!"

As usual, Natalia's colleague was perfectly groomed, blond highlights symmetrical. She wore a filmy gray blouse, tasteful yet sexy under a black suit jacket, and slacks.

"Yes," the countess said. "How are you my dear? How's Mama?"

"Difficult as always," Dr. Agari replied warmly.

The countess moved away to let the detective and the doctor confer.

"Mama?" Natalia said, as she pulled on rubber gloves.

Two mortuary men entered near the hedges.

"Over here!" Dr. Agari called. "She and my grandmother were great friends. I had my tenth birthday party here in this garden."

Mortuary staff earned a good living in their coveted jobs. Nepotism abounded: The husky men looked to be brothers.

"They'll need another ladder." Natalia returned to the countess.

"There's one in the tool shed," she said and escorted the men toward the far end of the garden.

Natalia searched the perimeter. Fancy topiary abounded: bushes shaped like turrets, azalea trimmed to a perfect circle around the base of an olive tree. Something interrupted the perfect symmetry. She stepped closer. It took her a moment to understand what she was seeing: a cotton work shirt. This one appeared old, the kind once worn by laborers in the fields, patched and mended many times, laid out across a bush as if to dry. It may have been white when new, but this morning—except for the rust-colored sleeves—the shirt lay dark and stiff, heavily stained, its fabric torn.

Natalia called for an evidence bag, slipped it in, and returned to the corpses. Dr. Agari was peering in and around the bodies, looking for signs of sexual union between the two. Soon, Natalia thought, she would peel away, remove, examine and weigh their secrets, as Dr. Agari would their flesh and organs.

There were no discernible tracks in the hard earth along the walks. They'd kept to the grass.

A dove regarded Natalia from its patch of dirt beneath a flaming bougainvillea. Checking for footprints, she followed the pebble walkways radiating from the fountain. A profusion of flowers—giant lilies, amber and rose—enveloped her path, their sweet scent thick. A bee anchored the velvet petal of a petunia.

Such a strange place for a gruesome murder. Out of the way, certainly. The countess's paradise seemed light years removed from the rest of the city. Someone had gone to a lot of trouble to stage it here, someone familiar with the garden.

The countess had taken refuge under a large awning that shaded a stone patio and the table where she took her coffee. Lilies, thistles and wild flowers surrounded her. The mortuary men had taken down the bodies and laid them on gurneys. Dr. Agari stood over the corpses, securing her swabs and evidence envelopes.

Natalia approached the countess. "Would you mind taking a look?" She indicated the dead men. Francesca approached across the lawn.

"She's going to try to identify the other victim," Natalia said.

"Nella, are you sure?" Dr. Agari came and put her arm around the countess.

"My dear, you know me better than that."

The mortuary men stepped away. The countess bent from the waist and studied the unidentified corpse. He was short and stocky. Not as young as the other victim, but no more than forty. Prematurely bald, cheeks ashen.

"Carlo Bagnatti," the countess said, standing.

"The gossip columnist?" Natalia asked. "Are you sure?"

"He writes for *Rivelare* and is carried in *La Stella*. I've seen his photo and once or twice on the chat shows." She looked exhausted.

"Perhaps you should lie down inside," Dr. Agari suggested. "Here." She held out an arm to escort her.

"No, I'm fine. Really. I can sit on the terrace." The countess and her friend made for the house.

"Excuse me," Natalia called.

The countess looked back. "Yes? What?"

"I'll need to ask you a few more questions. Would you mind?"

"Of course not."

Francesca touched the countess's shoulder. "Are you sure?"

"I'm fine. Don't let me interrupt your work, *cara*. We'll talk later, yes?"

"*Certo*," Francesca said. She joined the photographer, and they spoke quietly.

The countess led Natalia to a bench obscured by a large magnolia.

"So, you knew Carlo Bagnatti as well?" Natalia said.

"Only from his column," she said. "Vile trash. Stories that might shock even you, Captain. Really salacious stuff and, more often than not, he was accurate, unlike the usual tabloid nonsense."

"So, you knew Vincente Lattaruzzo from the museum and had encountered him at their functions?"

"A number of times, yes."

"And Bagnatti? You never ran into him at social affairs?"

"No. Though he did contact me once—he was looking for dirt about someone I was acquainted with. Naturally, I was of no help."

"The way the murdered men were posed," Natalia asked, "do you have any idea if the victims were involved? Romantically, I mean?"

"I don't know about that. I do know Vincente lived with

a significant other. I believe that's the correct term. A male. About Bagnatti's personal life, I have no idea."

"Would you have Mr. Lattaruzzo's address?"

"Certainly. I'll get it for you."

Natalia closed her notebook. "I will have more questions later today or tomorrow."

"Of course. Just call ahead. My calendar isn't full."

Natalia returned to the victims.

"She okay?" Dr. Agari said.

"Seems so. What do we have?"

"Shotgun blast," Dr. Agari said, indicating Lattaruzzo. "Small gauge. The other victim the same."

A small gauge shotgun—the traditional execution weapon of the rural mafia, a stubby weapon for hunting small game and two-legged mammals.

"Victim One," Francesca said, "also has ligature marks around his throat."

"He was strangled?"

"More likely hung."

"The other victim too?"

"No. Both also show signs of having been tortured."

Natalia squatted to look at the wounds more closely and played her flashlight on Lattaruzzo's face. Vincente, he was lightly made up.

"Is Bagnatti wearing makeup, too?" she asked.

"Both are, yes. Cheeks rouged, a faint white dot at the outside corner of each eye, lashes thick with mascara, eyebrows penciled. Across the lips, the slightest suggestion of color."

"Were they killed here?" Natalia said.

"I don't think so. Not enough blood present."

"Any clues as to where?"

"You might look for wherever Mr. Lattaruzzo left his privates."

Other Titles in the Soho Crime Series

Michael Genelin
(Slovakia)
Siren of the Waters
Dark Dreams
The Magician's Accomplice
Requiem for a Gypsy

Timothy Hallinan
(Thailand)
The Fear Artist
For the Dead
The Hot Countries
Fools' River

(Los Angeles)
Crashed
Little Elvises
The Fame Thief
Herbie's Game
King Maybe
Fields Where They Lay
Nighttown

Mette Ivie Harrison
(Mormon Utah)
The Bishop's Wife
His Right Hand
For Time and All Eternities
Not of This Fold

Mick Herron
(England)
Slow Horses
Dead Lions
Real Tigers
Spook Street
London Rules
Joe Country

Down Cemetery Road
The Last Voice You Hear
Why We Die
Smoke and Whispers

Reconstruction
Nobody Walks
This Is What Happened

Stan Jones
(Alaska)
White Sky, Black Ice
Shaman Pass

Stan Jones cont.
Frozen Sun
Village of the Ghost Bears
Tundra Kill
The Big Empty

**Lene Kaaberbøl &
Agnete Friis**
(Denmark)
The Boy in the Suitcase
Invisible Murder
Death of a Nightingale
The Considerate Killer

Martin Limón
(South Korea)
Jade Lady Burning
Slicky Boys
Buddha's Money
The Door to Bitterness
The Wandering Ghost
G.I. Bones
Mr. Kill
The Joy Brigade
Nightmare Range
The Iron Sickle
The Ville Rat
Ping-Pong Heart
The Nine-Tailed Fox
The Line
GI Confidential

Ed Lin
(Taiwan)
Ghost Month
Incensed
99 Ways to Die

Peter Lovesey
(England)
The Circle
The Headhunters
False Inspector Dew
Rough Cider
On the Edge
The Reaper

(Bath, England)
The Last Detective
Diamond Solitaire
The Summons

Peter Lovesey cont.
Bloodhounds
Upon a Dark Night
The Vault
Diamond Dust
The House Sitter
The Secret Hangman
Skeleton Hill
Stagestruck
Cop to Corpse
The Tooth Tattoo
The Stone Wife
Down Among
the Dead Men
Another One Goes Tonight
Beau Death
Killing with Confetti

(London, England)
Wobble to Death
The Detective Wore
Silk Drawers
Abracadaver
Mad Hatter's Holiday
The Tick of Death
A Case of Spirits
Swing, Swing Together
Waxwork

Jassy Mackenzie
(South Africa)
Random Violence
Stolen Lives
The Fallen
Pale Horses
Bad Seeds

Sujata Massey
(1920s Bombay)
The Widows of Malabar Hill
The Satapur Moonstone

Francine Mathews
(Nantucket)
Death in the Off-Season
Death in Rough Water
Death in a Mood Indigo
Death in a Cold Hard Light
Death on Nantucket

Seichō Matsumoto
(Japan)
*Inspector Imanishi
Investigates*

Magdalen Nabb
(Italy)
*Death of an Englishman
Death of a Dutchman
Death in Springtime
Death in Autumn
The Marshal and
the Murderer
The Marshal and
the Madwoman
The Marshal's Own Case
The Marshal Makes
His Report
The Marshal
at the Villa Torrini
Property of Blood
Some Bitter Taste
The Innocent
Vita Nuova
The Monster of Florence*

Fuminori Nakamura
(Japan)
*The Thief
Evil and the Mask
Last Winter, We Parted
The Kingdom
The Boy in the Earth
Cult X*

Stuart Neville
(Northern Ireland)
*The Ghosts of Belfast
Collusion
Stolen Souls
The Final Silence
Those We Left Behind
So Say the Fallen*

(Dublin)
Ratlines

Rebecca Pawel
(1930s Spain)
*Death of a Nationalist
Law of Return
The Watcher in the Pine
The Summer Snow*

Kwei Quartey
(Ghana)
*Murder at Cape
Three Points
Gold of Our Fathers
Death by His Grace*

Qiu Xiaolong
(China)
*Death of a Red Heroine
A Loyal Character Dancer
When Red Is Black*

James Sallis
(New Orleans)
*The Long-Legged Fly
Moth
Black Hornet
Eye of the Cricket
Bluebottle
Ghost of a Flea*

Sarah Jane

John Straley
(Sitka, Alaska)
*The Woman Who
Married a Bear
The Curious Eat Themselves
The Music of What Happens
Death and the Language
of Happiness
The Angels Will Not Care
Cold Water Burning
Baby's First Felony*

(Cold Storage, Alaska)
*The Big Both Ways
Cold Storage, Alaska*

Akimitsu Takagi
(Japan)
*The Tattoo Murder Case
Honeymoon to Nowhere
The Informer*

Helene Tursten
(Sweden)
*Detective Inspector Huss
The Torso
The Glass Devil
Night Rounds
The Golden Calf
The Fire Dance
The Beige Man
The Treacherous Net
Who Watcheth
Protected by the Shadows*

*Hunting Game
Winter Grave*

*An Elderly Lady Is Up to
No Good*

**Janwillem van de
Wetering**
(Holland)
*Outsider in Amsterdam
Tumbleweed
The Corpse on the Dike
Death of a Hawker
The Japanese Corpse
The Blond Baboon
The Maine Massacre
The Mind-Murders
The Streetbird
The Rattle-Rat
Hard Rain
Just a Corpse at Twilight
Hollow-Eyed Angel
The Perfidious Parrot
The Sergeant's Cat:
Collected Stories*

Jacqueline Winspear
(1920s England)
*Maisie Dobbs
Birds of a Feather*